CW00983517

Separation

Andrei,
Thanks for
reading ♡

STYLO FANTÔME

Separation
Published by BattleAxe Productions
Copyright © 2014
Stylo Fantôme

Editing Aides:
Barbara Shane Hoover
Leticia Sidon

Cover Design:
Najla Qamber Designs
http://najlaqamberdesigns.com/
Copyright © 2014

Formatting by Champagne Formats

This book is licensed for your personal enjoyment only. It is the copyrighted property of the author, and may not be reproduced, copied, re-sold, or re-distributed. If you're reading this book and did not purchase it, or it was not purchased for your use only, then this copy must be destroyed. Please purchase a copy for yourself from a licensed seller. Thank you for respecting the hard work of this author.

ISBN-13: 978-1501086434
ISBN-10: 150108643X

Dedication

This is for all the Ladies in our street team. Not only do you help make it so I can continue doing this – you make me laugh, you make me feel better when I'm down, you support me AND each other. You just make the world a better place to be. Thank you.

And of course to Sue – thank you for assuring me that this book wasn't meant to be scrapped.

Sanders

PEOPLE OFTEN THOUGHT "*SANDERS*" WAS Sanders' last name; it wasn't – his last name was Dashkevich. Sanders was the name of some long forgotten relative. Kind of exotic, really. But he never explained this story, he just let people think what they wanted. That always seemed to work out best for him.

He was thirteen when Mr. Jameson Kane found him, starving on the streets of London. He had tried to steal from Jameson. He had been very bad at pickpocketing, and Jameson had grabbed him by the collar, held him against a wall. But then he'd looked at Sanders in the strangest way, and instead of getting angry, he had offered to buy Sanders lunch.

After the meal, Jameson informed him that if Sanders was at the same spot every day, he would continue buying meals for him. Sanders was sure to be there, every day. After two weeks, they finally got to talking. Jameson asked why he was starving, living on the streets.

"I ran away from home," was Sanders' only explanation. Jameson had nodded.

"I know how you feel."

"You ran away, too?

"Sort of. I did something very bad to someone back home."

"And you felt bad, so you ran away?"

"No, I *didn't* feel bad, and *that's* why I ran away."

They kept meeting for lunch. Jameson would have him run the odd errand, then pay him for it. Jameson would laugh — *"you're my assistant now, Sanders, so we have to work out a salary."* Rented out a hotel room for Sanders to stay in, bought him new clothes.

Sanders couldn't figure it out. Who was this guy? What did he want? For a long time, Sanders thought it was sex. He kept waiting to hear his hotel room door open, see a silhouette in the light. It's what had always happened to him, in his old home. But it never happened with this man. It became very obvious, very quickly, that Jameson was not attracted to him, *at all*. Sure, Jameson was very adventurous, and Sanders could see that he lived by a *"I'll try anything once"* kind of credo – but he wasn't gay. Jameson loved women.

"The perfect woman, Sanders. That's what I'm on a quest for — the perfect woman. Don't know if I'll ever find her," he had slurred late one night, very drunk.

"Have you ever met a perfect woman?" Sanders asked. Jameson thought long and hard about it.

"I think I might have. But I didn't know it at the time. And she wasn't quite perfect yet."

"Was it a long time ago?"

"Not long enough."

Sanders wasn't gay either, but he didn't really have any interest in sex. He'd never done it. Well, at least not consensually; and never with a girl. He had always been too busy hiding his secret. Then after Jameson came along, Sanders had been too in awe of his new world, too in shock, to think about girls.

He told Jameson about the family he'd grown up with – his aunt's family, in South London. Sanders was originally from Belarus, but his parents moved to England when he was five. His family got deported, but they managed to leave him at his mother's sister's house. He never heard from his mother or father again. His aunt's husband was an Englishman, and not a very nice one. Sanders didn't want to tell Jameson that whole story.

So how could Jameson have known?

He had wanted to do something nice for Sanders. Wanted Sanders' family to see how well their nephew was doing, the kind of life he was now leading. Let Sanders show off a little. His family owned a small bed and breakfast, and Jameson surprised him by getting them rooms there for a night.

Something snapped in Sanders. When his uncle came to his room, tried to hold him down, tried to tell him that he would never be more than what he was in that moment, Sanders fought back – the first time he had ever done so. He was much smaller than his uncle, but rage completely overtook him. It wasn't until Jameson was standing over him, pulling him away, that Sanders even realized he had completely beaten his uncle's head in against a radiator.

His life would be over. He would at best be deported back to Belarus. At worst, and most likely, spend the rest of his life in prison. Sanders sat in the middle of the blood and gore, and just sobbed. Jameson knelt down and grabbed onto him, held him still against his chest. Told him everything would be okay, that he didn't have to worry, that Jameson would take care of everything. And when Sanders finally calmed down, Jameson kept his promise. He managed to magically have the body disposed of; cleaned up the room. Left a large sum of money with Sanders' aunt, who never even seemed to question her husband going missing. Apparently he wasn't a nice man to anyone else, either.

They never spoke of that night again. Jameson didn't even ask, just arranged for Sanders to come back to America. Paid for him to attend the best private schools. Sanders was *very* smart, it turned out. He spoke fluent English, Russian, Belarusian, Polish, and German; as well as conversational French and Spanish. He could play the piano, and got as high as a Master level in competitive chess before he gave it up. Took classes in sharp shooting. Learned how to rebuild automobile engines.

While in school, Sanders was also diagnosed with a mild form of Asperger's syndrome. It explained some of his intense focus, why he never really wanted to talk, and his minimal OCD. He hadn't thought much of it, and Jameson had just laughed, said it would give him a leg up in the world.

Because of Jameson, Sanders was able to do anything he wanted; was *allowed* to do anything he wanted. Jameson never questioned his choices. When Sanders turned eighteen, Jameson offered to pay for him to go to college, but he declined. He wanted to stay with Jameson. He wanted a real job with him. He wanted to be wherever Jameson was, and the best way was to take a real position as his assistant.

They'd never had an entirely normal relationship, anyway. Jameson was more comfortable, in general, treating everyone like they worked for him. That appealed to Sanders' meticulous and cold nature. Their relationship worked for them. They didn't speak a whole lot, and even when they did, they weren't prone to long conversations. But there was a bond that no one could possibly understand. Sanders loved him. Hadn't known it was possible to love a person as much as he loved Jameson Kane.

That's why it killed him to see Jameson so unhappy. Jameson didn't realize he was unhappy, but Sanders could tell. All the women, all the sleeping around, all the debauchery. Something was missing in Jameson's life, that much was clear.

Girls came and went. Some stayed a little longer than others. Most ignored Sanders. He ignored all of them. There was an opera singer from Rio that he had almost considered liking, but before he could make up his mind, she was let go. She hadn't been up to Jameson's speed, anyway. None of them were, when push came to shove.

4

Then Petrushka Ivanovic entered the picture. How Sanders had hated her. She was the only one who ever truly got under his skin. They would have arguments in Russian – so Jameson couldn't understand what they were saying. She called Sanders a useless, dirty, immigrant who was just leeching off of Jameson. He called her a tasteless, fake, bitch who was just another notch on Jameson's very well marked bedpost. It took a lot longer, but eventually she went away, too. He was *very* glad.

It wasn't too much longer before Tatum O'Shea came along. Jameson had mentioned her a couple times, usually after many late night drinks. It was obvious that she had been the reason he had run away so many years ago, that she was that "*not quite perfect yet*" woman. It was also obvious they hadn't known each other well – they hadn't seen each other in over seven years. It was a while before Jameson explained the history to him.

Sanders wasn't sure what to make of Tatum, at first. He had expected just another silly girl. Another woman who thought she could keep up with Jameson, but ultimately wouldn't be able to keep up at all. Or one of those types of women who only wanted Jameson for his status and money.

Not Tatum. She took everything Jameson threw at her and rolled with it. Asked for it. Wanted more of it. And she seemed oblivious to, and uncaring of, the fact that he had more money than God. For a short while, and by mutual agreement, the relationship was purely physical, and she actually seemed to like it that way.

Unusual girl.

She also completely ignored Sanders' weird, awkward, social habits. He didn't like to talk very much. Tatum liked to talk *a lot*, and just talked to him anyway. She paid attention to him, spoke to him, asked him how he was, how his day was going. Seemed to look right into him sometimes.

She also touched him – no one ever did that. Sanders usually hated to be touched, and it had bothered him a lot, at first. But Tatum was very persistent. She held his hand, hugged him, tried to tickle him. It almost seemed as if she touched him more just because she knew he didn't like it. She was so comfortable with him, right off the bat. The same way Jameson had been. One day, she even kissed Sanders. It was a joke, a ruse, but something snapped in him. Sanders was twenty years old and had never kissed a girl, and here was a girl, laying one on him. He took the opportunity and kissed her back.

But Sanders wasn't attracted to Tatum, not like that. He could recognize that she was a very, *very* sexy woman. She was not shy about her body or her sexuality, and she flirted shamelessly with just about anything that moved. He wasn't entirely immune to her charms; he was heterosexual, after all. But for the most part he didn't view her that way. She was something different to him. Something special.

On top of that, it was clear from day one that she was different to Jameson, too. Also something special. No one else would have been able to tell, but Sanders could tell. She made Jameson happy. She made *Sanders* happy. He grew very attached to her.

When the relationship between Tatum and Jameson started to become strained, she would seek Sanders out. Their bond grew stronger. She would come into his room late at night, play chess with him, talk with him. She never rushed him to talk, just waited for the words to come out. Eventually, they did. She never asked questions, never judged anything he had to say. He fell a little in love with her. Not romantically, not sexually. He didn't know how to explain it. He just loved her.

If necessary, he would probably kill for Jameson Kane.

If asked, he would probably die for Tatum O'Shea.

When the relationship between Jameson and Tatum ended – and it ended *badly* – Sanders had mourned it. Jameson had been in the wrong. It was the first time he had ever asked Sanders to do things that made him uncomfortable. Things that he found repugnant. He didn't like lying. It all went to hell. He thought Jameson would admit his fault, admit he'd been wrong, then apologize. But Jameson wouldn't. It had shocked Sanders. He held Jameson to a very high standard. It was like hearing his father damn himself to hell. Sanders would have to save him.

Sometimes, Sanders felt like he had to fix *everything*.

Right After

A POUNDING NOISE BROUGHT JAMESON OUT of unconsciousness. Just blackness. He squinted and stared up at the ceiling. Where the fuck was he? It took him a second to realize he was in his library. It started to come back to him. He had passed out on the leather sofa that was tucked against a wall. He couldn't remember the last time he had even used the sofa, let alone slept on it. Then he remembered that a little over a month ago, he had put the sofa to very good use.

Tatum.

He groaned and sat up. There was more banging and he pressed a hand to his head. He couldn't remember how much he'd had to drink. It had been a lot. A glance at his liquor cabinet showed it to be wide open and completely empty.

There was more pounding.

"Sanders!" Jameson yelled, rubbing his face. There was no answer and he lifted his eyes to the ceiling. "*Sanders!* Get the goddamn door!"

Silence, followed by *bang bang bang*.

He growled and stood up, started marching across the room.

There was a crunching sound, and before he could fully realize what was happening, something sliced through his heel. He hissed and lifted his foot. A chunk of glass was imbedded in his heel. He yanked it out and glared at it. Then he looked down and lost his glare.

Glass was everywhere. No, not glass. Crystal. Broken crystal, scattered all over the ground. A wide swath of floor, from the liquor cabinet to the wall across from it, was coated in broken tumblers and bottles and decanters. It all came back to Jameson. He had broken every piece of glassware in the room, after Sanders had left.

After *she* had left.

The pounding wasn't going away, and now that he knew why Sanders wasn't answering the door – *because he wasn't there* – Jameson made his way to the front of the house. Someone was knocking, over and over. Jameson stomped up and yanked open the door.

"What?" he barked.

A police officer blinked at him. Jameson was surprised, but he didn't show it. He kept his glare in place. The officer was young and tall. Taller than Jameson. He looked gangly and nervous, like it was his first day at basketball camp. Jameson raised his eyebrows, glancing between the cop and the police cruiser that was parked in the driveway.

"Um, is this the residence of …" the cop checked a notepad. "Jameson Kane? Or Sanders Dash … Dashke …"

"*Yes,*" Jameson cut him off.

"Are you —,"

"I'm Jameson. This is my home. What do you want?" he demanded. The cop swallowed nervously.

"Uh, we wanted to let you know, we found your car," he answered. Jameson's eyebrows went back up.

"My car?" he asked, not having a clue what was going on. The cop looked down at the notepad he was holding.

"Uh, a Bentley, registered to a Jameson Kane and a Sanders

Dashke ... uh, yeah. License plate WXC1—," the cop started to prattle off. Jameson held up a hand.

"Yes, I know my own license plate. What about the car?" he pressed. Now the cop looked surprised.

"Um, it was reported stolen," the cop explained.

"*Stolen?*"

"Yes. Mr. ... Mr. Sanders reported it stolen, last night. It's being towed here, right now. I just had some questions," the cop told him.

"Sanders reported our car stolen?" Jameson clarified.

Someone had stolen the Bentley? He hadn't even known it was gone, and if he had, he would've just assumed Sanders had taken it. He was practically the only one who ever drove it; it was more his than Jameson's.

Who would want to steal the Bentley? After Sanders had put in his "notice", Jameson had kicked everyone out. Just walked into the main lounge and yelled at everyone to get the hell out of his house. Petrushka Ivanovic, his ex girlfriend, had argued to stay, but he had practically thrown her out onto the porch and then slammed the door in her face.

Then Jameson had locked himself in the library and drank himself stupid, cursing both Tate and Sanders while he destroyed all his crystal. Was it possible that one of his disgruntled party guests had stolen his car? Most of them were wealthy in their own right; they could buy their own Bentleys.

"Yes, last evening," the cop continued. "We found it soon afterwards. There's some minor damage to the vehicle, but it was like that when we found it. We took pictures, but you'll want to contact your insurance company."

At that moment, a tow truck started rumbling up the drive. Jameson stared in shock as his car was pulled around, right in front of the porch. The entire passenger side of the Bentley was scratched up, as if it had side swiped something and then dragged along it. The sideview had been ripped clean off.

"What the fuck happened? Did you find the person who stole it?" Jameson demanded, stepping out onto the porch. The cop flipped through some paperwork.

"Yes. Actually, that's how we found the car. An officer who had responded to a 9-1-1 call noticed the car idling in the middle of the road, he called in the plates," the cop read off the notes.

"Did you arrest the thief?" Jameson asked.

"Not yet. From what I understand, it was a woman. She was found unconscious in a pool in the Beacon Hill Athletic Club," the officer explained.

Tatum.

"Unconscious?" Jameson repeated, his voice soft. More pages flipped in the notepad.

"Um, that's how she was found, that's what the officer at the scene reported. Uhhh, let's see … okay, the report says that when paramedics arrived, she was having generalized seizures. A man on the scene said she had vomited prior to —,"

Jameson didn't hear any more. He turned around and walked back into the house without saying a word. Walked straight back into his kitchen and opened a cupboard next to the fridge. Pulled out a bottle of Jack Daniel's. Twisted off the wrapper and cap, chugging as much as he could before he had to breathe again. There was a creaking noise behind him and he became aware that the cop had followed him. Jameson took one more drink before leaning against the counter.

"Is she okay?"

"Do you know the —,"

"*Is she okay?*"

"Uh, um," the cop stuttered, and Jameson heard notepaper rustling. "I—I don't know. The last report I received was that she was checked into an emergency room, still having seizures, and with an irregular, slow, heart beat and low oxygen levels. I haven't heard anything else, Mr. Kane."

Mr. Kane. Someone should've told him my real name is Satan.

"Leave," Jameson whispered, staring at his granite counter tops.

"Excuse me?"

"I said *leave*. Get out of my house," Jameson snapped, finally turning around. The cop looked stunned.

"We have some paperwork, I need you to —," he started to stammer. Jameson strode forward and pushed past the officer.

"The car belongs to Sanders, track him down," he grumbled.

"But you —, *sir!* Sir, did you know you're bleeding!?" the cop exclaimed, hurrying after Jameson and pointing out the bloody footprints he was leaving behind him.

"Yes," Jameson snapped back. A large man in coveralls was hovering in the open doorway, holding a piece of paper.

"Hey! Who gunnah pay for dis tow job? I need fiddy bucks," the guy drawled in a thick Boston accent. Jameson growled again and stomped up to an end table that flanked the front door. He yanked open a drawer and pulled out a stack of money. Both the cop and the tow truck driver gaped at him.

"All of this is yours, just be off my property within the next five minutes," Jameson said as he led them out onto the porch, all the while flinging hundred dollar bills to the ground.

"Ay, ay, no problem, buddy," the guy said, quickly dipping down and picking up what had to be $800. He was a large guy, but he ran back to the car and had the Bentley unloaded and was driving off in his tow truck, well under the five minute time limit.

"We still have to —," the cop started. Jameson glared at him and stepped back into his doorway.

"Call Sanders. He reported it stolen, not me. He can deal with this mess," he snapped, then slammed the door shut.

The cop banged on the door for a while, but Jameson was very good at ignoring things. He took his stairs two at a time, his heart thumping louder than his footsteps pounding down the hall. He felt like he was going to explode. Like his heart was going to pound right out of his chest. Or rather, whatever organ it was he had in place of a heart.

Tatum.

He didn't know why he thought he'd find answers there, but Jameson went straight into Sanders' bedroom. A large walk-in closet stood open, all clothing gone from it. Sanders didn't mess around. Something had been left behind, though, and Jameson sighed as he walked up to the foot of the bed. Sitting there, stacked neatly and packed in even bundles, was $32,000 in cash. Jameson knew it was exactly $32,000 because the night before, he had taken the cash out of a safe in his own room and brought it into Sanders' room. Brought it to *her*.

A note sat on top of the money. Only one word was written on it, in Sanders' neat script:

"*Satan.*"

At least he spelled my name right.

A light was on in the bathroom and Jameson walked towards it. Very little actually disturbed him, but the sight he took in kind of made him want to vomit. Not because it was too ugly, but because it showed him what a terrible person he really was deep down. Through and through, to his core.

Sometimes, he forgot.

All the drawers on the vanity had been pulled open, stuff hanging out of them. The mirror had a large spider-web crack on the right hand side, closest to the door. One crack shot off all the way down to the sink, and some blood and strands of hair were in the very center of the spider-web. Long, black hair. Bloodstains were smattered across the vanity top and what looked like bloody fingerprints were smeared down the whole length. Jameson closed his eyes. Took deep breaths through his nose. Went back in time.

Petrushka had cornered him in the kitchen. Said unkind things about Tate. Jameson had been angry at Tate at the beginning of the night – angry at her for over two weeks before that, but after confronting her, after seeing her reaction, his anger had started to fade away. Started to turn into something else. Something unfamiliar. Something he hadn't felt in a *long* time.

Guilt.

Pet was a massive bitch who didn't even know Tate. She had come along with Jameson just to watch the fireworks. Petrushka was almost a bigger sociopath than he was; Tate didn't deserve it. Not from Pet. Jameson had treated Tatum poorly enough.

She had been so upset. Maybe, just maybe, there was the tiniest possibility that he had been wrong about her. Wrong about her relationship with the baseball player. It happened on occasion, sometimes even Jameson Kane was capable of making a mistake. He hadn't wanted to wait till the end of the night to find out; he'd sought Tate out the minute he shook Pet loose.

Jameson hadn't seen how it had started, just how it had ended. When he'd walked into Sanders' room and saw a man in a suit bent over Tate, he had thought it was actually Sanders, at first. Talk about upsetting. Sanders was like a son to Jameson, he didn't want to have to kill him.

But it wasn't Sanders. It was Wenseworth Dunn, Jameson's business partner. A man Jameson had gone to school with, a man he had known for a long time. Dunn knew that Tate was off limits. Tate knew that Jameson didn't want her to sleep with any of his friends or colleagues. Breaking rules was apparently par for the course that night. Jameson had wanted to murder them both, but he'd settled for beating the shit out of Dunn, and then kicking Tatum out of the house. He hadn't bothered to look in the bathroom. He never bothered to look at anything, *ever*. He didn't have to – he didn't care.

Right? *Right?*

She had bled. How could I not notice that she was bleeding? Even I never made her bleed.

Jameson pressed his back against the door, then slid into a sitting position. Put his head in his hands. He was a Yale graduate. He owned multiple businesses, in multiple countries. He played the stock market like he'd invented it, and owned real estate so pricey, even Donald Trump was interested. He was considered by many to be a very smart, calculating man.

But suddenly he felt very stupid. Brought down by a woman with black hair and dark eyes. A sexy wit and a sexier body. A bartender, coupon clipper, temp worker. A college drop out turned party girl, with loose morals and legs that rarely closed.

So much better than him, in every way, shape, and form.

Her only downside was thinking she could use sex as a weapon. She'd always been too naive to realize that sometimes, weapons can backfire.

It had certainly backfired on him.

It took him a lot longer to find her than he would've thought. Sanders wasn't answering his phones calls, which was actually a surprise, even after everything that had happened. Jameson left several very angry, hostile voicemails. Regardless of his "work" position, Sanders was still family and this was an emergency.

Angier Hollingsworth, Tatum's best friend, wouldn't answer his phone, either, but that wasn't a surprise at all. Ang had never liked Jameson, and chances were the younger man already knew about what had happened. Was probably already on his way to avenge Tate. Or was possibly already with her.

Jameson finally tried Tate's phone, but it didn't even ring – just went straight to voicemail. Kind of ominous.

Hospitals are not very generous with patient information. It was evening before he found where she had been admitted, and even then, it was only because he'd lucked out – the hospital she was staying in was one his New York offices had made substantial donations to; Jameson's name was on one of the wings. Upon realizing that, the nurse was ready to give him any kind of information he wanted.

Actually getting to her room proved even harder, though. Jameson wasn't family, and he wasn't her husband. He wasn't *anything* to Tate, technically. They wouldn't even tell him what her room number was; he would have to wait till regular visiting hours, and even then, only if the patient requested to see him. He didn't really foresee that happening.

He saw Ang at one point, but Jameson kept his distance. He knew it wouldn't be pretty when they met up, and both of them had bigger things to worry about than defending her honor. The other man looked haggard. Tired. His clothing was rumpled and ruined. The cop had mentioned that there had been a man on the scene, someone who had seen her before she had started convulsing. Jameson had thought maybe it was Sanders. Now he was realizing it must have been Ang.

How else could Angier know she was here?

It was hours before Jameson found a nurse who would take a bribe in exchange for Tate's room number. Ang was nowhere to be seen, but it was well after visiting hours, so Jameson asked to be shown to the room. The nurse chattered away in a nervous manner, obviously a little awed by him. He ignored her, all his focus on one thing.

Tatum.

"Is she still unconscious?" Jameson asked as they stood in front of the room door.

"Oh no, she regained consciousness earlier today. The pain meds put her to sleep a little while ago. Would you like me to wake her?" the nurse asked, and then pushed her way inside the room.

"No. No, that won't be necessary."

Jameson stayed standing in the doorway while the nurse fussed around the room. Only one small, fluorescent light was on behind the bed. The rest of the room was dark. There was a curtain separating Tate's bed from the neighboring bed. He frowned. That wouldn't do. She needed a private room.

"I didn't get to talk to her myself, and I shouldn't be saying this, but the doctors said she's going to be just fine," the nurse assured him, all the while checking different machines that flanked the bed. Jameson cleared his throat, but still didn't enter the room. Something about that doorway. He felt like he was walking through the gates of Hell.

Abandon all hope, ye who enter here ...

"I thought she was in here because ... because she ingested some xanax. What does she need pain medication for?" Jameson asked, his eyes skimming over the foot of the bed. He still couldn't look directly at it.

Be a man, for god's sake. When has anything ever scared you? Go in there.

"They had to pump her stomach. It can be quite a painful procedure, and from what I understand, they had a problem getting the tube down her throat. Nothing permanent," again, the nurse's voice was comforting and reassuring. Jameson had an epiphany.

She thinks I'm a concerned boyfriend. How cute.

"So she won't wake up, if I sit next to her, or touch her?" Jameson asked. The nurse finally glanced at him, and then did a double take, obviously surprised that he hadn't even entered the room.

"I doubt it. I mean, if you don't want to disturb her, I wouldn't start a conga line or anything, but just sitting and holding her hand

17

should be fine," she told him. He nodded.

"Thank you. You can leave."

"Would you like me to bring you —,"

"*No*. Just leave."

He didn't enter the room till after the nurse had left. He was slow in making his way to the foot of the bed, his footsteps soft in the quiet room. Jameson stood there for a while, staring at her feet. Then he slowly lifted his eyes, following her form under the blankets. A form he had gotten to know very well. A form that he felt belonged to him, something he had molded, *created*, with his own two hands.

Tatum.

She was ghastly pale. Jameson hadn't gotten a very good look at her the night before, and he hadn't seen her for a month before that, so it was very possible that she had lost her tan in the onset of fall.

Still. This wasn't a normal pale. She almost looked gray. Her lips were a neutral shade, blending into her face, and they were pressed tightly together. Her eyelids were twitching, and he wondered what she was dreaming about; wondered if it was a nightmare he had created. She had IVs in both arms and a hospital gown was visible, peeking out from under her blankets.

She looked small. Vulnerable. *Damaged*. Jameson tried to remember how angry he'd been at her, how mad he'd been when he'd first seen those pictures of her with the baseball player. He couldn't seem to recall it, though; all the anger was gone. All the jealousy, all the meanness. Tatum could be stupid sometimes, he wouldn't deny that, but Jameson was the goddamn devil.

And that was much, much worse.

He pulled up a chair and sat next to her, studying her face. He didn't like to say it to her, because he wasn't that sort of man, but Tate was a very beautiful girl. Even without makeup, she was still stunning. Seven years ago, she had occupied his fantasies. Now all this time later, she occupied his mind.

His heart.

I didn't want to like this woman.

He reached out and gently grabbed her hand, pulled it towards himself. She twitched once and Jameson held still, but when it was obvious that she wasn't going to wake up, he brought her hand closer. Ran his finger tips across her palm. She had long, delicate fingers. Almost graceful. The thought almost made him laugh – graceful wasn't normally a word he would have used to describe Tate.

"I'm so sorry, baby girl," he whispered, before bringing the back of her hand to his lips and kissing it.

"I never thought I'd hear you say those words."

Jameson chuckled to himself and looked up. Of course. Sanders was standing in the doorway. His hair was immaculately done, his suit looked freshly pressed; though if Jameson had to guess, he would say it was the same suit Sanders had been wearing since yesterday.

"How long have you known she was here?" Jameson asked in a soft voice, lowering her hand to the bed and lacing their fingers together.

"Since right after she was admitted. I heard about the Bentley and the pool on my police scanner, then I called Mr. Hollingsworth," Sanders explained, making his way into the room.

"Did you really?"

"Yes. He wasn't very nice at first. He told me to tell you that you can rot in hell. After I said I was no longer affiliated with you, he told me that she was here. I have been here ever since," Sanders replied. Jameson nodded.

"Will you tell me what all happened?"

"Will you actually listen?"

"Just this once, I think I will."

Jameson continued on as if nothing was wrong. He went to work like normal – no one even asked a single question when Dunn's name was taken off the building, and Jameson didn't respond to any questions about Tatum or Sanders. He went to work at eight in the morning, and was out of the building by six o'clock sharp, every evening. He was nothing if not meticulous.

But his nights he dedicated to her. Tate was kept in the hospital for observation. He would turn up around midnight, meet with Sanders in the cafeteria to get some coffee and discuss how she was, and then the two men would head up to her room, where they would sit in silence. Sanders would read. Jameson would work a little. Stare at her a lot. Think about her constantly. Think about what he was doing there, what it all meant.

This is not a game. She is so much more than a game. Maybe she always was ...

When she was moved to a psychiatric wing, it cost him a lot more money to get in to see her, and then even more to find out *why* she had been moved. They thought she had tried to kill herself and wanted to hold her pending a psych evaluation.

At least she's in a private room now.

Jameson wasn't sure who was more upset, Sanders, or himself. But Jameson wasn't there during the days, when the doctors were making their rounds. Sanders had to be angry in his place, and Sanders had never done angry very well. If Jameson had been there, she wouldn't have been moved. Not that he blamed Sanders – the younger man was sick with worry over Tatum, he didn't need accusations and anger.

All those nights she and Sanders had spent together, all those afternoons, Jameson had always assumed it was just Tate babbling on about anything that popped into her head. She was a smart girl and had a lot to talk about, maybe Sanders had been her sounding board. Jameson didn't know, and at the time, he hadn't cared.

It turned out they had been sharing their souls. Sanders knew every single one of Tate's dirty secrets, knew every vile thought she had about herself, or anyone else. Knew just about every single moment she and Jameson had ever shared. And Sanders was nothing if not fair, so he claimed he had told Tate everything. All about how he and Jameson had met, his life in England before Jameson, and even his time in Belarus.

Jameson didn't know what to think. Tate hadn't shared all her secrets with him, and he'd never pried into Sanders' past. Two of the most important people in his life, and Jameson was suddenly painfully aware of the fact that he didn't know much about either of them. It had never bothered him before; or at least, that's what he had told himself.

Now it bothered him a lot.

So, of course, Sanders knew everything that had happened. Tate had told him. About how she and Nick really were *just friends*. She hadn't so much as kissed him. How she had waited all month for Jameson, had looked forward to him coming home. How betrayed she had felt by Sanders, when she found out Jameson had brought his ex girlfriend home. How *hurt* she was by Jameson. It hadn't been a game to her anymore. She had *genuinely* cared about him. Had been perilously close to falling in love with him.

Well, I certainly solved that little problem.

She had gotten drunk to deal with the party. She had taken the xanax to numb the hurt. She had been completely wasted when Dunn offered to sleep with her. She admitted to saying yes, but he had knocked her into the mirror and then held her down. She had regretted it before it had even started. Of all the things that happened that night, Tate said it was the thing she wished she could take back the most. Jameson paying her off and kicking her out; drunk driving twenty miles into town; floating in a pool high on xanax; well, that had all just been icing on the cake.

I should have killed him. Killed him, kicked everyone out, and just gone to bed with her.

Sanders had reported the Bentley stolen in hopes of finding her, maybe stopping her, before she could crash or something. He had a police scanner in his room, and it wasn't long before he heard a response to a 9-1-1 call where the cop mentioned a Bentley. Then Ang's name was put through for a background check. Bingo.

Tate couldn't say why she went to the pool, because she couldn't remember. Almost everything after she'd gotten in the car was a blank. She hadn't tried to drown herself. When Ang had found her, she'd been floating, holding onto her bottle of Jack Daniel's, barely clinging to consciousness. But not suicidal, she insisted. She had never once said anything about wanting to die, to anyone. She swore up and down that she hadn't tried to kill herself.

Jameson didn't need convincing. Tatum O'Shea, the woman he knew, would never give up so easily. That would be the worst kind of cheating, and she wasn't a cheater. Besides, their game wasn't over yet, he had more hands to play. She wouldn't ever check out like that. She was too strong. And she certainly couldn't leave him alone in the world.

Not until he said so.

"So when are you coming home?" Jameson asked as he strode down a hospital hallway, almost a week later.

"I am not going to work for you," Sanders replied, walking next to him. Jameson snorted.

"I didn't ask when you were coming back to work. I asked when you were *coming home*," he stressed as they got on an elevator. Sanders looked uncomfortable.

"I didn't have any plans to come home," he replied.

"You're going to live at that hotel forever?" Jameson asked. Sanders glanced at him. "Oh, yes. I've known every move you've made since you left. Who do you think pays those credit card bills, hmmm?"

"I could get another job after —,"

"Don't be fucking stupid. Stay in the hotel, come home, I don't care. I just need to know one thing," Jameson started as the elevator doors slid open, revealing their floor.

"And what is that, sir?" Sanders asked. Jameson got out onto the floor, then turned back to stare at Sanders. It was strange, to have been in someone's life for so long, but to not know them as well as someone who had only been there for a couple months. Jameson didn't like the feeling.

"Are we okay?" he asked in a straight forward voice. Sanders blinked a couple times, the question clearly making him even more uncomfortable.

"I'm not sure. You ... you disappointed me, sir," he answered. Jameson nodded.

"I know. I should have listened to you."

"But you didn't. I have only ever tried to steer you right."

"I know. And I'm *very* sorry."

Sanders looked completely shocked, and Jameson felt it would be best to catch the man off guard while he had the chance. He grabbed Sanders by the arm and yanked him forward, into a hug. It was awkward for a moment, then Sanders relaxed. Leaned into him. Until Tatum, Jameson had been the only person to ever really hug Sanders. For two very un-affectionate men, sometimes it was very natural between them. Jameson was the closest thing Sanders had to a father.

Sometimes, Jameson lost sight of that.

"I appreciate that, sir," Sanders mumbled against his chest. Jameson laughed.

"Good. Now. Do you think *she'll* accept my apology?" he asked. Sanders pulled away, made a production of straightening out his suit.

"Honestly? No. She doesn't want anything to do with you," Sanders replied.

"We'll see about that; she doesn't have much of an option, not while she's stuck in here," Jameson laughed. Sanders shook his head.

"She's getting released tomorrow."

"*What?*"

"Tomorrow. She's been declared mentally stable and her throat doesn't hurt anymore. They have no reason to keep her anymore. She wants to go home," Sanders explained.

Home? But I haven't cleaned up the library yet ...

"But I thought I —,"

"If you are going to apologize, I suggest you do it tonight," Sanders interrupted, and then he reached out and hit a button, causing the elevator doors to slide shut.

Jameson was left at a loss. Of course, he'd known this day would come, but he'd thought he would have just a little bit more time.

Jameson Kane *always* had more time.

As he walked to her room, he prepped himself with the realization that she probably knew he was coming, was maybe even waiting. Sanders didn't pull any punches for Jameson, but there was no doubt he would have prepared Tatum. Jameson had thought his little midnight visits were a secret, but now he doubted it. She had probably known the whole time.

"May I come in?" he asked, once he got to the doorway.

Tate was laying flat on her bed, but he could tell she was awake. She took a deep breath, let it out as a sigh. He held very still, waiting for her voice. It felt like it had been a lot longer than a week since he had last heard it.

Probably because I never really listened.

"You never asked permission any of the other times, so what's stopping you now?"

Jameson strode into the room and went to his chair, which was pulled up to the left side of her bed. He took off his jacket and draped it over the back, before sitting down. She still hadn't turned to look at him. He cleared his throat.

"Do you want to do this now?" Jameson asked. She nodded her head.

"Like a band aid, just rip it off," she replied.

"*I'm sorry.*"

Tate looked shocked. She glanced at him, and then her hand fumbled around on the mattress, looking for the bed controller. She found it and pushed a button until she was sitting almost upright. She had some color back in her face, though she was still much paler than she had been a month ago. It made her dark eyes and hair stand out. He couldn't stop staring at her.

Have I ever just looked at her?

"For what?" she asked. He wasn't quite sure how to answer her, wasn't sure if there were enough words, even. If there would be enough time, enough space, enough air, to express just how sorry he was to her.

"For … everything," he finally answered. She managed a laugh.

"Sounds like a cop out. You don't have to apologize just to make me feel better. I'm okay, I don't —," she started, but his anger at himself boiled over and spilled onto her.

"I'm sorry I hurt you," Jameson snapped. "I'm sorry I was too stupid and pigheaded to just call you. I'm sorry I didn't stop you from leaving. I am *really* sorry I tried to give you that money, and I am *very* sorry I didn't go after you that night, but most of all, *I'm sorry I didn't kill Dunn.*"

"Thank you. That means a lot," she told him, but her voice was flat. He narrowed his eyes.

"You don't believe me."

He said it as a statement, not a question. Tate shrugged.

"I don't know. I'm trying not to think about it," she replied.

"I never stop thinking about it. Thinking that maybe I —,"

"Why are you here, Jameson? You kicked me out. You brought her home to embarrass me – mission accomplished, by the way. I quite literally almost died from embarrassment," she chuckled. His heart skipped a beat.

Dead? Never. You can't leave me.

"*Not funny,*" Jameson growled. "I was so upset with you. I thought you had gone back on your word. I saw those pictures of you, with that guy, and I just got so angry. *So stupid.* Jesus, what a fucking night. I even impressed myself with how much of a bastard I was."

He groaned and leaned forward, putting his face in his hands. He wasn't the kind of man who could be easily intimidated, but suddenly the thought of meeting her gaze made him feel nervous. Sick. Made him feel *ashamed.*

Because I'm not worthy of her.

"Is this a game?" Tate whispered. Jameson shook his head.

"No, baby girl. No games," he whispered back.

"What are we, if we don't have games?"

"*Something else.*"

"I hate you," she sobbed, and Jameson lifted his head. She was back to staring at the ceiling, but now tears were streaming down her face. He frowned.

"I want you to know that I —,"

"*I fucking hate you!* What about that statement don't you get!?" she was suddenly screaming at him. He sat back, a little stunned.

"I *am* getting it, loud and clear. I just think —,"

"No! *No!* You don't get to think! I almost fucking died, Jameson! And I'm not blaming that on you, but you sure didn't fucking help! So I don't give a flying *FUCK* about what you think! I just want you to get out," she sobbed, pressing her hands to her eyes. He stood up, but he had no intention of leaving. He moved closer to her bed, leaned over her.

"You and I have unfinished business, baby girl," he told her softly.

She swung her arm in a wide arc. For someone who had "*almost died*", she certainly had a lot of strength. She walloped him right in the ear. She let out a shriek and continued swinging her arms. Jameson didn't move away, just ducked his head and struggled to hold onto her arms. Her whole body thrashed around on the bed, and it took him a few moments to pin her wrists to the mattress.

"You and I *are* finished business, *Kane*," Tate hissed, refusing to meet his eyes.

He remembered the night they had fought in his kitchen. When she had broken all the dishes and he'd held the scissors to her throat. The look in her eye that night was something he had never wanted to see again; had *hoped* to never see again.

Now, the look was back, only worse. Much, much worse.

I should've been the one in that pool.

"You and I will *never* be finished, Tate. Haven't you figured that out yet?"

"*Get out.*"

"No. Not until you tell me what I can do, what you want me to do, to fix this," he replied, squeezing her wrists. She had to tell him, he had to know. Jameson Kane could fix anything, solve any problem – she just had to tell him how. *He had to make this right somehow.* She started to laugh and it turned into sobs.

"You wanna know what I want? What I *really* want? I want you to leave me alone. I want you to go away. I want to have never met you. *I wish* I had never met you. I wish that I hadn't catered that stupid party, and I wish I had never gone to your apartment that night. I want you to *not exist* anymore. I want you to just *go away,*" Tate cried, trying to pull her wrists free.

Not exist? But I made her. She's mine. You can't exist if I don't, stupid girl.

"Alright, alright," Jameson said in a soft voice, pulling away when she seemed on the verge of hyperventilating. He had never seen her so upset. "If that's what you really want, I'll go."

She continued sobbing while he grabbed his jacket off the back of the chair. She pressed the heels of her hands into her eyes, trying to stop the flood gates that had opened. It hurt his heart to see her that way. Hurt his pitch black soul. He realized she was saying something, so he walked back up to the bed while he slipped back into his coat.

"*Just go, just go, just go, just go,*" Tate was whispering, over and over again. Jameson sighed and brushed the hair away from her face, before leaning down and kissing her on the forehead. She didn't move, didn't say anything. Just cried. He turned away and forced himself not to look back. If he looked back, he would be lost forever, and if he was lost, he certainly wouldn't be able to find her again.

And Tatum most definitely needed finding.

"See you around, baby girl," he called out as he strode towards the door.

"No, you won't," she said after him.

History really does repeat itself.

He couldn't resist a laugh. He was, after all, Satan.

"*I will if I want to.*"

1

"*WHAT ARE YOU DOING?*"

Tate glanced over her shoulder, trying to find who owned the voice that was hissing at her. Her best friend, Angier, stepped out of the shadows, joining her at the edge of the balcony. She sighed and went back to looking out over the city.

"I was trying to escape," she replied. He glared down at her.

"I meant, what the fuck is this? I thought you said you weren't going to do this anymore."

"*You* said I wasn't going to do it anymore. I never said anything."

Tate took a long drag on her cigarette and blew the smoke up at him. Ang was much taller than her, almost by a foot, and the smoke mostly dissipated before it reached him. He glared some more and waved his hand around.

"Of all the things I've ever seen you do, this is by far the most disgusting," he told her. Tate laughed.

"Wow. Considering all the things you've seen me do, that's quite a statement," she snickered. He finally smiled at her.

"Exactly."

Ever since her midnight swim/xanax-whiskey-cocktail, Tate's relationship with Ang had been strained. She was more grateful than she would ever be able to express, and she was so horrifically embarrassed by the whole episode, she could barely look him in the eye. Ang had seen her at her worst, at her absolute lowest – so low, she hadn't seen a way up again. So bad, she couldn't even remember it.

However, Ang *could* remember it. In vivid, technicolor, high-definition recall. After Tate had gotten out of the hospital, she had stayed with him for a couple of nights, and it was hard to say who had worse nightmares, her or him. She had scarred him a little, and she would never be able to forgive herself for that.

Even knowing all that, though, knowing everything Ang had done for her, and everything she had done *to* him, didn't stop her from being annoyed with him. It compounded her guilt, but it was the truth. She couldn't deny it. Tate had never been good at lying to herself.

Ang mothered. He hovered. He watched her with a wariness in his eyes, like he was expecting her to leap off a ledge at any moment. She lived with him for a week, but when she caught him hiding the knives, she moved back out. She wasn't suicidal, and he claimed that he knew she wasn't suicidal – but his actions said otherwise. She moved back in to her old apartment, squeezing in with her sister, Ellie, and her old roommate, Rusty.

The fighting started not long afterwards. They would argue over everything. Over nothing. Ang would show up unannounced, and Tate would walk into her bedroom to find him rifling through her stuff. They'd be out at dinner, and he would try to set her up with random guys. She'd be laying in bed, and he would show up at one in the morning to drag her to a party.

SEPARATION

Not cool.

Ang just couldn't understand that she wasn't the same old Tatum. Part of that girl had stayed in that pool. Stayed in that house in Weston. She didn't want to go to parties, and she didn't want to hook up with random guys, but most of all, she didn't want her best friend staring at her like she was a nut job.

She moved out of her apartment, stopped answering her phone for a while. Then Ang seemed to return the favor – Tate was hardly ever able to get a hold of him, and even when she could, he was rushing her off the phone, or giving her all sorts of reasons for why he couldn't hang out with her. The stress would have been enough to drive her to drink, but she hadn't touched alcohol since that night in October.

So she took up smoking.

Jameson would kill me for doing something like this.

Her hospital stay hadn't been very enjoyable, either. Ang had been two steps away from having a nervous breakdown. Her sister wasn't any better – a pregnant woman in the process of leaving her abusive soon-to-be-ex-husband; Ellie had enough problems without having to deal with her estranged-sister's alleged suicide attempt.

Sanders had visited every single day, but he was always quiet and taciturn. Tate's little episode had really upset him. And then the day when she had found out that *he* had been visiting her. A night nurse, going off duty in the wee hours of the morning, had let it slip.

"You're very lucky to have such a handsome man visiting you all the time."

"Sanders? Yeah, I know."

"Well, yes, he's good looking, too, but I meant the other one."

"Ang?"

"No, the one who comes at night."

"At night!?"

31

"Yes. The man with those blue eyes. I swear, it's like he's looking straight through me."

Pretty accurate description. Tate had almost had a panic attack. She hadn't seen Jameson, or heard from him, at all – he had asked her to leave, she had gone. She figured that had been the end of it. He didn't care about her. In fact, it was now painfully obvious that he had *never* cared about her.

You're such a stupid girl – only you would fall for the devil. Only you would be stupid enough to think he'd fall for you, as well.

Tate hadn't wanted to talk to him. The whole situation made her feel ill. Made her feel like passing out. Jameson. Petrushka. A pool. *Everything.* She had never been entirely normal, but Jameson had driven her straight to the center of crazy-town and dropped her ass off. How could a human being do that? Punish someone, just for liking him? Talking dirty to her in bed was one thing; hurting her soul was quite another. As slutty and masochistic as she was, even Tate had her limits.

She knew she had to claw her way back to some semblance of normal, so she gathered as much courage as she could – which wasn't much – and waited up for him on her last night in the hospital. It hadn't gone well. She hadn't been able to handle the strange, sad look in his eyes. He wasn't allowed to be sad, not when he was part of the problem. Tate may have driven herself straight into that pool, but Jameson had driven Petrushka between them. *He did not get to be sad.* She pretty much just broke down in the middle of it all and screamed at him to leave her alone. To get out of her life. To stop existing.

And for the first time ever, Jameson had respected her wishes.

"I will if I want to."

It was the same old story, all these years later. Only much, much darker. The first time Jameson had said those words to her, she had secretly been delighted at the idea that he would want to see her again. This time around, not so much. It was a whole bevy of emotions, tangled together. He was bad. He was wrong. He was the devil. *She never wanted to see him again.*

And yet it was a month before Tate stopped hovering over her phone, hoping for his call.

It was so fucked up. Jameson had done something that was so horrible, she still couldn't even wrap her brain around it. Still didn't really understand it, understand *why*. And Tate knew, *she knew*, if he could do it once, he could do it again. Most likely *would* do it again. Had probably *enjoyed* doing it. Had probably laughed all the way back to his bedroom about it, right along side his gorgeous, fabulous, Ukrainian-Danish, supermodel, sex slave, homewrecker-slut-whore-mother-fucker-cunt-shit-fuck. *Fuck.*

What is wrong with me!?

One good thing did come out of her hospital stay, though. Tate was propped up in her bed one day, trying to gather the courage to rip out her IV so she could make an escape, when a nurse walked into her room. The lady fussed around her, put extra medical tape around the needle and smacked it down hard before standing back by the door.

"You have a very special visitor today," she had said.

"Who is it?"

"Only my favorite athlete! If you don't mind, I would love an autograph before he leaves. Think you could help me with that?" the nurse had babbled.

Tate had stared at her in shock, her mouth hanging open. The nurse finally just walked away, and two seconds later, Nick Castille walked into the room. The first baseman for the Boston Red Sox. The guy she had slept with in her bar, after having only known him for two hours. Sure, they had become friends before her overdose, gone to dinner a bunch, the movies once or twice, but really, nothing more than that.

Nick had gone looking for Tate at her apartment, and Ellie had told him she was in the hospital, though not why. Tate didn't want him to have anymore delusions about her being a nice, normal girl, so she had laid it all on him. Told him about Jameson, how they had "met", how they had gotten reacquainted. Told Nick about the night she had spent with him, how she had been upset about Petrushka, how she had used him. Told him about the party – though she did leave out the parts with Dunn and Jameson paying her off. Told Nick about the crazy drive in to town, the xanax, and the pool. She had wanted to scare him off.

It didn't work. Tate may have been a succubus, but Nick truly was a nice, normal guy. He didn't abandon his friends, and he considered Tatum to be a pretty good friend.

What is wrong with him?

When Tate finally realized she would have to move because she couldn't stand living somewhere Ang had complete access to, Nick offered for her to live with him. She made it very clear that she was in no way interested in a relationship; romantic, sexual, or otherwise. Nick assured her that his intentions were noble and good, and that it was just a place for her to stay, as long as she liked.

He wasn't home much during the weekdays. It was the off season and he spent most of his time at a cabin on Lake Ontario. But during the weekends he always came down to Boston, first thing in the morning on Saturdays. Tatum couldn't cook at all, but he taught her how to make French toast and omelets. Nick was a good old country boy, from Iowa. His momma had raised him right. He took Tate out to dinners, stayed in and watched movies with her, and most importantly, he never, ever, once asked her how she was doing. He never looked at her like she was crazy.

An invaluable gift to Tate, at that point in her life.

"You're doing it again."

"Huh?" Tate snapped to attention. Ang was leaning close to her, looking into her face.

"That thing, where you stare off into space. Are you thinking about *him* again?" he demanded. She frowned.

"No."

"Tate. We talked about this," Ang said, his voice full of warning.

"Ang. Stop. You're not my dad," she warned him right back.

"But he's the one who —,"

She reached over and singed his hand with her cigarette. Ang hissed and yanked his arm back, jumping out of her reach. She laughed and flicked the cigarette over the ledge before wiping her hands down the front of her skirt.

"I wasn't thinking about him. Let's have a good night, just this once," she pleaded, before grabbing his hand and leading him inside.

"I can't stand all these yuppies," Ang whispered under his breath as they made their way through a crush of people. Tate elbowed him.

"They're not yuppies," she mumbled back.

"They all have more money than I'll ever have. In my opinion, that makes them yuppies."

"Snob."

"Why did you tell me to come to this thing?" he complained, pulling at the tie he was wearing. She stepped in front of him and batted his hands away.

"I haven't seen you in a couple weeks, I thought it would be nice to hang out," she replied, adjusting the Windsor knot for him.

"What, so you can show off all your *new friends?*" Ang said, his tone snide. Tate glared at him and yanked the knot up high. He made a choking sound.

"*Shut up.*"

Nick had invited her to a party, some shindig that was being thrown for the whole team, in a fancy hotel suite. She hadn't really wanted to go, but even Nick was beginning to worry about her spending so much time at home. Tate had originally asked Sanders to go with her, but he didn't like parties. Or people. Or places. So she had figured what the hell, why not try to mend fences with Ang?

It wasn't going too hot.

"I gotta go soon anyway," he told her as they made their way to a table full of food. She looked up at him.

"Where? I told you this thing would be going for a while," Tate reminded him, a little surprised. Ang shrugged.

"I know, but I had other plans. Sorry, kitty cat," he replied, rubbing his hand up and down her back.

She frowned, but didn't argue. The same thing had happened the last couple times they had made an effort to hang out. Ang always had "other plans"; something he else *had* to do. It was frustrating. Hard to mend a friendship when one person was depressed, and the other was checked out all the time.

"Hey! I was looking everywhere for you!"

Tate felt a strong arm wrap around her shoulders, then she was pulled sideways into a solid chest. She smiled and looked up at Nick. There were many times over the last six weeks that she had argued with herself about him. Told herself that she should like him. Or at least fake it until it happened for real. He was really good looking, semi-famous, wealthy, nicer than any normal person should be, and it also didn't hurt that she knew he wasn't bad in bed, either. Maybe not quite her tastes, but she was sure she could learn to live with it.

But Tate hadn't been able to talk herself into it. She knew she was a horrible liar, and she didn't want to do that Nick, use him like that; at least, not yet. Maybe after a couple more weeks of feeling like she wanted to claw her skin off, she would be able to do it. She was working on hardening herself.

"She's been with me," Ang replied around a mouth full of hors d'oeuvres, not bothering to look at Nick. He didn't like the other man, though Tate couldn't figure out why. Nick was like a kitten, only in sexy-human-man form. Who wouldn't love him?

Besides her, that is.

"I'm glad you guys came. Tate said she didn't want a birthday party, so I thought maybe this could be like a substitute," Nick laughed. Tate managed a smile. Her birthday was the next day. That meant Christmas was three weeks away. More depression.

"Yeah, *awesome* birthday party. Tate just loves high rises and yuppies," Ang grunted. Tate scowled and kicked him in the ankle.

"*Ang*," she hissed. Nick glanced down at her.

"It's alright. I know it's not really your guys' scene. It's not really mine, either. I grew up in a town of less than 2,000 people – I still don't know how to put on a tie right," he chuckled. She smiled up at him.

"Good for you. I gotta go. Tate, walk me out," Ang said, shoving a last sausage roll in his mouth before grabbing her hand and dragging her away from Nick.

"*Rude, much!?* And you said soon! I didn't realize you meant *right now!*" Tate snapped as she was pulled out the front door.

"I can't be around these people, that guy," Ang replied, letting go of her hand once they were in the hallway.

"What's with you and him? He is one of the nicest people I've ever met, what could you possibly not like about him?" Tate demanded. Ang frowned and stared down the hallway.

"It's not him, he's fine. I mean, kind of boring, but yeah, nice. I just ..." his voice trailed off. Tate crossed her arms. She was fed up.

"Just *what*, Ang? We never see each other anymore, and the few times we do, you're always rushing off somewhere – but not before being a complete dick. Is it me? Just say it. I'll stop calling. Is it him? Cause that's not —," she started, but suddenly Ang stomped right up to her. Got in her personal space, forced her to back up into a wall. She pressed herself flat, staring up at him. He looked *mad*.

"It *is* you. It's the way you dress now," he gestured to the fancy skirt and blouse she was wearing. "It's this party, it's those people, it's the way you act – who the fuck is this person!? You didn't die in that fucking pool, Tate, but you sure fucking act like it. You don't have to become someone else!"

Oh, Ang. I became someone else the moment I walked into Satan's house.

"Look, I'm sorry I'm not that person anymore. I'm sorry that I can't go back. Don't you think I wish I could!? I wish I could just close my eyes and the last four months wouldn't have happened. I wish I could go back in time, back to when I first met you, and I could've told you '*Yes, I'll shoot that porno with you, why, I love fa-cials!*', and then you and I could be married-millionaire-porn-stars with a hundred babies, and I would've never met him again! But I can't go back, *so get the fuck over it!*" Tate screamed at him.

They stared at each other for a second, breathing hard. Then Ang burst out laughing. Tate was right behind him, laughing so hard she fell into him, pressing her face into his chest. His arms wrapped around her, pulling her into a full body hug. It had been a long time. She laughed till tears were running down her face and she dug her fingers into his back.

"God, I knew it. I knew you secretly loved getting facials," he snickered in her ear. She snorted and pulled away a little.

"Shut up, that shit's impossible to get out of your hair," she told him, wiping at her nose.

"Don't I know it."

She laughed again and looked up at Ang. Really looked at him.

Took in his gray eyes and wild hair. She really did wish she could go back, to when things were easy between them. When she wouldn't think twice about curling herself around him and getting lost in his skin, in his touch. But it wasn't that way anymore. Tate hadn't had sex, *real sex*, since her little accident.

Since Jameson.

"I love you, Ang. Quite possibly more than I love myself," she laughed, her eyes watering up. He sighed, pushing her hair off of her shoulders and then putting his hands on the back of her neck.

"I know, sweetie pea. I love you, too. And I know I give you a hard time, and I know things can't be the same, I just … I don't want you to give up. I can see it in your eyes. He's an awesome dude, I know, but I can practically feel you trying to talk yourself into, like, marrying him, or something. Nick's not the right guy for you. *Don't settle,*" Ang urged her. She sniffled.

"I'm not settling. I'm just …" she mumbled, staring at his chest.

"And you don't need *Satan,*" he whispered. She shuddered.

"I *definitely* know that. Look, I'll get out of my funk. I will. And I promise, I won't settle, or anything else. When I decide to jump back into the sea of men, you will be the first boat I choose to ride," Tate assured him. Ang laughed and stepped away from her.

"Baby, maybe this boat has already sailed," he teased.

Tate started to laugh, but then something clicked. Her eyes got wide. Ang was moody. He was never around. He always had to leave early. He was constantly checking his phone. Oh god. The unthinkable had happened. She gasped.

"Oh my god. Ang. Do you have a girlfriend?" she asked. His laughter died instantly.

"What? Why would you say that? I just —," he started, but she knew him too well. Even after all their problems, and everything they'd been through, Tate still knew him. Ang was a worse liar than she was, he got all twitchy and nervous.

"You do! You have a girlfriend! Holy shit! Have you *ever* had a girlfriend!?" she exclaimed. He glared at her.

"Of course I have, have you looked at me!?" he snapped back. She laughed and clapped her hands.

"What is she like? Does she come to your movie sets? God, did you meet her on set!? This is amazing! Who is it!?" Tate demanded. He rolled his eyes and started to walk backwards down the hall.

"I'm not talking about this right now. Someday, we'll get over our weird shit, and you'll throw yourself at me – *naked* – in some sad, desperate, attempt to get back in my good graces, and maybe then I'll tell you. But not now," Ang said, backing into the elevator doors. Without looking, he reached out and hit the down button.

"But I'm dying, Angie-wangy! Please!" she begged. He laughed.

"Beg harder!" he yelled.

"*Pleeeeeeease!*"

He kept laughing as the elevator doors opened. He saluted her, then disappeared.

And then she was alone. Tate glanced at the door to the suite, but she didn't want to go back to the party. She pressed her back to the wall and slid to the floor. Ang's words sat heavy in her brain. *Don't settle.* What was she supposed to do? Jameson had wrecked her a little bit. Wrecked her *a lot*. Ang didn't feel familiar to her anymore, and even if he had, now he had a new playmate. Nick was one of the only people she felt comfortable around anymore. Sure, she didn't feel like herself, but she couldn't win 'em all. Who else was left?

As if to answer all her questions, her phone rang. Tate dug it out of the waist of her skirt and smiled when saw Sanders was calling. When she had practically been living in the same house as him, Sanders had never called her – back then, he wouldn't even use her first name, she was always "*Ms. O'Shea*" or "*ma'am*". Now he called at least once every other day, like clock work. If she felt comfortable when she was around Nick, than she felt like she was *home* when she was around Sanders.

"I miss you," she breathed into the phone, in a Marilyn Monroe-style voice. She snickered when he cleared his throat.

"I saw you yesterday," his clipped voice responded. Tate laughed.

"Sandy, I miss you whenever you're not next to me. How are you?" she asked, stretching her legs out and crossing her ankles.

"I am well. And you?" he responded. So prim and proper.

"Lonely without you. When are you going to let me move in with you?" she demanded. He cleared his throat again.

Tate had been trying for weeks to get him to let her move into his hotel suite. Sanders lived in a large, two bedroom hotel suite, there would be plenty of room for her, and they got along ridiculously well. But he kept resisting, and Tate couldn't figure out why. Money couldn't be the issue – not only would Sanders give her the shirt off his back, but her sister had given her a hefty chunk of change as a sort of "get well" present. Ellie had made out very well in her divorce. Tate hadn't gone back to work since she'd gotten out of the hospital.

"It's your birthday tomorrow," Sanders stated. Almost like she might have forgotten.

"Yes, I know."

"I was wondering if you'd like to have dinner with me," he asked. Tate laughed again.

"Sandy, you don't even need to ask. What should I wear?" she asked back.

Tate had learned very quickly that the way a person looked was very important to Sanders. It wouldn't necessarily stop him from going somewhere, but she knew it made him a lot more comfortable if she looked like she matched him. Which meant it always had to be something *nice*.

"A nice dress, but no tall heels," he informed her.

"Ooohhh, there's that vanity," she snickered into the phone. It bothered him when she wore heels that made her taller than him.

"I don't know what you're talking about, I'll pick you up at seven." Then he hung up the phone. Sanders never said goodbye at the end of his phone calls, just cut the line. It didn't really bother her, but it did remind her very much of someone else. She held the phone cradled in her hands, staring down at the screen.

What's wrong with me? How can I miss someone who only wanted to hurt me?

"Are you okay?"

She jerked her head up to find Nick standing over her.

"Yeah, just said goodbye to Ang. Sorry about him – he's all flustered because he has a new girlfriend," Tate said quickly, focusing on Nick's smile, on his pretty white teeth. Trying to banish someone's fangs from her mind. Nick squatted down next to her.

"God help the woman," he laughed.

"I know. How long are we gonna be here?" she asked. He glanced back at the door.

"It's getting kind of rowdy in there. Wanna take off?" he replied, holding a hand out to help her up.

I should like this man. I really, really should.

"Please, god, yes," Tate groaned, letting him pull her to her feet.

They went back inside to find jackets, but they were both waylaid. Nick was congratulated on having such a nice girlfriend, then there had to be a whole explanation about how she wasn't his girlfriend. Awkward. She had been around him long enough to have met most of his teammates, but they still didn't seem to get it. Either they assumed the two of them were sleeping together anyway, or they tried to hit on her.

Ew.

They collected their belongings and headed back into the hallway. As they waited for the elevator, she looked at her reflection. Ang didn't like the way she dressed. Most of Tate's clothing was in the house in Weston, and she wasn't about to go get them back. So while she was in the hospital, she had asked her sister to go shopping for her. They were all nice clothes but … they were kind of boring. No more leather leggings or see-through tank tops or booty shorts for Tatum.

"Are you okay?" Nick asked, putting a hand on the small of her back to guide her into the elevator. She struggled not to skitter away from his touch.

"Fine, fine. Just thinking. But hey, good party, huh?" she changed the subject. He smiled at her as they started their descent.

"It was okay. Sorry I dragged you guys along," he told her. She snorted.

"No, it was a good idea. I needed to get out. I think I was becoming one with the couch. Another night and you'd have to surgically remove it from my butt," she joked. He laughed out loud as the elevator stopped, the doors sliding open again.

"You're so gross."

"Hey, I can't help it if Judge Judy —," Tate started to get off the elevator, but he grabbed her elbow, holding her in place.

"Shit. I didn't think this would happen."

She stared at him, worried about what he was gonna say next, but then she realized he wasn't even looking at her. Nick was looking past her, out the front windows of the lobby. She turned her head to follow his gaze and gasped at what she saw.

Outside the glass doors was a sea of what looked like reporters. A crowd of men and women, some video cameras, tons of digital cameras, microphones, the works. All of them were looking in the glass, into the lobby. A line of uniformed bellmen and doormen were attempting to keep them at bay. Tate's jaw hung open and she turned back to Nick.

"What the fuck is going on!?" she demanded. Nick winced.

"A teammate of mine is in some trouble. Last night, the shit hit the fan. He was using all these crazy drugs, brought some hooker to a hotel room, and his girlfriend caught him. I guess a massive fight ensued. All three were arrested. The press here in Boston is having a field day. I guess they caught wind of this party," he explained.

"Yeah, well, obviously they did. How do we get out of here?" Tate asked. He sighed.

"My car should just be on the other side of them. We'll plow through, just keep your head down and please, don't say anything," Nick asked, then started walking forward, keeping her next to him with his grip on her elbow.

"Plow through them!? Nick, there's like fifty people out there!" she snapped. He laughed.

"Not that many. And look, there's hotel security out there – they'll help us through," Nick pointed out, and at that same moment, a large guy walked in the front doors. He walked up to them and shook hands with Nick.

"I'm Barney Noughby, head of security. Very sorry about this, Mr. Castille. One of the guests at the party, I guess, called one of the papers, and now they're all here. Want me to bring your car around back?" Barney offered. Tate nodded her head yes, vigorously, but Nick just waved the suggestion away.

"We're right here, let's just get this over with," he replied.

"Alright. Don't worry about a thing, ma'am, it'll be over before you know it," Barney assured her. She held onto her purse strap and nodded.

Barney nodded one more time, then yanked open the doors. The sound was deafening, all the reporters and paparazzi shouting Nick's name, asking questions. Did he know about his teammate's drug use? Did Nick use drugs? Did Nick use prostitutes? Who was the woman he was with? Did *she* use drugs? Was *she* a prostitute?

Tate had to resist the urge to punch one reporter in the throat. Barney stuck by her side for the most part, and she kept her face pointed at the ground. But then a paparazzi grabbed Nick's suit jacket, yanked him into the mob of people. A scuffle started, Nick trying to pull away, more people grabbing at him. Barney leapt into the fray, pulling Nick back and shoving at the reporters. Tate fell a few steps behind, and a reporter grabbed her.

"Miss! Miss! Were you and Nick at the party last night!?" a man screamed in her face.

Flashes were going off all around her and she felt claustrophobic. Tate tried to push away, but someone had a tight grip on her coat. She yanked away again, bumped into someone behind her, then got shoved forward. She lost her footing and started to fall forward, shrieking as she went.

Well, this isn't exactly how I wanted to end this night – flat on my face in front of a million reporters.

But she didn't land on her face. There was a loud shout, commotion around her, and someone grabbed her arm. Yanked her upright. Tate stumbled forward and was pressed flat against a very solid chest. A strong arm wrapped around her shoulders. Tate looked up to see it was Nick who had saved her from complete embarrassment. He was holding her against him while he shouted angrily at the reporters behind them. She had never seen him look so mad.

So much for being like a kitten.

"Are you okay?" he asked, finally looking down at her. Everyone was shouting around them, but he was speaking softly to her.

"Yeah, I'm fine. Thanks for saving me," she joked.

"I should've had them bring the car around back. I'm so sorry," he told her, then brushed a hand over her hair, letting his fingers trail through the dark locks. She swallowed thickly.

Maybe falling on my face would've been better.

"Nick, we should —,"

He was kissing her then, and she turned into a statue. Tate hadn't kissed him since the one time they'd slept together, and even then, they hadn't spent much time locking lips. It had been a purely sexual thing.

But there didn't seem to be anything sexual about this kiss. The arm around her waist squeezed harder, and one of his hands moved to the back of her head, holding her tighter against him. She had acknowledged to herself that Nick had a crush on her, but she hadn't thought it was anything more than that. His kiss was now saying otherwise. All his longing, all his desire for her; she could feel it all. And more. This was a man who desperately wanted her.

Tate pressed her hands against his shoulders, but didn't know what else to do. It seemed like thousands of flashes were going off all around them. She was frozen. She didn't want to shove him away and embarrass him further, but she couldn't kiss him back. Not in the same way he was kissing her. Her heart just wasn't in it.

Poor, poor, Nick. Never could tell a succubus when he saw one.

When Nick finally pulled away, a thousand more questions were screamed out by the reporters, but he ignored them. He stared down at her for a long moment. Tate licked her lips nervously, forcing herself not to look away. He frowned, traced his thumb down the side of her cheek, then he was turning away, leading her to the car. Tate kept her head down again, shielding her face with her hand.

Why can't I lead a nice, normal life?

2

ATE WAITED OUTSIDE FOR SANDERS the following night, trying to smoke as many cigarettes as she could before he got there. Sanders hated her new habit, so she never smoked around him. But her nerves were still a little on edge.

The car ride home the night before had been awkward, to say the least. Nick apologized for kissing her, explained that he hadn't planned on it, that it had just happened. He liked Tate, *a lot*. But he understood that she was still hung up on her past. Still hung up on Jameson. He promised he wouldn't press his attentions on her.

Thinking about it gave her a headache, so she lit up another cigarette.

She glanced at her cell phone, then looked down the street. One more minute, and he'd be late. Sanders was never late. She thought about trying to call her sister while she waited. Tate figured it was probably a good time to think about moving. Her sister had moved into a much nicer place than Tate's old apartment – Tate figured she could hole up there while she looked for a job.

What the hell do I even know how to do, besides sling drinks, walk dogs, and give good head? Though that does make for one hell of a resume ...

Her phone lit up and she pressed it to her ear.

"You're late," she sang out, chucking her cigarette into a gutter.

"I am never late. I am coming around the corner, I wanted to make sure you were outside," Sanders replied.

"Yes, kind sir, I am patiently awaiting your arrival," she laughed.

Tate's laughter got caught in her throat, though, when a large, black car pulled up to the curb in front of her. She stood completely still, didn't make any move towards it. Not even when Sanders got out and came around to stand in front of her.

"Happy birthday," he said, his voice softer than normal.

"What ... what is this?" she asked, glancing between him and the car.

"I thought it was time."

It was a Bentley Flying Spur. Inky black and shiny, blending in with the city. Tate had known the make and model the minute she saw it; the same way she knew the interior was all buttery leather, and that it always, *always*, had that "new car" smell. She had been in it many, many times. She had some pretty incredible memories in that car.

And some pretty fucking awful ones.

"Time for what? What does that mean?" Tate asked, starting to panic a little. If Jameson climbed out of the car ...

"It means I finally got my car back. There were a lot of problems with getting the work done on it. My name isn't the only one on the title, I ran into some issues. Please, we'll be late for dinner," Sanders informed her, putting a hand on her back and urging her forward.

Sliding into her seat was like sliding into a panic attack. Tate had never sat in the front while Sanders was driving, only ever the back seat. *With Jameson.* And there was one time she sat behind the wheel. Almost her *last time* behind a wheel.

I hate this fucking car. It's like a goddamn hearse.

"Why didn't you just get a new one?" Tate croaked out when he got into the driver's seat.

"I didn't want a new one, I wanted mine back. Seatbelts," Sanders reminded her, then leaned across her so he could buckle her in.

"Why are you doing this?" she whispered. He glanced at her. His eyes were large, and an interesting gray-blue color combination. Like there was always a storm brewing in them.

"If I may be blunt, I am tired of pussy-footing around you. This is my car. I like my car. I want to drive my car. You do not own a car, so if you need me to take you somewhere, then it will have to be in *this* car," Sanders replied.

She was so shocked, she started laughing.

"This is going to be one hell of a birthday, isn't it?" Tate laughed. He snorted and pulled the car into traffic.

"It's just dinner. How was your party last night? I saw The Globe today," he told her.

"God, don't remind me, I've been getting a million texts about it. Rusty is already planning my wedding," she groaned, trying to sit as straight as possible so she wouldn't touch the leather any more than was necessary.

Remember the time he took the car without telling Sanders and drove you all the way to Provincetown, then when you got there, you didn't even get out, he just took off your – SHUT UP! SHUT UP, SHUT UP, SHUT UP, SHUT UP!

"Care to explain?" Sanders asked.

"It was an accident. The party was boring, and Ang and I had kind of a fight, but then a breakthrough thing, I don't know. Then Nick and I went to leave, and there were all these reporters, and I got knocked down, and he saved me, but then he kissed me, and …, and I didn't know what to do! I couldn't shove him away, not in front of all those cameras," Tate explained quickly. Sanders nodded.

"I see. Did you want to shove him away?" he asked for clarification.

She paused for a moment, really thinking about it.

"Yes. I mean, kissing is great and all, I just ... don't want ... *that*, right now. From anyone," Tate replied.

"So it wasn't because it was him?"

She glanced across the car.

"Sandy, are you jealous?" she teased. The back of his neck turned pink and she laughed.

"No, I am not jealous. Your relationship with Mr. Castille has never made sense to me, I am just trying to figure it out," Sanders replied while pulling the car up in front of a swanky restaurant.

"Why doesn't it make sense? We're friends. Or I mean, I thought we were friends," she told him before getting out of the car. A valet ushered them to the front doors.

"Exactly. Clearly, Mr. Castille sees it another way. And I know Mr. Hollingsworth doesn't care for the relationship," Sanders pointed out.

"Oh, Ang is just worried about me. Hey! Did you know he has a girlfriend?" Tate changed the subject while a maître d' led them to a table. They had barely been seated before a bottle of champagne was brought out to them with great flourish. After Sanders approved of the taste, the waitstaff scurried away and they were left alone.

"Yes, I know he has been seeing someone," Sanders answered her question. She was surprised. While not exactly friends, Ang and Sanders had met, and got along on a basic level. Neither asked the other a lot of questions, and that seemed to appeal to both of them.

"Who is she?" Tate pressed. Sanders raised his eyebrows.

"He hasn't told you?"

"No, I just found out last night, and he wouldn't say her name."

"He hasn't said anything to me, I just know that he has been seeing someone."

"Sandy, you're so good at getting people to talk, maybe you

could just —,"

"*No.*"

"But I'm dying to know!"

"No, I am not asking him."

"*Sandyyyyyyyy!*"

"Not this again."

"Sandy, please! Please! Please!" she whined in a high pitched voice. He pressed his lips together.

"No. It's none of our business," he reminded her.

"*Fiiiiiiiine,*" Tate groaned.

"Besides. I thought maybe *I* could ask some questions tonight," Sanders said.

She was blown away, *again*. He just kept shocking her. Sanders talking in whole paragraphs was monumental enough, but asking questions? Being *engaging*? She almost felt dizzy. She *definitely* felt nervous.

"Of course, of course, go right ahead," she offered.

"I want you to know," he started, his eyes staring straight down while his posture remained as straight as an arrow. "I admire you a great deal, for how you've handled this whole situation, this last month."

She instantly teared up.

"Sanders, I —,"

"And I wanted you to know that I understand how you feel, about *him. I understand* why you feel that way. I know that things cannot be taken back, once they have been said and done," Sanders continued.

Always about Jameson.

"Thank you," Tate responded, waving a hand in front of her eyes to keep the tears from spilling.

"*But* – he is a large part of my life. I don't want to have to choose between the two of you. I have avoided talking about him or anything to do with him up until now, just for your sake. This cannot always be, I owe my life to him. I am not proud of what he did, I am not making excuses for it, but his home is my home. He is the only family I have," Sanders reminded her. She nodded her head.

"I know that. I would never make you choose, Sandy, he's your family, I'm just —," she tried to assure him.

"You are very important, too," Sanders assured her first. She laughed and wiped at her eyes.

"Thank you. Thank you for telling me all this, but I've gotta say, it makes me nervous. He's not gonna pop out of a cake or something, is he?" she joked.

"I shall notify the kitchen to cancel dessert."

Tate didn't stop laughing until a waiter came to pat her on the back.

"I'm not gonna lie, it's not easy. I don't like … thinking about him, or those days. I don't talk about him. But I don't want you to feel like you can't be around me just because you also need to be around him. I wouldn't do that to you," she told him again.

"Thank you."

She thought he was going to continue on, maybe tell hilarious anecdotes about his and Jameson's life in the country as bachelors, now that Tate was out of the picture. Oh, the shenanigans they probably got into together! To get through it, she would probably have to stab herself in the thigh with a fork, but she would suffer through it. For Sanders.

But he didn't. Their appetizers were brought out, and they chatted over normal things. Sanders was an avid horse rider, and Tate had ridden all through school, so they talked about horses and stables, the best places to ride. He complimented her hair and she complimented his suit. He promised that after dinner he would take her to McDonald's, so she could get a Happy Meal with a toy – she should have something to unwrap on her birthday, after all, and she could never resist a milkshake. She hugged him from across the table.

"This was awesome, Sandy, thank you so much for taking me out," Tate said as she scraped the last little bit of cake off her dessert plate. It was promptly whisked away, and two tiny glasses of port appeared in front of them.

"Of course. I always enjoy our dinners. Which leads me to ask, I was wondering something. You can say no, I won't get mad. It was just an idea I had," he started, sipping at the dark wine. Her defenses immediately went up. Apparently the conversation from earlier wasn't over.

"Alright. What is it?" she asked slowly.

"I am a fairly accomplished cook. I thought it would be nice to make you dinner one of these nights," Sanders told her. She raised her eyebrows.

"Of course! Just tell me when, and I'll come over to your place —,"

"I moved out of the hotel," he said quickly. Her breath caught in her throat. There was only one other place he would go.

"Sandy, *I know*, I know he's your family, but I can't. I just can't go sit and have dinner with him. I'm not making you choose, really, I just can't be in that house, with him. I can't, *I can't*," Tate was speaking at supersonic speeds. Sanders reached out and rested his hand on her arm, and she was instantly soothed. He *never* touched anybody, so any display of affection from him was a massive one.

"He's not there. He left the country. He hasn't been home for almost six weeks," Sanders explained.

Six weeks. Tate had been out of the hospital for almost exactly six weeks. Apparently when she had said she wanted him gone, Jameson had taken her very literally. She was such a stupid girl, her stupid heart had believed him again. So much for seeing her around. Kind of hard to do from 3,000 miles away. Or was Berlin 4,000 miles away? She wasn't sure.

Goddamn fucking stupid Danish beauty FUCK. FUCKER.

"Oh. I just ... I don't know. Let me think about it? It's hard, Sandy. It's ... hard," Tate's voice fell into a whisper.

Jameson's house had become home to Tate, in the short period of time she had stayed there. It was where she had met Sanders, a soulmate. It's where she had met her match, in Satan. More than her match, it turned out. She had left a piece of herself in that house, imbedded in the structure, buried in the foundation. She wasn't ready to get it back yet.

"Of course, no pressure," Sanders assured her. She smiled.

"You could always come cook at our place. Nick has a really nice, commercial grade stove," she told him. His lips quirked to the side.

"May I ask you one more question?" Sanders ignored her suggestion.

"Yes."

"Will you *ever* be ready to see him again?"

Sanders just would not stop with the surprises. She wondered how long he had been planning this; Sanders would never do something without extensive planning, especially if it involved him going out of his comfort zone. This was so far out of his zone, he was practically a new person.

"I don't know. I'm ... he ... I don't think I can explain it. I thought ... I told him I felt a certain way. I didn't ask for anything back, but he led me to believe there was something. It was all a lie. A joke. *A game.* He didn't care about me, he just wanted to hurt me. *Me*, my heart. Why would a person do that? Why would he be so cruel to a person, just because she liked him?" Tate asked, wiping at tears again.

"You know when I tell you something, it is completely unbiased, yes?" he asked. She nodded.

"Are you even capable of being biased?"

"No. And I am telling you, it was not all a joke to him. It was not a game. He didn't lure you into *'falling for him'* just so he could play some cruel prank on you. It wasn't like that. He is very stupid, I will agree, and he acted like a child, that is certain. As I said, I am not proud. But I also know that *he cared about you,*" Sanders stressed.

Tate squeezed her eyes shut tight and tried to remember the pool. Sometimes, she almost thought she could. Coldness, surrounding her, coming from everywhere. From inside of her. Like being dead. She knew that Jameson wasn't the one who put her there – she had done that to herself, she was the only one to blame. She had debased herself, she had *degraded herself.* She had done a lot of low down, dirty things in her adult life, but that night had taken the cake.

But Jameson had been a part of it. Tate may have been responsible for her drunk driving descent into madness, but Satan hadn't helped, either.

"I'm sorry, Sandy, but I just don't believe that. It's just wishful thinking."

"You are entitled to think what you want, but that does not make it accurate. So. If you don't believe he ever cared for you, then there is no chance of you two making amends, sometime in the future?" Sanders questioned further. Tate almost laughed again.

"Is this for real? No, Sandy, I don't think there is any chance that we will '*make amends*' sometime in the future. I can't even imagine speaking to him, and *clearly* he doesn't want to speak to me. It's better this way. It was a pretty toxic relationship, whatever it was – I think I need to just calm down for a while. Show a little restraint. Maybe try out a normal relationship for once," she told him. He quirked up an eyebrow.

"A normal relationship? Like something with Mr. Castille?" Sanders asked. She laughed.

"You know what, yeah. Maybe. Maybe something *exactly* like that. Nice and normal," she replied.

There was a very long pause, during which Sanders stared at her the whole time. The table was cleared and the check was brought, but he still stared. She began to wonder if she should pay when he finally looked down to grab the bill.

"Would you like your birthday present now, or at home?" Sanders asked in a lightning quick shift of topics. She blinked in surprise.

"Oh, uh, whenever is fine. You didn't have to get me anything, dinner was fabulous," she told him, standing up. He came around the table and guided her back to the front of the restaurant.

"A birthday is not a birthday without at least one real present," Sanders replied. Tate laughed.

"Did you make that up?" she asked. He shook his head and held the front door open.

"No. Jameson taught me that, after I came back to America with him," he replied. She tried not to choke while he gave instructions to the valet driver.

"It's a nice rule to have," she managed to croak out. Sanders turned to face her and reached inside his jacket.

"Besides, I bought this long before I made the dinner plans, so it *is* your real present," he told her, then pulled a long envelope out of his pocket and handed it to her.

Tate couldn't make sense of it at first. It was just a simple e-mail that had been printed out. It took her eyes a second to sort out the tiny lettering, but when she did, she was shocked. She gasped and looked between Sanders and the paper.

"Is this for real!?" she exclaimed. He nodded.

"Yes. We would leave three days after Christmas, because New Year's —,"

"You bought me tickets to *Spain!?*" Tate squealed. Sanders glanced around, obviously embarrassed by her outburst.

"I bought *us* tickets to Spain, for New Year's. The winters here become too much for me, and I thought you would enjoy a vacation," he explained matter-o-factly.

She shrieked again, startling him, as well as several other customers. Then she pounced on him, wrapping her arms around his neck and hugging him as tightly as possible. He squirmed and grumbled into her ear, but he finally hugged her back.

"This is going to be so much fun. *So much fun.* We will have the best time. I am going to turn you out. Thank you so much," she breathed. Sanders pulled away a little, looking down at her.

"I think, after everything you've been through, you *need* this trip, Tatum," he assured her.

Her name. He said her name. It didn't come out often.

She figured that deserved another present, so she kissed him, as loudly and sloppily as possible.

Three days after Christmas, Tate stood in Logan Airport, feeling very uncomfortable.

She had finally gotten a hold of her sister, and Tate, Ellie, and Ang all met up for Christmas dinner. It was one of the most awkward experiences of her life – which was really saying something. Ang and Ellie barely spoke to each other. Tate had originally wanted to get everyone together to open presents Christmas morning, as well, but she threw that idea out the window and called Sanders, instead.

She tried. She had really tried. He didn't really do Christmas, but Sanders said he would buy a tree and everything, if Tate spent the morning at his house. At *Jameson's* house. She finally agreed. Sanders picked her up, drove her out there, held her hand as they walked to the house. But she didn't even make it to the front door – halfway across the broad porch, she lost it, and had to lean over a railing and puke.

Sanders didn't bother hiding the grossed out look on his face, but he didn't push her, either. They ate breakfast at an IHOP.

The weeks leading up to her trip, she had been so excited, she could barely contain herself. What to pack, what to wear, what to buy. Looking up all sorts of things that she wanted to do. They were staying in Marbella, one of the southern most cities in Spain, close to Gibraltar. It was probably one of the warmer spots in Europe during the winter, which made her happy. She packed her bikini.

But when Tate woke up the morning they were supposed to leave, she felt nervous for some reason. She didn't have any reason to, she had seen Sanders almost every single day since her birthday. He had shown her their flight itinerary to Spain, the pictures of the hotel they were going to stay in – had even bought tickets for a weekend trip to Paris. What wasn't there to be excited about?

Something wasn't right, though; she just couldn't put her finger on it. As she waited on the other side of security for Sanders, Tate could feel it weighing heavy in her stomach. He had only checked one small bag, which seemed light for Sanders. The entire time she had known him, she had never seen him wear anything twice, so how could he go a whole week or two with just one suitcase full of clothing?

Wait, one week, or two weeks? Holy shit, I have no idea when our return date is.

"Sandy," Tate started when he finally joined her. He glanced at her, straightening his tie as they walked away from security. "I can't believe I never asked, but when are we coming home?"

"I haven't booked return tickets yet."

"*What!?*"

She pulled him to a stop.

"I haven't booked them yet. I figured when you grew tired of Spain, I would simply buy you a ticket home. Very simple. Can we continue?" Sanders asked, trying to pull his arm free of her grip.

"That's *insane*, I don't even want to think about how much that ticket would cost, let alone the swanky resort you booked. How much is all this costing you?" Tate demanded. His eyebrows furrowed together.

"This is a gift, I won't discuss the price. Just know that cost is never a problem for me. I had to cancel the hotel reservations, anyway. A more suitable location became available," he informed her. She wouldn't let go of his sleeve, so he just started walking forward. Tate was forced to follow.

"What? That place looked amazing – where are we staying that's better than that?" she asked, her mind whirling.

"The area we are going to is referred to as the *Costa Del Sol*, renowned for its boating. I thought a yacht would be more in order," Sanders replied.

Tate knew what the Costa Del Sol was; her father had never taken them there, but she was well aware of its reputation. She wondered if she'd even be allowed in the town, or if they would request bank statements first.

"You rented a *yacht!?* For just the two of us? This is insane," she repeated her earlier sentiment. Sanders finally managed to pull his sleeve free.

"This is all very carefully planned, just for you. I would ask that you trust me on all things," he said, cutting his eyes towards her.

Tate pressed her lips together and glared at him, but didn't say anything else. *Ooohhh,* Sanders was a clever man. She trusted him implicitly, but that was also a scary thing. Tate never wanted to offend him by not showing her faith in him, so of course, she went along with anything he said. She would go along with him for now.

But something was most very, *definitely,* off.

The plane ride was long, and she slept fitfully through most of it.

They had to switch planes in Paris, and she seriously considered making a run for it. Or asking Sanders if they could just stay there. But as they walked through Charles de Gaulle Airport, Tate couldn't help but notice something.

Sanders looked happy. Sure, he wasn't smiling, but he had a lighter step. His eyes didn't look so intense. If she hadn't known any better, she would almost say he seemed *excited*. While she loved Sanders with her whole heart, and knew that he cared a great deal about her, Tate couldn't fathom him being excited about taking a trip with her. Half the time, she almost felt like he stuck around to make sure she didn't stick her finger in a light socket, like a babysitter.

"How many times have you been to Marbella?" she asked as they waited to board their flight to Malaga. From there, he told her that they would drive to their final destination.

"Many times, though I haven't been there in over a year," Sanders replied.

"Do you speak Spanish?"

"Enough to get by."

"How many languages do you speak?"

"Enough to get by."

She punched him in the arm.

Sanders had booked them first class the whole way, but the plane they took to Malaga was so nice, Tate almost wondered if she should take her shoes off before stepping inside. She sank into her cushy seat and sighed, rolling her head back and forth. When she opened her eyes, Sanders was staring at her.

"You do trust me, don't you?" he suddenly asked. She blinked, and guilt washed over her.

"Of course I trust you, Sandy. You're the most open, honest person I know. Sometimes, I don't feel worthy of your friendship," Tate replied, reaching over and holding his hand. He squeezed her fingers back.

SEPARATION

"You are very worthy of it, but thank you. I am glad you trust me. Everything I have ever done has been to help you, since that night," he assured her.

Where is this going?

"I know that."

"Good. Just … I just wanted you to know that," Sanders stammered a little, and then looked away from her. But he didn't let go of her hand.

Tate hadn't really slept on the seven hour flight to Paris, but she conked out for the first hour of their next leg. When she woke up, the flight attendants were bringing around drinks. At first they tried speaking to her in Spanish, then switched to English.

"Would you care for some champagne?" the attendant inquired in a lilting French accent. Tate shook her head.

"No, no thank you."

"And your husband?"

Tate almost burst out laughing, glancing at Sanders. He had his head tilted back and his eyes closed, dead asleep. His arms were folded across his chest. Prim and proper, even in his sleep.

"I think he's fine. He's not my husband, just a good friend," Tate explained. The attendant laughed.

"Oh, madam, he is much too handsome to be just a friend," she laughed, then winked at Tate before moving on down the aisle.

Tate took another look at Sanders. He was a very good looking man. He had a slender frame and wasn't particularly tall, but his face had that *Look* – like a Louis Vuitton runway model. Fair skin, full lips, defined jaw. *Almost* androgynous, but not quite. Pretty was a word that often came to her mind when thinking of him. Sanders was a very pretty man. She had never been physically attracted to him herself, but she thought it was funny when she was with him, watching other women do double takes. It was the same thing with Ang. Apparently Tate only surrounded herself with good looking men, because Satan was the best looking of them all, and Nick was no slouch, either.

Nick. She sighed and glanced at her phone. He had texted her, during their brief stop in Paris. He had not been happy about her leaving. After their highly publicized little lip-lock, he had gone back to Iowa to spend Christmas with his family. He had invited her, but Tate had figured that was a bad idea on a cosmic scale.

Apparently saying he wasn't going to press his attentions on her *really meant* he wouldn't bother her about it unless she was out of his sight. Now Nick was making his feelings known, very vehemently. He cared about Tate. He thought they made a great team, a great couple. They already knew they were physically compatible. What was the problem? Was it him?

The problem was … she didn't know what her problem was, Tate just knew she couldn't be with him. Not that way. She hadn't told Sanders any of it, because she knew he would just tell her to end the friendship. And she didn't want to do that. She opened her text messages.

Please tell me you have spent at least half as much time thinking about me as I have about you.

Tate hadn't texted him back, because she hadn't been thinking about him. God, she was an awful person. A horrible, awful person. She cared about Nick a lot, but just as a friend. She had no desire for it to be anything more.

She looked around at the other men sitting in first class. She wondered if she would *ever* want "*anything more*" with someone else. She hadn't slept with anyone in almost three months. Her longest dry spell since she had run away to Boston, seven years ago. Men and sex were so far off her radar, she was practically a nun.

She actually laughed out loud at that thought.

When they got off the plane in Malaga, Tate teased Sanders about falling asleep. He was such a highly strung person, imagining him nodding off in front of people was hard, but he'd been out like a light for the whole ride. He wouldn't meet her eyes as they picked up their luggage.

"I have been under a lot of stress lately," he replied. She stopped smiling.

"Really? Is it because of the trip?" she worried out loud. He shook his head.

"No. Just some … work issues," was all he said, then he started heading out of the baggage area.

It wasn't until they were through customs and actually walking outside that she was able to question him about his "*work issues*" – as far as she knew, Sanders didn't have a job. He had worked as Jameson's personal assistant, but the title was more for him than out of necessity. Jameson paid for everything. The Bentley, Sanders' clothes, his living situation, *everything*. And after Jameson had kicked Tate out of the house, Sanders had quit. Moved out. The two had made up, but Tate knew Sanders had refused to work for him again. So what was he talking about?

She never got an answer. Sanders left her outside, in front of the arrivals area, while he took off for a parking garage. She was a little surprised. She had assumed they would just take a taxi or a shuttle to get to their hotel – or yacht, now – after they landed. But after about ten minutes of waiting, a white, convertible, older model Rolls-Royce pulled up in front of her. It was in perfect condition. Tate gaped as Sanders got out of the car and came around to grab her luggage.

"You rented a Rolls-Royce!?" she exclaimed. He cleared his throat.

"It's a Corniche III. 1990," he replied, loading up all their belongings into the trunk.

"It's beautiful, but it's a bit much, considering I plan on spending

90% of my time on the beach," Tate laughed. He glanced at her and then went back to the driver's side.

"Well, I don't. Let's go," he urged.

The interior was all leather and wood paneling. It screamed old money to her, reminded her of cars her father had owned. Normally, those kinds of things made her uncomfortable, but sitting in that car, cruising down a highway in Spain, did wonders for her inner-abused-child.

Spain was having an unseasonably warm winter. Though it wasn't really considered hot out by the locals, to Tate's winter acclimatized-body, it felt like heaven. Temperatures in Boston had been in the thirties when they left; now she was sitting in over sixty degrees. She loved it.

"This was such a good idea!" Tate had to yell over the wind. She had begged him to take the top down.

"Good. I'm very glad you're happy. That's all I ever want," Sanders replied. She laughed and turned to look at him. He had taken off his suit jacket and put on a pair of sunglasses. Dressed down for him. It was almost like seeing him in his pajamas, or something.

"Well, mission accomplished, sir," she laughed, then reached out and rubbed her hand against the back of his neck.

They drove like that for a while, Tate with her fingers in his hair, scratching up and down lightly. He kept twitching his head to avoid her touch, but eventually he gave in, like he always did. By the time they were entering Marbella proper, he was actually resting the back of his head in her hand.

"Tatum," Sanders said, sitting upright. Tate pulled her hand away and sat up as well. "I, personally, feel that I have infallible judgement. If more people would just listen to me, I think things would run a lot smoother."

"And modest. Don't forget that you're modest," she teased. He took off his glasses and glanced at her.

"Modesty isn't necessary. I pride myself on being logical," Sanders replied.

"Cut to the chase, Sandy. What's up?" she asked.

"I just wanted to say that, just so you'd know," was his explanation. She snorted.

"Alright. So you're smarter than all of us. Awesome. I can moonwalk better than anyone I know, so we're practically equals," she pointed out. He barked out a laugh.

And now I can die happy.

Sanders pulled up in front of a large building and asked her to step out of the car. Tate waited while he went and parked in some underground garage. She had thought she would be more jet lagged, but she wasn't. She was excited. It was late morning, and there were a lot of people walking around, sight-seeing. It made her itch to get moving and looking around. Finally, Sanders joined her, pulling their luggage behind him.

"Alright, let's go," was all he said, surging ahead of her when she tried to grab her suitcase.

"So where is this yacht? Are we gonna stay on it the whole time?" she asked while they crossed the street.

"The yacht is in the marina right in front of us. How long we stay is entirely up to you," he replied. Tate laughed.

"What if I get sea sick and want to leave an hour after we board?" she joked. Sanders snorted.

"Then I will fetch you a sick bag and you can learn to deal with it."

Tate knew where they were, though she didn't tell him that. They were entering Puerto Banus – nicknamed "*The Millionaires Playground*", because it was the marina of choice for many celebrities and wealthy people.

She managed to keep her composure while they walked amongst the rows of mammoth boats. She didn't see any famous people, but she looked as hard as she could. Tate came from a wealthy family, but she hadn't been around much opulence. Her father was a very conservative man – yachts on the Costa Del Sol weren't really his style.

She was trying so hard to see everything, that she wasn't paying attention to what was right in front of her. Tate was vaguely aware that someone was walking down the gangplank of a yacht a couple sleeves down from them. Though it was a beautiful boat, it certainly wasn't the biggest, so she figured whoever it was couldn't have been a celebrity, and she kept looking over the other boats.

Sanders actually tipped her off. His steps got tighter, his back straighter. It was like watching someone pull a string on a marionette. One right twitch, and everything locked into place on Sanders. It was a sign of some sort of distress. Nervous, or anxious, or upset, or angry. She wondered if they were finally at their boat and something was amiss.

"Sandy, I was just kidding, you know I'd love anything you'd —," Tate started, turning to look ahead of them, following his gaze. Her voice died in her throat.

Eight weeks. Four days. Eleven hours.

She stopped walking.

Seven years.

Stopped breathing.

Not long enough.

"It took a lot of trouble to get you here. The least you could do is smile, baby girl."

3

BEFORE JAMESON EVEN LEFT THE hospital, he'd had a plan. She had said she wanted him to go away. To leave. To be gone.

But she never once said anything about not seeing him again. He considered that a loophole.

Sanders was waiting outside, as Jameson had expected. He would have known that it wouldn't end well. Jameson strode past him, heading straight for the parking lot. Sanders followed behind.

"Are you alright?" he asked. Jameson nodded.

"Of course. She asked me to leave. I left," he replied.

"That's it?"

"There were a few more curse words, some screaming, but yes, that's pretty much it."

"And you're just going to go?"

"What other choice do I have?" Jameson asked, glancing down at the other man.

"You could fight for her," Sanders pointed out. Jameson laughed.

"Let's not get radical. Besides, you and I both know that wouldn't work. She wants me gone, so I'm going to go. I'm going to head back to

Europe," he said. Sanders narrowed his eyes.

"With **her?**" he practically hissed. Jameson shook his head.

"No, Pet's already gone, I kicked her out that night. I'm not going to Berlin. I was thinking Spain. We haven't done Spain in a long time. Sunshine is good for the soul," Jameson explained.

"I am not going to Spain with you," Sanders said quickly. Jameson laughed.

"Of course not. I need you here," he replied.

"I won't work for you."

"I'm not hiring you. But I will need you to do me some favors," he told him. Sanders stopped walking.

"Last time you asked me to do something for you, someone very close to us almost died," he reminded him. Jameson's smile vanished and he turned to face him.

"I am very aware of what I have done, I don't need you reminding me. Listen. I am going to Spain. I am going to be gone for a while. But when I call – and I **will** call – you have to promise me that you will do everything in your power to fulfill my wishes," Jameson said. Sanders shook his head.

"No, I won't risk her —," he started to argue, when Jameson held up his hand.

"Just trust me, Sanders. Surely one mistake won't erase a lifetime of you trusting me," Jameson snapped.

"Seven years is hardly a lifetime."

Jameson felt as if he had been slapped. He stepped up close to Sanders. So close, he had to tilt his head straight down to look at him.

"There is nothing in this world you could do that would make me stop trusting you. After everything we've been through, I thought the feeling was mutual," Jameson growled.

Sanders stared at him for a moment and then sighed, his eyes sliding to the ground. Jameson let out a breath he had been holding and stepped away. That had actually made him nervous for a moment.

"*I can only promise to do what you want **if** I deem it appropriate,*" Sanders amended the promise. Jameson nodded.

"*I can live with that,*" he agreed. He started to walk away, then turned around. "*Oh! I need one more favor.*"

"*Oh god. What is it?*"

"*I was wondering if you could call ahead and see to having the boat put in the water and prepped to sail,*" Jameson told him. Sanders' eyebrows shot up.

"*The boat, sir?*"

"*The boat.*"

"***The** boat?*" he clarified. Jameson smiled.

"***The** boat.*"

He had never been pale, but Jameson Kane normally had fair skin. Tate had always liked it because it set off his intense blue eyes and thick black hair. Made him look sharp, like his edges would cut when put to skin. When not at home, he was always immaculately dressed, whether they were going out to eat, or shop, or take in a movie. Always clean shaven – five o'clock shadow was only seen in the wee hours of the morning, before it was scraped away.

Seeing him again, but now with a deep tan, dressed casually wearing shorts and a light t-shirt, his jaw covered in at least a few days worth of stubble, was too much. Seeing him, *period*, was too much.

He was always too much.

Tate felt like she was going to faint, so she sat down heavily on the cement dock. Sanders dropped the bags and immediately knelt down next to her. He was saying something, but she couldn't hear anything. She had her hands pressed against either side of her face and she was trying to remember how to breathe. A pair of feet came into her vision.

He owns a pair of sandals!?

A short argument broke out over her.

"Go inside."

"No, I'm not going to —,"

"*Go inside.* Take her bags."

"What if —,"

"You promised. Remember?"

There was some grumbling, but Sanders stood up. Grabbed the bag that she had dropped and their suitcases. He rolled away, and she watched his feet disappear onto the gangplank. Tate still couldn't look up. Not even when she realized that Jameson was slowly squatting down, directly in front of her. She was sitting lotus-style, and his hands came to rest gently on her knees.

Her body temperature immediately shot up past 100 degrees.

"Is this real?" she whispered.

"Yes. Are you alright?" he asked. She shuddered.

"You planned this? You and Sanders?" she asked.

"*I* planned this, a long time ago. Sanders just helped me execute it," Jameson explained.

She felt betrayed. She felt confused. Obviously, over the past two months, Tate had wondered what it would be like to run into Jameson again. She had never thought it would go the way it had; she felt like she was on the verge of a heart attack. Or a psychotic break. A little of both.

"Why? Why are you doing this?" Tate asked.

A finger under her chin. Like flames. Her whole body was igniting.

"Because I wanted to talk to you. You wouldn't let me in the hospital. So I gave you time. Time is up, baby girl," Jameson informed her, slowly tilting her head up to face him.

When they locked eyes, it was like an explosion in her chest. She gasped on a sob, and a tear streamed down her face. He smiled sadly at her, but she refused to believe it. The last time she had seen him, *really* looked at him, he had been angry at her. Staring down at her. Throwing money at her.

I'm in hell. I died in that pool, and I'm in hell. That's why I'm so hot. That's why I'm sitting in front of Satan.

"What if I don't want to talk you?" Tate whispered. Jameson chuckled, smoothing his hand over her hair.

"Now when have you ever known me to care about a silly thing like that?" he whispered back.

She surged to her feet. He couldn't talk to her like that, not anymore. No boyfriend-voice allowed. Not after all the time that had passed, all the damage that had been done. His voice was like silk, smooth and strong. Flowing over her. Covering her. Strangling her. She had to get out of there.

"You can't just do this!" she shouted.

Jameson slowly stood up as well. Tate couldn't look at him. It split her in half. Her brain knew one thing. Her heart recognized another. And good god, her body was completely mutinous.

Why does he have to be so tan!?

"Do what?" Jameson asked.

"Kidnap somebody! Use Sanders! Use *me*! I'm not some puppet you get to jerk around!" she snapped at him.

"Buying you a ticket to Spain for your birthday is hardly kidnapping," he pointed out. She let out a frustrated yell.

"*Why!?* Why did you bring me here?" she demanded.

"Because I've missed you."

"Bullshit," Tate snorted. "Mr. Kane doesn't ever care about anyone enough to miss them."

"He missed *you*. I wanted to see you, talk to you, maybe —,"

"You made it *very clear* that you wanted nothing to do with me.

I have obeyed those wishes. Why can't you respect mine? What do you want?" she asked.

"I'm trying to explain, I want to —,"

"You know what? I don't care. I really don't. And I don't have to stand here and listen to you. Our transaction is done, over with; you paid for my '*services*'. I am no longer required to be in your presence," Tate's voice was dripping with venom by the end, and she went to brush past him. He grabbed her upper arm, holding her in place. Her eyes snapped to his.

"*I* say when it's over," he replied.

She was shocked into a stand still. Jameson touching her, talking to her like that, it was like getting knocked back in time. Back to when she knew her place in the scheme of things, back to when life was simple enough to revolve around being with him. A shiver ran down her spine, and Tate forced herself back to the present. Forced herself to remember what having her stomach pumped felt like, forced herself to remember what it felt like to be so cold, she couldn't feel her entire body.

"*Do not touch me,*" she hissed at him, and he let go of her.

"I'm not trying to hurt you," he assured her.

"You *always* try to hurt me," she snapped back. He frowned.

"I never tried to hurt you, not until the end. Can we please go inside and discuss this?" Jameson asked. She laughed, a loud, abrasive sound.

"I wouldn't get on that boat if you paid me to! Do you have any idea what it's like for me? Being here, seeing you like this!?" Tate demanded.

"I can imagine."

"You probably can't. Seeing you, is like … like somebody taking off a piece of my skin with a potato peeler. Seeing you is just a big, neon sign. A reminder of … of how low I got. How horrible I became, of how awful I was, of … a reminder of how much I hated myself. Which is really unfair, because I should've hated *you*," she told him, turning away.

"But you don't," Jameson pointed out. She sighed, struggling to hold in the tears.

"I want to. It's what you deserve. You hated me. I should at least get to hate you back."

"I *never* hated you. I was angry, and I was stupid, yes, but I didn't hate you," Jameson assured her. Tate laughed.

"If that's how you treat someone you like, then I'm scared to see how you treat people you actually do hate. You wanna know what the worst part is? I don't blame you. You didn't pour the alcohol down my throat. You didn't make me get in that car. Worst thing that ever fucking happened to me, and I can't even blame you. Just me. All my fault. Always my fault," her voice was a whisper and she kept looking away from him. Out to the ocean. To the water. The cold, cold water.

"You can blame me, Tate. *I* blame me," he told her. She managed another laugh.

"Just so you can feel better about yourself? No. I could've died that night and you wouldn't have even noticed," she guessed. He stepped up close to her, but she refused to turn and look at him.

"I would have noticed, Tatum. I would have *felt it*. When the police came to my house, and I found out what had happened, I —," Jameson started to explain, but she held up a hand.

"It's already bad enough that I had to live it, I don't need you making me feel worse about it."

"I wasn't going to make you feel bad about it," he told her. Tate laughed and finally glanced up at him.

"You love to make me feel bad," she replied. He took a step closer, so he was almost touching her. Flames almost burning her.

"And you used to love it when I made you feel bad, but this isn't one of those times."

Tate couldn't handle it. Just couldn't take it anymore. She choked

on a sob and turned around, walking away from him. He didn't follow, but that didn't surprise her. Jameson Kane never did anything
he didn't want to do.

It took her a couple hours of milling around, but eventually Tate
calmed down. She sat in a little cafe, wondering what she should
do with herself. She felt kind of silly. It was pretty hard to run away,
when all a person had was the shirt on her back. Sanders had taken
all of her stuff onto the boat, including her purse. Her wallet, passport, cash, *everything*, was on Jameson's goddamn yacht. All she had
was the little bit of money in her pocket, which wasn't much, after
the coffee and sandwich she had bought herself.

But even if she'd had her stuff, it wasn't like Tate could just fly
home. He was very clever, Mr. Kane. This wasn't like his party, she
couldn't just drive off in a drunken rage. She was stuck in another
country. Her Spanish wasn't very good, and even if she could make it
to the airport, she was pretty positive she couldn't afford a last minute, one-way ticket to Boston.

Sanders had to have known how she would react, so it was safe
to assume he wouldn't just buy her a plane ticket at the first sign of
tears. No, he had probably prepared himself for this little episode. It
was also probably the reason why no one had come looking for her.
Tate had stormed away from the boat around eleven that morning.
It was after five o'clock at night, the sun was beginning to go down.

She was *exhausted*. She didn't want to fight with anyone. She
didn't want to feel so upset anymore, so emotionally charged all the
time. In a way, the whole situation reminded her of the time Jameson
tricked her into visiting her parents. Tate had hated it at the time,
had hated him. But in the end, it had been a huge act of closure for

her. Maybe that's what this trip could be, *closure*. She'd been a bundle of nerves, wondering and worrying about Jameson. Now that problem was solved.

She could move on; she could get on with her life.

By the time she found her way back to the marina, the sun had almost completely set. There was just a burnt orange line on the horizon, surrounded by a heavy blue. It suited her mood. She wandered down a couple docks before she found the right one, and then made her way towards his boat.

Tate had to admit, she was very impressed. It wasn't the largest boat in the harbor, but it was one of the sleeker looking ones. The exterior of the boat was white – of course – with black lining and piping. The boat on the other side of the sleeve was a sharp looking speed boat, obviously a mate to the larger yacht, as it was done in the same style and colors.

She was just standing there, staring up at his boat, when she heard a whistle. Tate turned in a circle, looking for the source, when it came again. She finally spotted it. A man, leaning over the rail of a ridiculously huge yacht, was whistling at her. She slowly made her way down to him. She could hear that some sort of huge party was going on inside the boat.

"Are you lost?" the man asked in a heavy British accent. Tate shook her head.

"No, I just found it," she assured him, gesturing back to Jameson's boat. The guy whistled again.

"A guest of Mr. Kane's! Outstanding. I haven't had the pleasure of meeting him personally, yet. Would you care to come on board for a drink? We're having a pre-pre-pre-New Year's party," he laughed.

Tate laughed as well, and was about to decline, when she stopped herself. Why couldn't she say yes? It wasn't like she really wanted to be on Jameson's boat. And she hadn't been to a party, a *real* party, in forever.

It's not like there's somewhere else I'd rather be.
"Why not? Sounds like fun."

Sanders was practically going out of his mind with worry. He wasn't saying anything, but Jameson could tell. The younger man would fidget. Adjust his tie, adjust a vase, adjust a chair. Adjust, adjust, adjust. Pace from one end of the boat to the other. Adjust some more stuff. When Jameson couldn't take it anymore, he went to go get her.

I have never chased after a woman in my life, and now it feels like I spend most of my time chasing after Tatum O'Shea …

But she was worth it. Jameson could admit that, now.

The last time he had seen her, Tate had been in the hospital, looking damaged and broken. Something he had smashed on the ground under his foot. So sad. Seeing her walking down the dock, smiling, *laughing*, looking almost like her old self, had been wonderful. He wasn't prone to sentimentality or romanticism, but she was like sunshine. And Jameson's life was very dark.

Of course, the sunshine hadn't lasted long. Tate had been very upset when she realized he was behind everything. He had expected that, of course. She had run away, and he had expected that, too. But without any money or her passport, he hadn't expected her to be gone for so long. It was after nine o'clock at night. It was dark out. Where in the hell could she have gone? What could she be doing?

Jameson stood between his two boats for a few moments, contemplating where she would go. Once upon a time, she had been a very smooth operator. She was looking much more like a Stepford-wife now, but Tate might just still have it in her to talk her way into a free hotel room.

But then something else got his attention. A boat a couple

sleeves down from his own was having a party. A very loud, raucous one, by the sounds of it. On a hunch, Jameson made his way down to it. No one was guarding the stairs that led to the plank, so he made his way inside.

On board, the deck was covered in wall to wall people. He found her on the far side, leaning against a railing. She wasn't alone. She was talking, laughing, with some man. He looked vaguely familiar. Jameson scowled. He hadn't seen her smile in so long, and the first time he really got to see it again, she was giving it away to someone else. He walked up slowly, so he was right behind her. She didn't say anything, but he knew that she was aware of him.

"Oh, looks like he found you!" the man laughed. Tate laughed as well, but still didn't look behind her.

"I knew he would. He always does," she teased, but Jameson could hear the edge under her voice. He almost laughed as well.

Better remember that, baby girl.

"And you are?" Jameson asked, staring at the other man.

"Bill. Bill Matthews," the man said, holding out a hand. Jameson shook it.

"Your boat?" he asked. Bill nodded.

"Yes, yes. We haven't met, but I've heard of you, Mr. Kane. Glad to finally meet you," he said. Jameson managed a smile.

"Thank you. Now if you'll excuse us, I'm sure Tatum would like some rest. She's had a long day," Jameson explained, reaching out and gripping her elbow. She jumped at his touch, but didn't pull away. Bill looked surprised.

"Oh, sorry, didn't mean to keep her from you. I —," he started, but Jameson just walked away, pulling Tate along beside him.

"I see your manners haven't improved," she growled at him.

"Why would they have?"

When they were back on the dock, she yanked her arm free and surged ahead of him. He lengthened his stride to keep up with her.

She was still refusing to look at him, but he could tell that something was different. She had made some sort of peace with his little ploy. He figured he was safe, at least for the night. She wasn't going to run away quite yet.

"So what, I'm a prisoner, now? I have to stay locked in your stupid boat?" Tate snarled as they walked up behind his yacht.

"Of course not. But Sanders has been worried. I had to find you, or he would've driven me insane," Jameson explained.

She stomped down the plank. He had thought maybe she would comment on his boat, on the style or size, but Tate didn't say anything. She continued moving, striding across the deck. Sanders was coming out at the same time, and the relief was obvious on his face. Tate steamed right up to him.

"I'm very happy to see you. I was so worried that —," he started, when she slapped him across the face.

Jameson was shocked, but he didn't hesitate. He immediately moved between them, grabbing her by the wrist in case she tried to swing again. Sanders looked completely bewildered. He had a hand pressed to his cheek, where she had hit him, and his eyes were huge as he stared at her. Tate glared right back at him, struggling against Jameson's grip.

"You're a traitor! You told me not to make you choose, but it's kinda obvious you already had your choice made! I never even stood a chance! *Traitor!*" she yelled at Sanders. His jaw dropped open.

"*Hey!*" Jameson barked, and everyone's attention snapped to him. He forced Tate backwards, out of reach of Sanders. "None of this was his fault. I asked him to help me. Apologize to him, *now,*" Jameson growled, glaring down at her.

She burst out laughing, and he was surprised.

Someone's gotten braver since I saw her last.

"Are you fucking kidding me?" she cackled. Jameson nodded.

"You can hit me all you want, but if you touch him again, I'll

throw you off this fucking boat," he warned her. Her laughter esca-
lated for a moment.

"*Ooohhh,* what a threat, being thrown off a boat *I don't even
want to be on,*" she hissed.

Before Jameson could respond, Sanders whirled around and left
the deck. Disappeared inside, walking so fast, he was basically jog-
ging. Jameson could see the shock on Tate's face, and then it fell away.
Replaced by sadness. Guilt. He let go of her wrist.

"Whatever kind of relationship you think you have with Sanders, you should remember, *I* am practically his father. The only family he has got anymore, so of course he is going to help me when
I need it," Jameson warned her. Her bottom lip trembled, and she
continued staring at the door Sanders had gone through. "But you
should also know that Sanders would *never* do anything to hurt you,
even if it meant disappointing me. If he brought you here, even under false pretenses, it's because he thought it was for your own good."

Tate still refused to look at him. She strode towards the doorway, ignoring his existence. He let her go. There were only so many
rooms on the boat, she would find her own.

Jameson sighed and sat down heavily in a cushioned deck chair.
Things hadn't gone as badly as they could have, but they sure as shit
hadn't gone well, either. Sanders had warned him that her feelings
hadn't changed, that she was trying very hard to hate him.

It didn't matter to him. Two months was a long time. During
the short amount of time they'd spent together, Jameson had grown
ridiculously attached to the stupid girl. All his preaching and ranting
and warning, telling her repeatedly that she should never expect him
to be anything more than he was – he should've listened to himself
once in a while.

While he had been so busy trying to warn her away, he hadn't
even noticed himself falling into her. Now Jameson couldn't tell
where she began and he ended. The thought of Tate dying, it hurt his

heart. Being away from her for two months, not allowing himself any contact with her …, it had been difficult. Jameson was forceful and impulsive by nature – not tracking her down and simply demanding that she forgive him, demand that they go back to the way they were; it had all been hard.

He hadn't seen her in *two months*, but the moment he had seen Tate walking towards him, it was like no time had passed. Suddenly, he was right where he needed to be, and any questions he'd had about what he was doing, any doubts he'd had, flew out the window. Good or bad, wrong or right, Jameson needed Tate. He wasn't exactly sure when it had happened, but it *had* happened, all the same. No point in denying it.

Now, all he had to do was convince her that she needed him, as well.

No one ever said hell was an easy place to live.

Around two in the morning, Tate couldn't take it anymore. She threw back the covers. Her room was nice, with a queen size bed, but even better – it was one of the furthest rooms from Jameson's. It was the first one she had looked in, when she'd huffed off to go to bed.

But she hadn't been able to fall asleep. Guilt was eating her alive. She couldn't believe she had hit Sanders. She felt like she had hit her own child. She climbed out of bed and didn't bother to put on any pants, just tip toed out into the hallway in her tank top and under-wear. It wasn't like it was something Jameson or Sanders hadn't seen before; if anything, it was actually like getting back to normal.

Tate had figured the big door at the end of the hall, the one that would lead to a room directly under the bow, was Jameson's quarters. She tried the room next to hers, but it was empty. She tried the room across the hall next. Turned the knob as slowly as possible, then pushed the door open an inch. Tried to peer inside to see if there was a lump on the bed.

The sound hit her first. She couldn't tell what it was for a moment, then it hit her. Right across the face. Someone was crying. Tate slid into the room and quietly shut the door behind her. Didn't even think about it, just went to the foot of the bed and crawled up it till she was right next to him. Sanders was laying on his back, so she pressed herself against his side. Wrapped her arm around his chest, her leg around his leg.

"I'm sorry, Sanders," she whispered. "I'm so, so, sorry."

"No, no, you don't need to be sorry, ma'am, I shouldn't have … I didn't realize you'd …, tomorrow, I'll —," he started in a jerky voice, but when he said 'ma'am', reverted back to calling her by a stranger's title, her heart ripped in half. She pressed her hand over his mouth.

"I do need to be sorry. I really, really do. I never should have hit you. I love you, Sanders. I love you so much. I was just mad, I shouldn't have done it. I'm so sorry," Tate breathed, pressing her face into his shoulder. She felt his hand come to rest on her arm, patting at it tentatively.

"It's okay, Tatum. Everything will be okay. I promise."

Sanders didn't handle any kind of contact well. She knew that; even handshakes were difficult for him. So a slap, she knew that must have been like a gun shot. A bullet, ripping right through his psyche. She knew his past, *knew* the kind of abuse he had been through, and still. Tate was the one who pulled the trigger.

I'm no better than Jameson.

"I don't want to be here, Sanders. But I'll do it. For you," she whispered into his ear. She felt him nod and she let out a sigh. Kissed him on the cheek. Settled back into his side. He squirmed a bit. Now that he had stopped crying, it was clear that her closeness was making him uncomfortable.

So she held on tighter.

Finally, he gave in and wiggled his arm loose. Wrapped it around her shoulders. Held her even closer. She fell asleep against his chest, listening to his heart beat.

Jameson sat on his front deck the next morning, staring out over the ocean. He had a spot on the outside of the marina, so he didn't have to face any other boats. A must, for him. All that was between him and a view of the open ocean was a rock jetty.

He had gone to check on Sanders in the morning, and had been in for a little shock. Tate was in bed with the younger man, and they were spooning like it was something they did everyday, Sanders' arms locked tight around her waist. Even Jameson had never slept with her like that; had never even thought to try.

Now he felt left out.

The pair of them didn't emerge until after ten. By then, Jameson had showered and gotten dressed, even went to get a newspaper for himself. They didn't say anything to him, but it was obvious that whatever had transpired between them the night before, it had made up for the slap. Good. If the two of them didn't get along, then there was no hope for him.

"Hungry?" Jameson asked when Tate wandered up to where he was sitting. She shrugged and sat across from him, picking a piece of toast up off of his plate.

"How long do I have to be here?" she asked, looking out over the water while she nibbled at the bread.

"You're not a prisoner. You're free to go whenever you want. Sanders can drive you to the airport right now. I just thought you were tougher than that," he told her. She snorted.

"You thought *wrong*."

"Look," he sighed, leaning forward and taking off his sunglasses. She kept hers on. "Whether or not you want to admit it, you and I *do* have unfinished business. I made a big mistake, yes. You made a mistake. It doesn't have to break us."

"There wasn't ever an *us*," Tate pointed out. Jameson shrugged.

"Whatever we were. Friends," he suggested. She laughed.

"We were never friends," she replied.

"We were something."

"We were *nothing*."

"Why do you need everything to be so clearly defined? Because society says *A* plus *B* equals *C*, then we're nothing? Sometimes *X* divided by *4.3* equals *fuck all*, Tate. Bad things happened, but there were moments of good," Jameson reminded her. He *needed* her to remember. She snorted again and turned away so she was fully facing the water.

"I seem to have forgotten those moments. Probably when my oxygen supply was cut off, right after my seizures," she snapped at him.

"That's not funny."

"No, not even a little bit," Tate agreed. He took a deep breath. Dug down deep into his heart to find a shred of kindness. Of honesty.

"I'm very sorry for ever hurting you," he said in a soft voice. It was obvious she was struggling not to cry.

"Someday," she started, clearing her throat, "you will find someone who is better at these games. Better than *you*, and you will finally know how it feels."

"How will I find this someone else if I'm not looking?" Jameson asked.

"Maybe you should start looking. You're not getting any younger," she pointed out.

"I have the person I want," he said bluntly. She choked on a gasp of air.

"You don't have shit," Tate managed to cough out. He laughed.

"You're so easy to rile up now. This should be fun," he said. She shook her head.

"I don't want to play your games," she insisted. He leaned against the table, crossed his arms on top of it.

Finally, we can cut to the chase.

"How about just one last game. No-holds-barred, winner takes all," he offered.

"How about that's a really bad idea," she replied, but he could tell that she was intrigued.

"Give me a month," Jameson started. Her eyebrows raised above her glasses and she turned towards him.

"A month to what?" she asked.

"One month to convince you that I'm not the devil," he stated. Tate burst out laughing.

"A leopard can't change his spots, Jameson. But go head, explain your little game. I could use some cheering up," she snickered.

"One month to convince you that I'm not the devil, that things can be as good between us as they ever were," he continued.

"Hmmm. Not very appetizing, I'm not really winning on this deal," Tate pointed out, still smiling to herself.

Jameson got up from his chair. Slowly walked around the table. She stiffened up when he got next to her, but she didn't move away when he leaned down close to her head. Pressed a hand to the side of her face to bring her in close to his lips.

"*One month to make you forget your ballplayer even exists,*" he whispered against her ear. Oh yes, he knew all about the ballplayer. Jameson had an online subscription to The Boston Globe.

But he could feel something. Her body was connected to his, in some inexplicable way. It always had been, ever since their very first time together. She didn't move at all, but he could feel her skin come to life. Like it was vibrating, humming with energy.

"It's cute that you even think that's possible," Tate whispered back, but he was already grinning. He knew she was bluffing. He let go of her and stood upright.

"One month, Tatum. Here, with me and Sanders."

"Ooohhh, I get Sanders in the deal, too?"

"Looked to me like you already had him."

"Jealous?"

"Don't be stupid."

"But what do I get out of this?" she pressed him. Jameson sighed.

"If after one month, you still don't want anything to do with me, you have my promise that I'll leave you alone. No showing up at your home, or your job, or talking to your friends. Any of that bullshit, I'll even do split custody with Sanders. I'll let you go. Once and for all. We let this go, whatever *this* is," he told her, gesturing between them.

Tate was silent for a long time. If it hadn't been for the stern set of her mouth, he almost would've thought she'd fallen asleep. But after a long time, she opened her mouth. Closed it. Thought for a second longer. Opened it again.

"You have to know, you won't win," Tate warned him.

Looks like I already have.

"Won't know for sure until I've tried. But you have to be honest with me, you can't fake anything or lie. You have to let me do whatever I want," Jameson amended the deal.

"I was always honest with you, and you should never be allowed to do whatever you want," she replied. He laughed.

"Fair enough. Do we have a deal? One *whole* month, starting today?" he asked.

"You won't win," she warned him again, but she held out her hand. He took it in his own.

"Baby girl, I never lose."

Inside her brain, Tate was freaking out. She wasn't sure what she'd gotten herself into – an all expenses paid, luxurious vacation in the South of Spain? *Check.* Psychotherapy under the guise of hitting a dear friend? *Check.* A deal with the devil that could potentially mean losing her soul? *Double Check.*

The end result was too tantalizing to turn down, though. It would be over. No more wondering, or worrying, or what ifs. Just *over.* Dead. No more Jameson and Tate, whatever they even were, anyway.

But she couldn't quite figure out his angle. Jameson didn't care about her, that much was clear. If he did, he wouldn't be offering her some silly game – he'd be offering his heart. Was he really so obsessed with sleeping with her that he needed to drag her all the way to Spain? Play *more* games with her? She would only ever be just a game to him. Maybe that had been fine before, but it wasn't fine now. She wanted more for herself, and she certainly wasn't going to get it from him.

Jameson could play all the stupid games he wanted, Tate wasn't about to fall for them again. She was not going to make the next thirty days easy for him. They would go around in circles for the next month, then it would be goodbye, *forever.* And hey, if he happened to grow a heart in the process and lose it to her, why, that would just be gravy on top. But either way, he *would not* be winning this time around.

Easy as pie.

4

AFTER MAKING HER DEAL WITH the devil, Tate went to her room to change. If she was going to be busting balls, she couldn't be doing it wearing Ellie's style of clothing. For god's sake, she was wearing *khaki*. Barf. Tate felt like she was really waking up, for the first time since the hospital.

And the first thing she wanted was a really tight pair of pants.

They hadn't spoken much after they'd woken up, but Sanders hadn't seemed bothered by their little slumber party, so she convinced him to go shopping with her. They were treated exceedingly well in all the stores they went to – Sanders' expensive, tailored-to-fit suit, and Jameson's black American Express card, ensured prompt service.

In the old days, she had spent Jameson's money sparingly. Tate didn't mind being taken care of, but she also wasn't a *complete* whore. She never bought herself clothing or jewelry or gifts, or anything else of that nature. But those days were gone. She felt like Jameson owed her, and until she could take it out of him in skin, she would burn his money.

She bought everything. Anything Tate saw that she even remotely liked, she bought. Every store had a stack of purchases, promising to have them delivered by the end of the business day. She even bought Sanders clothing, though it was very much against his will.

"C'mon, Sandy, admit it, you're having fun," Tate teased as they were leaving a restaurant. Sanders had begged for lunch after the first four hours of shopping.

"Yes, it is kind of fun. It reminds me of how we used to be," he replied. She looped her arm through his and leaned against him.

"How do you mean?"

"In Boston. When we would wait for Jameson to get off work," he reminded her. Tate frowned.

"This isn't like that. You know that, right?" she asked. He shrugged.

"We're all together again. That's all that matters to me," Sanders replied.

"I wish more people were like you, Sandy."

"Me, too."

They went shoe shopping for a while after that – Tate hadn't brought one single pair of heels with her, thinking she would be on vacation with just Sanders. Now that wouldn't do. Jameson was a tall man, around six-foot-two, and broad shouldered. Big. Much bigger than her. She could wear skyscrapers on her feet around him and still feel like a petite pixie. Heels weren't necessary to make an outfit sexy, but she didn't think they hurt, and she knew he loved her in heels. Loved her ass, her legs.

I want him gagging for it.

She only bought designer. Red bottoms, big labels, towering heels, double-platforms. The bills were enormous, more money than she had ever spent in her entire life. She loved it. She found herself regretting not taking advantage of it all when she had been living with him.

They stopped for coffee before heading home, and Tate finally bit the bullet and made some phone calls. Though she still hadn't been able to really pin him down before she left, she and Ang were in a much better position friend-wise. It was the reason why she hadn't called him the day before; she knew Ang was going to be pissed when he found out what had happened.

Turned out, pissed wasn't a strong enough word. *Atomic* was almost better. Ang freaked the fuck out. Was threatening to sell a kidney to fly over there and get her. When people at neighboring tables began to tune into the screaming coming out of Tate's phone, Sanders took it away and put it to his own ear. She wasn't sure how he did it, but Sanders had the ability to calm just about anyone down. Maybe it was his tranquil nature. She wasn't sure. Ang had been all kinds of mad, but after five minutes of talking, he was calm and willing to let her stay there in peace. *For now.*

Nick wasn't a happy camper, either, but he wasn't like Ang. He never tried to tell her what to do. He just wanted her to be happy, and careful. He told her his home would always be open to her. Tate wouldn't be back in Boston till the end of January, and by then he would be settling into his house in Arizona, gearing up for spring training.

She didn't tell either of the boys about the little bet she had going with Jameson.

When they headed home, it was a little after six. Jameson had told them dinner would be at seven, but he probably hadn't been expecting them to stay gone all day. She thought it was awesome. One day down, only twenty-nine left to go. Tate would win this game like she had invented it.

"Uh uh. No way. *Nooooo* way," Jameson was shouting at them as they made their way onto his boat.

"What?" Tate asked innocently, ignoring all the bags and boxes that were strewn across the deck.

"Have you seen these fucking bills? I like expensive shit, Tate, but goddamn, did you buy everything in the entire fucking town?" Jameson snapped. She suppressed the urge to shudder – she hadn't heard that tone of voice in a long time.

"Oh, I'm sorry. Money a little tight lately?" she teased as Sanders disappeared inside the boat. She'd had all day to talk herself up, build up her courage. Talking to Jameson now, she almost felt like her old self again.

"*Fuck you.* I could buy this entire fucking city and dump it in the goddamn ocean, and my bank account wouldn't even notice. And do you know why? *Because I earned that money.* I can spend it any way I fucking want – *you* need to work for it," he growled, waving the bills in her face. Tate shrugged.

"Restitution. *You owe me.* You're lucky I didn't buy a fucking $50,000 pearl necklace. You want me to stay? This is part of my new price. *Suck it up,*" she informed him. Jameson's eyebrows went up.

Now I've got his attention.

"New price, hmmm?" he questioned. He looked equal parts intrigued and wary.

"Oh yes. I am most definitely worth a lot more now," Tate assured him.

"That's a matter of opinion."

"*And yours doesn't matter,*" she mocked him. He rolled his eyes.

"I think I liked you better when you were all damaged and weepy."

"God, you're going to burn in a special place in hell."

"Probably. At least I'll have memories of you to keep me happy."

"Stop talking. Where are you taking us to dinner?" she demanded, wading into the sea of bags and boxes.

"Nowhere. I had planned on us eating here tonight," Jameson informed her. Tate turned back towards him.

"Seriously?" she asked, not hiding the disgust in her voice.

"Yes. Is my pathetic excuse for a yacht not good enough for her majesty to dine on?" he asked, folding his arms across his chest.

"It'll do, but I was hoping for lobster and champagne," she replied. He snorted.

"Tatum, the only time I buy a woman lobster and champagne is when I'm guaranteed pussy at the end of the night."

She turned away. This was the part she wasn't prepared for; she didn't know if she would ever be prepared. Snarky banter was one thing – sexy banter was a whole other. It was too close to him. Sex and Jameson were like … synonymous. Tate could flirt with him, dangle herself in front of him, but she wanted to avoid sleeping with him. It was too dangerous. During sex, it was like he owned her body, her mind. Like they weren't hers anymore.

Probably because they never were.

"Pity. Guess I'll have to find someone else to buy me lobster," she managed to sigh. Jameson barked out a laugh.

"Good luck with that. I don't know if you've noticed, but there are a million women here, all throwing themselves at anyone who looks like they've got money. So go ahead, give it your best shot," he offered.

Ooohhh, he makes me want to kill.

Tate turned around and walked towards him. She took a deep breath and reached a hand out, pressed it against his chest. Felt the muscles twitch under her palm. She chewed at her bottom lip and dragged her fingertips across his front. Slowly, she did a full circle around him, letting her nails scratch a path around his body. When she was back in front of him, she leaned in close.

"*Good thing I'm one in a million,*" she whispered.

Jameson turned his head towards her and her breath caught in her throat. They were very close together. She could barely remember the last time they had been so close. She let her eyes wander over his face, his newly sun-kissed skin, his dark lashes, his lips. Lips that she knew could treat her so well. Lips that were so close to her own.

He leaned a little closer and she could feel his breath against her mouth. So close ...

"*When is dinner?*" Sanders' voice boomed across the deck.

Saved by the bell.

Tate smiled and looked up, but only to find Jameson staring very hard at her. She looked into his eyes, *really looked*, probably for the first time since she had gotten to Spain. He looked angry. Or upset. Or maybe ... maybe even hurt.

Not possible.

Jameson cooked dinner. Tate thought she was going to have a heart attack. She had never seen him cook before, hadn't ever seen him even operate a microwave. She kept peeking in the kitchen, watching him as he made shrimp scampi. He caught her staring one too many times, though, and stood back from the stove, offering to let her cook. She snorted at him and sat outside.

The food was divine. Was there anything the man didn't do well? It was made even better by the fact that she was eating it on the Mediterranean. Tate was so caught up in all their drama, that sometimes she forgot she was in a whole other country. She toasted Sanders with her water glass, and then Jameson disappeared into the boat.

"I thought this would be more appropriate," he said when he reappeared, carrying a bottle of champagne.

Her breath got stuck in her chest as she watched him pour a glass for Sanders. She hadn't had any alcohol since her little episode. Tate didn't think she was an alcoholic, but it was also very obvious she couldn't trust herself around the stuff. One brush with death was enough for her to learn her lesson. Jameson poured a glass for himself, then raised his eyebrows at her.

"I don't think I should," she told him.

"Aright. But what do you *want?*" he asked. She bit her bottom lip. Champagne wasn't exactly something she got treated to very often. Nick was more of a beer kind of guy, and not only was Ang poor, he was more of a double vodka-black out drunk kind of guy. Tate held out her glass.

"Just a little," she instructed him.

After they had their celebratory glass, cheesecake was produced. They ate in silence, watching boats come and go. When they were finished, Sanders excused himself and went to his room, leaving her all alone with the devil. They sat in silence for a while, then Jameson lit up a cigarillo.

"Bother you?" he asked, glancing at her. Tate was shocked that he was even asking.

"No. In fact, I'm glad you're doing that," she replied, then scampered away to find her purse. When she had it, she sat back down at the table and dug through the bag till she found what she needed. She pulled it out and Jameson laughed.

"You've got to be shitting me," he chuckled. She shook her head.

"We all have our coping mechanisms. Got a light?" she asked, holding the Marlboro Light 100 out towards him. He shook his head.

"You are not smoking that *filth* on my boat," he told her. Now it was Tate's turn to laugh.

"You're smoking right now," she pointed out.

"*This* was imported from Cuba. It's a work of art. You're smoking something that smells like death. You'll stink, my boat will stink, *no*," Jameson stated. She glared at him and dug a lighter out of her bag. She put the cigarette between her lips.

"Just because we have a deal, doesn't mean you get to tell me what to do. Those days are long gone, and I am —," she started, when he got up and stood in front of her, pulling the cigarette out of her mouth. She watched as he broke it in half.

"I don't give a shit about our deal. You could be my Nana, and I wouldn't let you fucking smoke. No cigarettes on my boat," he stressed.

Did he just say Nana?

"This is the stupidest thing I've ever heard. You can smoke something because it was made in Cuba, but I can't smoke a stupid cigarette? Fine. *Fine.* What if I go find some fancy French imports? How about some German roll-your-owns? Fancy enough for Mr. High-and-Mighty?" Tate snapped, standing up and glaring at him.

"I don't care if they're from Middle Earth and rolled in gold. *No cigarettes,*" Jameson wouldn't budge.

"I'm sorry. Did you just make a Hobbit reference?" she asked, stunned.

"Yes. Don't change the subject. Give me your cigarettes," he asked again, holding out his hand.

"Are you joking?" she laughed, clutching her purse to her chest.

"No. I don't want to find out you've been sneaking them in your room, or in the bathroom. Jesus, you haven't gotten Sanders started, have you?" he groaned.

"No! I'm not some drug dealer, peer pressuring Sandy into smoking! And he's not that stupid anyway," Tate snapped.

"At least you recognize what you're doing is stupid. I'm not asking again – give me the cigarettes," Jameson demanded. She snorted and started to walk away.

"You can fuck right off, that's what you can do."

She hadn't made it far when she felt his arms wrap around her from behind. It was like a five-alarm fire instantly spread across her skin. She gasped and struggled against his hold. He simply picked her up, holding onto her tightly so her feet were dangling above his own.

"Give up yet?" he asked from behind her. She could feel one of his hands pulling at the bottom of her bag, so she crushed it to her chest.

"*No!* I promise I won't smoke on your stupid boat! Let me go!" Tate yelled.

"Stop yelling."

"I'll do whatever the fuck I want, you can't —,"

He shook her back and forth, and her fingers opened, letting her purse go. It slipped through her hands and past his, crashing to the deck. Most of the contents spilled everywhere, and when Jameson saw the pack of cigarettes, he kicked them hard enough to send them flying overboard. She gasped, and at the same time, he dropped her. She stumbled forward a little before turning to face him.

"I forgot how difficult you like to make things," he grumbled, rubbing at his lower back.

"You can't just do that! You can't just grab people, and shake them until they do what you want! You can't just —," Tate was shouting, when he reached out and clamped a hand over her mouth. She went to move away, but his other hand was at the back of her head, holding her in place. He forced her forward, till their foreheads were almost meeting.

"*Stop. Yelling,*" he growled at her. She tried to tell him off, but it all sounded like *womp wuh womp womp* from behind his hand. "I am going to take my hand away. You are going to be quiet. Yes?" She managed a nod, and he slowly removed his hand from her mouth.

"*DON'T YOU EVER FUCKING —,*" she started to shriek.

The hand on the back of her head bunched into a fist, and before Tate knew what was happening, Jameson was pulling her hair. Snapping her head back. The sting caused her to gasp and her hands flew to his chest. Not to push him away, but to keep herself from falling into him. She was stunned, and by the look on his face, he seemed more than a little surprised, too.

In their past life, it would have been normal. Even expected. Jameson telling Tate not to do something, or she'd be punished. She does it to get punished. He pulls her hair, she loves it. The way other people kiss cheeks or hug, Jameson and Tate had pain. Pleasure. It was second nature to them, a second language. How easy it was to fall back into old habits.

95

Being with Jameson is like doing heroin. Highly addictive and highly lethal.

She stared up at him, frozen in place. In all their time together, over the course of those two months, she had never felt out of her depth with him, or out of her league. But in that moment, right then, suddenly Tate was that eighteen-year-old girl again, standing with him in his bedroom. Excited. Nervous. *Scared.* Unsure of herself, of what was going on, of what he was going to do. Back then, there had only been one thing she had been sure of – that she wanted him to do *whatever* he wanted.

It was unsettling to know that deep down, she still felt that way.

"Scared, baby girl?" Jameson asked softly, his eyes roaming over her face. She cleared her throat.

"*Bored* would be a better word to use," she managed to reply. A smile slowly spread across his face, one she hadn't seen in a *long* time.

Satan, finally.

"It's nice to see there's still some fight left in you," he told her.

"You have no idea."

When he lowered his mouth to hers, Tate told herself she could handle it. It was just a kiss. She had kissed dozens of guys. Hundreds. Maybe more, who knew. This was just another man. Another mouth. She held herself still, closed her eyes.

She almost cried. That someone who caused her so much pain, could bring her so much pleasure, just wasn't right. Wasn't fair. His lips were soft, almost gentle, and made to fit her own. The hand he had tangled in her hair let go, his fingers massaging her scalp. She moaned and pressed against him. Tried to melt into him.

Who's winning now?

When he kissed her once more, twice, a third time, she didn't stop it. When his tongue ran along her bottom lip before plunging into her mouth, she didn't stop it. When his hand was back to tugging her hair, she didn't stop it. But when Jameson's free hand slid onto her hip, touched bare skin at her waist, it was like a cattle prod. Tate practically leapt out of her skin. Her eyes flew open and she broke the kiss, gasping in air as she stepped away from him. He chuckled.

"See? *Scared*," Jameson whispered, running his thumb across her bottom lip.

*Pool. You were half naked in a pool. You could have drowned. He may not have put you there, but he didn't help you get out, either. He doesn't care. **He does not care**.*

"No," Tate coughed out, then cleared her throat. "No, not scared. Just not that easy anymore."

"Oh god, then I might just be wasting my time," Jameson laughed. She glared at him.

"I already told you that you were. *Now pick up my shit*," she snarled, pointing at her purse before stomping away.

There. Who's tough shit now!?

She certainly felt like shit, when she woke up the next day. Tate felt like she had a hangover. Gross. Headache. Body aches. Self loathing really did a body in; she had tossed and turned for the better part of the night, resisting the urge to find Jameson and finish what they had started.

She had only been there for two mornings, but both times, food had magically been laid out in the galley, buffet style. He probably kept elves chained up in the bilge. She bypassed the eggs and settled on an ungodly amount of bacon and coffee, before heading out onto the bow to join him. He was looking fresh as a daisy, showered and clean shaven. She missed the stubble.

Fucker.

"Morning. You're looking particularly lovely," Jameson commented, not even bothering to look up from his newspaper. She grunted.

"Shut up. Where's Sanders?" Tate asked around a mouthful of bacon.

"He went on an errand, he'll be back later. Anything in particular you'd like to do today?" he asked.

"I don't know, aren't you supposed to be '*wooing*' me, or something? This is all pointless. I mean, so far I've been chastised for shopping, denied lobster, man-handled, and insulted. It's almost embarrassing, how badly you're failing at this," she taunted him. He folded the paper shut.

"'*Wooing*' is most definitely not the word I would use, and you used to love being man-handled," he reminded her as he sipped at his coffee.

"That was before I was man-handled straight into the deep end of a swimming pool." It was a low-blow, and completely unfair, but she couldn't resist the dig.

"I think we should make up some rules for our little game. No rubbing my past mistakes in my face every five minutes," Jameson told her. She snorted.

"Fuck that, cause it's not gonna happen. Have you ever had your stomach pumped? *Been committed?* I'll say anything I fucking want to," Tate snapped. He rolled his eyes.

"I guess we need to work on trust in our relationship."

"*We* don't have a relationship."

"Let's go on the boat," he suddenly said. A piece of bacon fell out of her mouth.

"Huh?"

"You don't have any plans today, neither do I. Let's go on a boat ride," he suggested.

"You're gonna take this behemoth on the water, by yourself?" she asked. Jameson laughed.

"I have, but no. I was talking about the *other* boat."

The way she was feeling, Tate didn't think a jaunt on a speed boat sounded like very much fun. But she knew if she protested, he would just get more pleasure out of it. She grumbled and ate more bacon.

"*Fine,*" she finally spit out.

"Wonderful. I'll get it ready," Jameson started as he stood up. He picked something up off the table and handed it to her. "Don't forget to put this away, you don't want to lose it."

She looked up to see him holding out her passport. She slowly took it from him, looking it over. She didn't remember ever giving it to him. Or even taking it out in front of him. It had been in her purse since she'd gotten off the airplane.

"Where did you find it?" Tate asked.

"On the deck, last night. Remember? You told me to '*pick up your shit*,'" he reminded her, smiling down at her.

Oh god.

"Oh. Yeah. Where's the rest of it?" she asked, glancing around. They were eating at the same table they had been dining at the night before, but she didn't see her bag anywhere.

"Well, since no one has ever said those words to me before, I couldn't quite figure out what they meant. I thought about waking Sanders up so he could explain them to me, but that seemed silly, so I figured I should just sweep it all under a rug," Jameson replied, strolling across the deck towards the back of the boat. She looked at the floor.

"Jameson. You don't have any rugs," she called out.

"I know. So I kicked your shit overboard."

Tate dashed to the railing and looked over the edge. Of course she couldn't see anything. She groaned and let her head fall forward. He had kicked her purse into the ocean. Of course. Stupid woman. She should've known better. She was lucky he had even bothered to save her passport. God, her keys, her money, her wallet, *everything* was now at the bottom of the harbor.

At the thought of her wallet, though, she perked up. Jameson's black American Express card was still in her wallet. *Ha ha ha.* And the day before she had bought three handbags, from three ridiculously expensive designers. The ocean could keep her Kate Spade knock off. Tate started laughing, and didn't stop till she was back in her bedroom.

A shower improved her attitude even more, and by the time she put on some new clothes and went upstairs, she felt human again. Better than human. She felt like *herself*, and she hadn't felt that way in a long time. She tried not to think about the fact that Jameson had something to do with it.

Like always.

He was sitting in the speed boat with the engine idling, leaning over the side to talk to their neighbor. Tate made her way down the plank thingy and then stood at the back of the smaller boat, waiting for Jameson to finish so he could help her on board. The man he was talking to finally noticed her and smiled, giving a tilt of his head before going back to his own boat. Jameson turned towards her, then stood still.

She was wearing a pair of extremely short denim cut-offs, paired with a slouchy, long sleeve, dolman style top. It draped off one shoulder and was cropped in the front, showing a slice of stomach. She had yanked her hair up into a messy ponytail and then shoved on a pair of aviator sunglasses, but hadn't bothered with shoes.

"Welcome back," Jameson blurted out. Tate raised her eyebrows.
"Excuse me?"

"You were hiding behind those Stepford-wife clothes. This is the real you. *Welcome back,*" he stressed as he walked towards her. She rolled her eyes.

"Clothes don't make a person, Jameson," she pointed out. He

held a hand out to her and she took it.

"No," he agreed, and helped her down onto the back of the boat. He wrapped an arm around her waist, holding her steady as the water rocked them. "But sometimes they can improve the scenery."

Tate snorted and pushed away from him. She couldn't be physically close to him, not after what had happened the night before; two more minutes of kissing, and she would've been on her knees. Bent over a table. Laid out flat. *All his.* She had to stay strong. She would win this game.

"Where are we going?" she asked, plopping into the passenger seat. He cast off from the dock and sat down to her right, behind the wheel.

"Just around. Thought we'd take her out, really open her up," he replied, easing the boat away from the yacht and slowly pulling away from the marina.

"Sounds oddly familiar," Tate mumbled, and Jameson laughed.

"Someone decided to be feisty today. I like it."

They were silent as he made his way around the marina and past the jetty. There were a couple of other boats out and about, some small ones zipping around, and a sailboat in the distance, but that was it. The water was actually pretty calm. It was Marbella's slow season, Jameson explained, that's why the harbor wasn't overflowing with people.

"How long have you been here?" Tate asked, talking louder as they picked up speed.

"About a month and a half," he replied.

"Living on the boat?"

"No, I have an apartment in town. I was having the boat resealed. It got finished about a week before your birthday," he said.

"Ah. That's when you planned all this."

"I had a back up plan," Jameson assured her. "If the boat wasn't going to be ready, Sanders was going to take you to Denmark."

"I've been to Denmark. I wouldn't have been as impressed," Tate replied.

"So you've been impressed. Good to know."

Dammit.

"How did you talk Sanders into all this?" she changed the subject a little.

"When I left, I made him promise that he would help me. When I told him I wanted you brought to me, he jumped on the idea. Almost everything else was his planning, his doing. I would've just hired a private plane, but he insisted on flying commercial," Jameson told her.

If they had flown private, Tate would have known Jameson was behind it. Sanders was clever.

"I'm still a little surprised by him, that he would trick me like that. We've … grown close," she started to explain. Jameson snorted and the boat jumped in speed. They were going so fast, they were skipping across the ocean like a stone. *Whump, whump, whump.*

"*Obviously.*"

"Not like that. We're friends. He knows how I feel about you. I wouldn't have thought he'd pull something like this," she tried to clarify.

"And how do you feel about me?" Jameson asked. Tate paused for a while.

"It's certainly not a good feeling," she assured him. He laughed.

"You know he wants this, right? We're like estranged parents that he's trying to get back together. It's all very sweet," he told her. She laughed as well.

"We were never together, so it's going to be pretty hard going for him."

"Tatum," Jameson's voice was serious as he looked over at her. They were zipping along at incredible speeds, but he kept his eyes locked on her face. "We were '*together*' for a lot longer than either one of us wants to admit."

He yanked the wheel to the left, hard, and she felt her heart drop down into her stomach. Whether it was from the boat, or his words, she couldn't be sure. Before she could ponder it, he whipped the boat in a tight circle, sending up a huge wave. Tate clung to the railing, struggling to keep from being thrown overboard. Before she could get her bearings, he gunned the engine, and the boat leapt forward, inertia thrusting her back into her seat. She felt like she was in a wind tunnel, a jet engine blasting air and water into her face.

This is amazing.

Jameson had always known how to show her a good time, and not just in the naughty sense. It was like without communicating, he just knew the things she would like; what clothing she would like to wear, what foods she preferred to eat, movies she would want to see. She had never really noticed it before, but when she found herself thinking a ride on a speed boat was the best time she'd had since September, she realized it. In his own backwards, domineering way, Jameson liked to indulge her. Tate was blown away.

This is going to be harder than you thought, stupid girl.

After scaring her a couple more times with some tight turns, and weaving in and out of buoys, Jameson finally slowed down. Took them well away from town and other boats, then threw out the anchor. Tate was about to ask if he was planning on killing her and dumping her body, when his phone rang. He took the call, standing at the very end of the boat with his back to her.

Tate crawled her way out onto the bow, dragging some cushions with her. She had thought they would just go out for a quick spin, so she hadn't brought her bathing suit. She stretched herself out and pushed up her sleeves, rolled up the bottom of her top so it was right under her breasts. Then she yanked up the legs of her shorts as absolutely high as they would go, before unbuttoning the top and rolling it down. She wanted to soak up as much sun as possible before she went home. Winters in Boston were cruel.

She didn't know how long she laid like there that, but it was long enough to almost doze off. She wasn't aware of Jameson until he was standing right over her.

"You can just get naked, Tate. I won't be offended," he offered. She managed a snort and put her hands behind her head, not opening her eyes.

"Keep dreaming, Kane," she told him.

"It is a sort of recurring thing for me lately."

"Dreaming about me naked?"

"Yes."

"Good. Cause that's all you'll ever have."

"You always make these threats, you realize," he started, and she heard him move. He knelt next to her. "That first time, threatening to walk out of my apartment. Then when you came to my office, warning me that we would never happen. You're like an anti-prophet. By proclaiming that it won't be, I think you're actually hoping it will."

Tate didn't answer him. Didn't want to think about it. With every person she'd ever had sex with, it had always been just that – sex. Every boyfriend she'd ever had, Ang, an accidental orgy, all just sex. Jameson was the only one it was different with; it had never been *just sex*. Tate could admit that, even if it wasn't the same for him. It had always been something else to her. If she slept with him again, she would be in danger of getting confused again. She had to keep her guard up.

"I think you like to interpret things however best suits your moods and opinions," she replied. Jameson laughed.

"Very true."

They were silent for a while after that. She didn't know what he was doing, because she was too scared to open her eyes and look at him. Then, suddenly, she felt his fingertips against her stomach. Tracing around her hip bone, then lightly up to the edge of her shirt.

Back down again. No nails, no scratching, so it was different coming from him, but it still caused her to shiver. She squirmed under his touch.

"How long did she stay?" Tate blurted out.

One of these days, I will have to develop a filter.

"Excuse me?"

"*Pet.* How long did she stay with you?" she asked, licking her lips nervously. Jameson was quiet for a long time.

"She didn't. I made her leave that night, with everyone else," he finally replied, his voice soft.

"Poor girl."

"It was better than she deserved."

"I saw you with her, in the kitchen."

"Really?"

"Yes. She was whispering sweet-nothings to you in German," Tate told him. She didn't know where this was all coming from, she hadn't intended on talking about anything personal with him.

"It's a good thing you don't speak German. There was nothing sweet about what she was saying," Jameson replied, and his voice was no longer soft.

"Looked pretty cozy to me. She was probably devastated. I know how I felt when I found out you were fucking another woman, it wasn't exac—,"

"*I never slept with her,*" he interrupted, his hand going flat against her stomach. Tate finally opened her eyes. He was still kneeling, but he was looking down at her with murder in his eyes.

"Now that I don't believe for an instant," she managed a laugh.

"If you will think very hard, you will remember that I never once lied to you. I may have withheld things, but I *never* lied. I am not lying now. I did not sleep with her. Not in Germany, and not at home," Jameson assured her.

Tate didn't want to think about it, so she closed her eyes and filed his confession away.

Under F, for "so fucked up I can't even handle it".

"Whatever, it looked sweet," she continued.

"She was telling me that I was wasting my time on filth like you," he explained.

"*Bitch.*"

"She's not a very nice person."

"Neither are you."

"No, but I never once thought you were filth. I told her to get the fuck out of my house," Jameson replied.

"So, you used her. You led her to believe you had something going, you brought her home to embarrass and hurt me, and then you kicked her out. You're doing a very poor job of convincing me you're not the devil," Tate pointed out.

"I've still got a couple weeks. You're going to have raccoon eyes," Jameson warned her, and she felt him fiddle with her sunglasses. She batted his hand away and sat up.

"Like the tan I'm going to have is going to be any better," she laughed, climbing to her feet and looking down at her mangled outfit.

"I told you. Just take your clothes off. There's no one out here, and it's nothing I haven't seen before," he pointed out, standing as well.

Tate looked up at him. Jameson was staring down at her, but at her body, not her face. She watched his eyes sweep over her frame, and she could see the blatant desire in his gaze. She found herself wondering when the last time he'd had sex was, wondered who it was with, if it was any good. The idea of him sleeping with other women used to turn her on. Now she just wanted to puke.

"*Alright.*"

Jameson looked a little surprised, but he didn't move as she slowly pulled her shirt over her head. His eyes got wider as he took in her white bra. Then she took her time peeling her shorts away from her hips, revealing skimpy, black panties. His eyes followed her movements, watching her hands and legs as she slid the material down her body, even watched her toes when she kicked the shorts into the back of the boat. If she hadn't known any better, she would have sworn he was holding his breath.

"That's not naked," Jameson informed her, in a tone of voice she knew well. A tone that meant he wouldn't tolerate any dissension.

"Are you sure you're ready for that?" Tate whispered, stepping up so she was pressed against him, pressing her hands flat against his chest. She almost felt dizzy, being that close to him.

"Baby girl, I was built ready for you."

"Too bad."

"Why?"

"Because you've never known how to handle me."

And with that, she shoved against his chest, as hard as she could. Normally, he was like a brick wall, unmovable. But he had been completely unprepared. Caught off guard. Jameson let out a shout and fell backwards, off the side of the boat. Into the water.

By the time he hauled himself back into the boat, Tate had stretched herself back out on the bow. She was wiggling her bra straps off her shoulders when she felt him stomp up to her. She didn't open her eyes, but smiled big, knowing he was watching her. Probably angrily. Probably so mad, he wanted to —,

THWACK.

She let out a shriek as something cold and wet landed across her, covering her from head to hips. She sat up and fought to untangle herself. When she finally got free, she realized Jameson had thrown his wet shirt on top of her. Her underwear and bra were now soaked, her hair plastered to the top of her head. She turned her head to glare at him, her sunglasses askew on her nose.

"Have you already forgotten everything I worked so hard to

teach you? You never get to have the last word, Tatum," Jameson told her, his arms folded across his broad chest. She growled and threw his shirt back up at him.

"Can we go back now? All this *fun* is making my head hurt."

She put her clothing back on, then managed to get her wet bra off from underneath her shirt – no free peep-show for Satan. Jameson just drove back without a shirt on. It didn't seem to bother him at all, but it was making Tatum very uncomfortable. She kept her eyes trained forward, not even glancing at him out of her peripherals. Of course she was very familiar with what he looked like shirtless, but she tried to keep those memories at bay. A good body and great sex didn't mean shit, when a person wound up floating in a pool, stoned out of her mind.

She just had to remember that.

They didn't talk, and when they got back to Puerto Banus, she thought maybe she had lucked out, that he was done pressing his attentions on her for the day. Jameson could only take so much social interaction, she knew, before he had to hide away. She managed to scramble off the boat before he could offer her a hand and she turned to walk back towards the yacht.

"Tatum," he called after her.

"Yeah?" she asked, starting to turn back to him. Something hit her in the face. She threw up her hands in time to catch her soaking wet bra before it fell to the ground.

Goddammit.

She didn't wait for his clever remark, just stomped her way onto the bigger boat next to them.

5

TATE KNEW SHE WAS MAKING things worse on herself. Her bitchy attitude was just antagonizing Jameson, making him try harder. Not good for her. The whole situation set her teeth on edge. Made her want to scream. Made her want to vomit. Made her want to run away.

Makes you want to give in.

She stayed below deck for a while and played chess with Sanders. "*Play*" was a generous term – he beat her every time, and the game only ever went on for as long as he wanted it to. But they would talk while they played. While he was lost in the intricacies of the game, his tongue would loosen.

"Sandy," she started, glancing at him. His eyes were focused on the board while he set the pieces back up.

"Pay attention. I'm going to teach you the Alekhine Defense. It's very common and will help improve your game," he told her. Tate nodded.

"I'm paying attention. But I wanted to ask you something," she continued. His eyes flicked to her before going back to the board.

"Go ahead."

"Do you think Jameson would ever marry me?" she asked.

Sanders stopped moving. He slowly lifted his eyes to hers, then leaned back from the board. They were sitting cross-legged in the middle of his bed, the chess board between them. He glanced around the room, then back at her.

"Why are you asking me this?" he asked back.

"Because it seems to me, and Jameson, that your whole goal in this little scheme is to get us together. Am I right?" Tate asked, picking up a Rook and toying with it.

"I … I just want things to be as they should," Sanders replied.

"So, Jameson and I sleeping together is how things should be?" Tate laughed. He cleared his throat.

"You were happy being with him. He was happy. I don't understand what the confusion is. If you would like to be happy again, then I think you should be together," Sanders tried to explain. Tate's laughter fell away. It was a very sweet sentiment.

"You have to know that he doesn't care about me. Whatever you're hoping for isn't going to happen. He wants to play a game, and I'm just trying to get out alive this time. I can't be with him, Sandy. Not after what he did to me," she told him. His lips pressed together for a moment while he thought.

"He made a mistake," Sanders' voice was soft. She opened her mouth to argue and he held up a hand. "A very large, very dangerous mistake. He wasn't thinking right. The fact that he got so upset, is a sign of *how much* he cares."

"His 'sign' nearly broke me."

"You can always go home. I will fly out with you, tonight, if that is what you wish. But it seemed to me that you were missing something. You haven't been yourself the past two months, but over the past two days, it has been like watching you come out of a coma. It's nice. I enjoy it. I had hoped that you realized it, too," he told her.

Tate frowned and looked down, putting the Rook back in its

place. She didn't like hearing things like that – Jameson always seemed to find a way to be responsible for all the good things in her life. She didn't appreciate it.

"I have," she whispered, then cleared her throat. "But that doesn't mean I'm stupid enough to fall for the same trick twice. Sandy, if I … if by the end of all this, by some magical chance, Jameson actually cares about me, actually wants to be with me, but I don't want to be with him, are you going to be okay with that? Would you be okay if I broke his heart and left him?"

Sanders actually laughed.

"How funny. If Jameson could finally prove to you how much he cares, why would you leave?" he asked.

Poor, simple, sweet Sanders.

"I know you love him, but the world doesn't revolve around Jameson Kane, Sandy. Just because he might fall in love with me, *does not* mean I will fall in love with him," Tate pointed out. Sanders cocked his head to the side.

"I've always wondered, how did you get so good at doing that?" he asked. She was thrown for a loop."

"Good at what?"

"Lying to yourself."

Before she could even process what he had just said to her, the bedroom door swung open. They both turned to see Jameson standing there. She hadn't seen him since their boat ride. She'd stuck mostly to her bedroom and he'd stayed above deck. Avoiding each other.

"Good evening, children. Just wondering if anyone had some suggestions for dinner," he said, wandering into the room.

Tate watched him as he prowled around. He had changed into a polo shirt and a pair of jeans. No shoes. The first time she had ever gone to his house in Weston, she had been shocked to see him barefoot. She had quickly learned that Jameson preferred to be barefoot whenever he got the chance. It was almost cute in a way. Her eyes wandered over him while he moved. His thick, black hair hadn't been cut in a while, and was a little wild on top of his head. His dark tan set off his blue eyes, even in the dim light of the bedroom, and she felt her heart beat quicken.

You're losing, you're losing, you're losing.

"Dancing," Tate practically shouted. Both men turned to look at her, and she licked her lips.

Note to self – SERIOUSLY, GET A FUCKING FILTER.

"Excuse me?" Jameson asked.

"I think we should go dancing. There's gotta be somewhere around here to dance. Let's do that," she suggested quickly, staring at him.

"You want to dance?" he clarified.

"Yeah, why not?" she asked.

"Do you know how to dance?"

"Do *you?*"

"I was thinking more along the lines of dinner up top," Jameson said. She groaned.

"I'm sorry, how is this any different than Boston? You never want to leave your little sanctuaries. How do you ever meet women?" Tate asked.

"I met you," he pointed out.

"By practically stalking me," she reminded him. He snorted.

"Alright, fine. We'll go out to dinner, then dancing. But when I say it's time to leave, it's time to leave," he stressed. She rolled her eyes.

"Yeah, yeah, I know. This is perfect, Sandy, I bought —," she started to get excited.

"No. No Sanders. Just you and I," Jameson said.

"Why not?" Tate whined.

"Sanders, do you want to go out dancing?" Jameson asked, and Tate had to laugh. Sanders looked ready to throw up.

"No, thank you."

"There. Be ready by eight," Jameson told her, and then walked out of the room.

She scrambled off the bed and high tailed it to her own room. That only gave her two hours to get ready, and she wanted to look nice. Wanted to look amazing. Wanted to make him regret ever losing the right to touch her.

Stupid fucker.

She pulled her hair up into a ponytail, but raked her fingers through the hair, giving it a messy, disheveled look; *sexy.* A look she hadn't gone for in a long time. She shimmied into a pair of tiny black shorts, then opted for a skin tight, long sleeve shirt. Something demure enough for dinner, but the plunging scoop-neckline also made it sexy enough for a night club.

Doing her makeup was harder. Tate hadn't really worn makeup since the accident. It seemed silly, but there hadn't been much of a reason to, no one worth being sexy for anymore. She didn't have her job, she wasn't going to sleep with anyone, and she had spent most of her time on a couch. What would have been the point of slutty eye makeup? But she laid it on thick now. She just barely talked herself out of false lashes. She wanted to look like a slut, not a two-dollar hooker. She finished off the outfit with a pair of high, thin stilettos. She turned every which way in front of a mirror, examining herself.

Eat your heart out, Satan.

Tate made her way upstairs, really wishing she could have a drink to settle her nerves. She hadn't been terribly nervous the first time she had gone to his house, and back then she had known they would end up in bed together. Now, not knowing how the night would turn out, only having hopes and wishes that she would get away unscathed – it was way worse.

"Do I look good?" she asked Sanders when she got out onto the deck. His eyes wandered over her.

"You look more like yourself," he replied. She laughed.

"That's not really an answer," she snickered.

"I know."

Tate laughed again and dug her finger into his side, causing him to jump and squirm away. His lips pressed into a hard line, obviously annoyed, but she just got closer and did it again.

"One of these days, you're going to push him too far," Jameson's voice warned from behind her.

"I could never push you too far, could I, Sandy?" Tate laughed, all of her fingers now traveling up and down his sides. He grabbed at her wrists.

"No, you could not," Sanders assured her.

"If you two are finished flirting, I'd like to leave."

Tate burst out laughing, and Sanders turned a little green. She was still snickering as she turned around, but her laughter caught in her throat, coming out as more of a snorting sound. Jameson was adjusting a watch on his wrist, not looking at her, which made her glad, because she didn't want to be caught drooling.

It was funny, but sometimes a person could wear really plain clothing, and it still looked expensive and rich. Jameson did this better than anyone she knew. He had changed into a very fitted t-shirt, which clung to his chest and shoulders in a way that made her mouth water. He had also tamed his hair, forcing it into a stylish mess that made her fingers ache to touch it. He finished adjusting his watch and put on his coat; a slim-fitted black leather jacket. When they had been together in Boston, if they ever went out, it was usually before or after work, so he just wore his suits. At home, he dressed to relax. Holy hell, she had never seen Jameson dressed to go out.

"You look nice," Tate blurted out, and he stopped in the middle of putting on his jacket, obviously surprised.

"I know, thank you," he replied. She snorted.

"You make it very hard to be nice to you," she told him, and he laughed.

"At least I'm consistent."

Her phone suddenly rang, and when she glanced at her screen, she couldn't believe the timing. Late Christmas present. Tate smiled slowly, and then looked up to find both Sanders and Jameson staring at her. She turned away a little before lifting the phone to her ear.

"Nick! How are you?" she exclaimed, her voice full of excitement. She could hear Jameson snort.

If she was using Nick when he wasn't actually present, it didn't really count, she figured.

*Maybe **I'm** really Satan, this whole time.*

"Good, good, how are you?" he asked.

"Doing good. Just about to go out and eat," she replied, crossing her legs at the ankle and fiddling with her ponytail.

"Nice. I was just checking in. It's kind of weird, isn't it? I mean, we've spent so much time together over the past couple months, and then to not see you or talk to you whenever I want …" he managed a laugh, but he sounded sad. Tate gave a sad laugh, as well.

"Awww, I miss you, too. Really," she told him.

There was another snort from behind her.

"Are you sure? I ran into Ang the other day, he seemed really concerned about you. I'm not here to judge you, Tate, I just … you know I'm always here, right? If you ever need me. If you need someone to come get you, I'll be there, in a heart beat," Nick assured her. She laughed.

"Always the gentleman. I don't need rescuing quite yet, but I'll be sure to call you if I do," she promised.

"I hope so. So. Are you having fun?" his tone lightened up.

"Sometimes. We went out on a speed boat today, it was alright," she started, laying it on thick and making it sound like it was the most boring thing she'd ever done. "But yesterday Sandy and I went shopping, and I bought anything I looked at, it was *awesome.*"

"Sounds like trouble. Did you buy clothing?" he asked.

"Yes, lots," she replied. He chuckled.

"Anything sexy?" he asked. Normally, Tate would stop the conversation right there. Whenever Nick tried to get flirty, she would put an immediate end to it. But she figured indulging him just a little bit this time wouldn't hurt anybody.

"Hmmm, define sexy," she told him, her voice low.

"Something other than khaki shorts and ankle-length-skirts," Nick offered. She laughed.

"I bought lots of shorts and skirts, but nothing khaki *or* ankle-length. You would love it, I bought this one skirt, it barely covers my —,"

Suddenly, her phone was pulled out of her hand. Tate barely had time to gasp before Jameson simply tossed it over the railing. She shrieked and dove for it, but it was too late. She got to watch her cell phone slowly sink into the inky depths, the screen flickering as it went.

"We'll be late," was all Jameson said before striding down the gangplank.

She was tempted to throw something at him, like a piece of furniture, but then she remembered – she was trying to be "nice" Tatum. Not vengeful, angry, spiteful Tatum. Not *punch-a-mother-fucker-in-the-head* Tatum. She took a couple deep breaths through her nose, then followed after him.

Jameson hadn't bothered waiting for her, and was halfway out of the parking area when she got off the boat. She glared at his back and started heading after him, but she refused to run. When he reached the street, he finally waited till she could catch up.

"That wasn't very polite," was all Tate said as she walked past him.

"Your phone call was *annoying me*. I wanted it to end," Jameson explained.

"You could have just *asked*, you didn't have to throw it in the fucking ocean," she pointed out.

"Oh, yes, I should have '*just asked*', because you've been *so compliant* up till now," he snapped back.

She suddenly burst out laughing, coming to a stop. They were in the middle of a crosswalk and Jameson had to grab her arm, yanking her forward. She stumbled on her heels, but managed to stay upright. He pulled her to a stop on a street corner.

"I'm sorry, I just realized something," Tate snickered.

"What?" he demanded.

"We argue and fight like an old married couple," she told him.

"Oh, jesus. Have you been drinking?"

"No. It's just, we never used to snap over stupid shit. It's kind of funny. When we were like a couple, we didn't act like it. Now that we're not anything like a couple, we *do* act like it," she wiped at her eyes.

"Maybe you should *start* drinking."

Jameson led her to an upscale restaurant that was near the marina. At first, when she saw the maître d' wearing a tux, she worried that she would be underdressed. But as they were taken to a table that sat on the third level, against a railing overlooking a huge dance floor, she saw that lots of people were dressed like her.

"When I said dancing, I was thinking more like a night club," Tate told him, sitting down as a waiter pushed in her chair.

"Then you thought wrong. *Señor* ..." Jameson started talking to their waiter in Spanish. She hadn't realized he spoke Spanish. She knew he spoke German – she had heard him speaking it to Petrushka. How many other languages did he speak? The waiter nodded and scurried away.

"What was all that?" she asked. He took off his jacket and sat across from her.

"I ordered for us," he told her.

"How do you know what I want?" she responded. Jameson laughed.

"Tatum, I *always* know what you want."

She swallowed thickly and looked away. She felt stupid. Since he had come back into her life, ever since she had catered for his party, she had been able to step up to Jameson. Sexy banter used to flow easily between them. Now she felt like her tongue was stuck to the roof of her mouth.

*Just fake it. Act like you're with someone, **anyone**, else.*

"You know what I think your problem is?" Tate asked, leaning low over the table. His eyes flicked down to her tits and she smiled.

"Enlighten me," he responded.

"You think what *you want* is what *everyone wants*," she told him. Jameson shook his head.

"No, *my* problem is I know what I want, and just *don't care* what anyone else wants," he corrected her.

"Sounds like a pretty big problem."

"Only for other people."

"Still sounds like I'm talking to the devil," she teased, and was rewarded with his eyebrows drawing together.

"Sometimes, while talking to you, I get the same feeling," he replied. Tate frowned and shook off his words. She leaned back in her chair and looked over the railing.

"This wasn't the kind of dancing I had in mind," she changed the subject. She watched as people moved across the huge ballroom floor, in what she assumed was a salsa dance. A live band played upbeat music, and it was nice, but not something that made her want to shake her ass.

"Once it gets late, it'll change. Stop worrying," he instructed her, then their waiter arrived. A scotch, neat, for Jameson. Sparkling water for Tate.

They watched people dance and made idle chit chat. It was

strained at first, but eventually it flowed. Jameson had always been easy to talk to, in a way. The only problem now was that they would be chatting along, and Tate would be enjoying herself, and then a memory would smack her upside the head, like a bad acid flashback. *Pool. Whiskey. Supermodel. All a lie. BAM.* Conversation dampener. It would take her a couple seconds to get back into the stride of talking, and he always looked at her like he knew exactly what she was thinking, which in turn made her more uncomfortable. She was grateful when the waiter finally showed up with their dinner, till she saw what was on the plate.

"You said you were craving it," was all Jameson said as he cut into the steak he had ordered for himself.

"You ordered me lobster," Tate said plainly, staring at what was probably the biggest lobster she had ever seen.

"Yes."

"You have awfully high hopes," she pointed out.

"Only the highest."

"This lobster could be plated in platinum, and you still wouldn't get any pussy," Tate warned him. An older couple at the table next to them turned around, but Jameson ignored them.

"I could make you wear that lobster as a hat and I'd probably still get pussy by the end of the night," he countered.

Tate decided to ignore him. She wasn't going to give anything up, but she did love lobster. And this one was delicious. She dipped the pieces in a buttery garlic sauce, savored every bite. Moaned out loud a couple times. Was contemplating lifting the shell to lick it clean when she realized Jameson was staring at her.

"What?" she asked, glancing down at herself to see if she'd dribbled butter down her front.

"You are the sexiest woman I know," he replied.

She coughed and laughed at the same time.

"I think there is a supermodel who would very much argue that point," she managed to choke out. Jameson sighed and pushed his plate aside so he could rest his forearms against the table.

"You love to bring her up, but then change the subject. Let's just get this over with so we don't have to keep going in circles. I left home. I went to Berlin. I ran into her at a function, she was there with a mutual acquaintance. I didn't see her again for a week. I saw pictures of you with your new *boyfriend*. Then old pictures of you with me. More with him. It made me angry. Then people, employees, were pointing them out to me. I got angrier. So I called her up, I took her to dinner, I took her shopping. I asked her if she wanted to come back to the states with me, for a vacation. She asked about you, I told her you would be fine with it – that's the only lie I've ever told about us," his voice got serious during the last part.

"Good to know," Tate whispered, looking anywhere but him. She did not want to be having this conversation.

"Before we even left Germany, I told Pet that there was nothing between her and I, that I just wanted to have fun. She agreed. I was so angry at you, Tate. I thought you had lied to me, about him, about how you felt about me, about everything. I felt played. I am not a man people do that to," Jameson explained.

"Clearly. I never even thought of trying."

"I didn't realize that, not until it was too late. Look, she was nothing to me, except a huge mistake. Every interaction I've *ever* had with her is a mistake. I have said this to her. It doesn't make up for what I did to you, but it's the truth. I didn't care about her then. I don't care about her now. *You're* the one sitting across from me," he informed her.

It certainly *did not* make up for it, at least not in Tate's mind. She sat there, still looking away from him, trying not to cry. It was blunt, and it made him sound like the worst kind of asshole, but in Jameson-speak, it was all very sweet. He had been jealous, angry, and upset. He had lashed out. He had been childish, petulant, and mean.

120

He had been *hurt*. She had unknowingly *hurt him*.

You can't hurt Satan. This is all part of his game. Note that he said he didn't care about her – but he never said anything about caring for you. Do not lose to him again.

"You know what I think?" Tate began, turning towards him and leaning against the table as well. He quirked up an eyebrow.

"I'm scared to ask."

"I think you wanted to hurt me. I think you planned it before you even left Boston. I think hurting my body was beginning to bore you – you wanted bigger game. You loved degrading me, now you wanted to do it in front of other people. I think it was fun for you, and I think you *enjoyed it*," she called him out. There. Now he knew *exactly* what she thought about the whole situation.

"Well then. Once again, you would be thinking *wrong*," Jameson replied, his tone cool, his eyes hard.

What does it take to get under this man's skin the way he gets under mine!?

"I'm going to dance," Tate said abruptly.

"Excuse me?" he asked, obviously caught off guard

"Dance. They've turned down the lights, the band is gone," she explained, scooting back from the table. He looked at her like she was crazy.

"Tate, I think we ne—," he started, but she held up her hand.

"I don't want to do this with you. Please. Let's just … be friends for tonight. Okay? Just friends," she stressed.

"Tate, in a million years, you and I will never be *'just friends*,'" Jameson replied in a low voice.

She got up and walked away from the table. She didn't think she could handle a heart to heart with Jameson. He already owned a large piece of real estate on hers, she couldn't afford to give him anymore. One more piece, and that pool in her memories would swallow her whole.

121

She went downstairs, moved straight onto the dance floor, shoved her way right into the thick of everyone. Wanted to get lost in the people. In the music. She moved her body, working her hips back and forth. It had been a really long time, but Tate still knew how to dance. Her skills had been legendary, back when she had been a bartender. She had spent many a night raking in the cash for shaking her ass. Ang had once tried to convince her to become a stripper, but she couldn't get into the idea.

It wasn't long before a guy moved up next to her. He wrapped his arm loosely around her waist and leaned in close, saying something to her in Spanish. She leaned away and tried her best to communicate via sign language, explaining that she didn't speak Spanish.

"*No hablas español?*" he yelled over the music. She nodded.

"No. I mean, yes. *Si, no hablo español,*" Tate finally got it right. He laughed.

"Ah. You are American, yes?" he asked. His Spanish accent wrapped itself around the English vowels. Tate felt a shiver creep across her skin, and she wondered what Jameson was doing, wondered if he could see her.

"Yes, very much so," she laughed again. The guy nodded.

"I like America, American girls. I was saying, do you want to dance?" he asked again. She flicked her eyes around the room, then nodded.

His name was Alvaro, and he was from Barcelona. He was in Marbella on vacation. He was only twenty-one, but he could dance really well, so she overlooked his age. They chatted while they danced, and when he grew bolder, he wrapped an arm around her waist, taking one of her hands in his free hand. He showed her some basic steps to a rumba. Dipped her once. Let his hand wander lower on her waist.

Tate pulled away after that, keeping it strictly PG-13. She caught sight of Jameson once, at the edge of the dance floor. A flash of angry eyes and a sharp smile, then he was gone. She figured she had pushed her luck far enough. If she went too far, he would drag her off the dance floor, and then she would pull back. Then they would fight again.

And not in the fun way.

Between songs, she made her excuses to Alvaro and left the dance floor. She wandered through the crowd, wondering where Satan had gone. She didn't see him anywhere, and after three circuits of the downstairs, she began to think he had left her. Not a complete shock.

Then she finally spotted him near a small hallway. He was talking to someone, another man in expensive clothing, with a watch even bigger than Jameson's. Through her bartending job, Tate had learned that she could tell a lot about a person by their watch. They could be wearing shit for clothing, but if a man was wearing an Audemars, he was the business.

She started heading towards them, pushing her way through people. But then, at the same time, someone broke away from the crowd and stepped up next to Jameson. A dark shape, a shadow. A nightmare.

I'm so stupid. How can I be Lillith? Lillith was first, and I certainly wasn't that.

Tate thought she was going to faint. Before Jameson, she had never been that kind of girl. Now, he was right. She *was* all damaged and weepy. She hated that feeling, but she couldn't stop it. The edge of her vision started going black as she watched Petrushka slime against his back, her harpy claw gliding over his shoulder.

He did it again. All of this, all a lie, all a game, he did it again, I knew he'd do it —,

Tate was shocked out of her reverie, however, when Jameson turned to look at who was touching him. He snatched Pet's hand off his shoulder, as if her touch burned him. He yanked her around till she was standing in front of him, and he *did not* look happy. In fact, he seemed to be yelling about something, as he held fast to her wrist. She tried to take a step towards him, but he held her at bay.

What the fuck is going on?

There seemed to be a lot of yelling. Pet was yelling at him, Jameson was yelling at her, the man in the suit was yelling at both of them. Tate wasn't near enough to hear anything that was being said, not with the music so loud. Jameson pointed a finger in Pet's face, before letting go of her wrist, forcing her backwards. Then he pointed his finger at the man, who just nodded and pulled out a cell phone. Jameson whirled around and stomped off in the opposite direction. The man was on his phone, glaring at Pet. She melted back into the crowd, and the guy yelled after her. Pointed in her direction as two large men in suits walked up.

Tate turned around and hurried across the dance floor, elbowing people out of her way. She wasn't sure what had just happened, but she could have sworn that it looked like Jameson had been telling Petrushka to fuck off. But what was Petrushka even doing there, if Jameson hadn't invited her? How could she be at the same restaurant as them? Didn't Pet live in Berlin? Didn't she have the *whole world* as her goddamn playground? Why couldn't Tate get away from this chick!?

Tate broke free of the dance floor and spied some leather couches tucked in a recessed corner, next to a tiny, narrow hall that lead to the bathrooms. She made a beeline for the sofas, just wanting to sit down and breathe. Collect her thoughts, figure out what was going on. But as she stepped down into the sitting area, a large man jumped out of nowhere, holding his arms open in front of her.

"No, go back the way you came," he grumbled at her with a thick Middle Eastern accent.

"Excuse me?" she bristled, trying to step around him. He matched her move for move.

"This area VIP," he informed her. Tate snorted.

"No one is even sitting in there," she pointed out. He shook his head.

"VIP. You go back the way you came," he repeated. She opened her mouth to tell him where *he* could go, when someone stepped in between them.

"Where the fuck have you been? I've been looking everywhere for you," Jameson demanded.

"Uh ..." Tate answered articulately.

"You cannot be here, please leave!" the security man was snapping.

"We're leaving," Jameson informed her, ignoring the guard and grabbing her by the elbow. She didn't budge.

"Good, yes, you leave now," the guard agreed, ushering them away.

"*Now*," Jameson growled.

"*STOP.*"

It came out as a shout, even though she hadn't meant it to. Both men stared at her, the security guard looking shocked. Jameson just looked angry.

"I don't have patience for your bullshit, Tate, not right now. I want —," he started.

"I want to sit down. *Please*," she asked. He blinked down at her, his lips pressed into a hard line. She could tell he wasn't happy. Could tell that he *really* wanted to drag her out of there. By her hair, if necessary.

"I don't think —," Jameson began again.

She brushed past him. He was blocking the security guard, so she made it all the way to one of the couches before all hell broke loose. The security guard started yelling, which set Jameson off. Jameson never yelled, not unless he absolutely had to, but he did stand toe to toe with the larger man, quietly explaining that he and his guest could sit *wherever the fuck* they wanted to sit. A second later, the man in the suit from earlier, the one who had also yelled at Pet, showed up. This seemed to settle everything. The security guard slunk away, followed by the suit-man, and then Jameson came and sat down next to Tate.

"Thank you," she said. He raked his hand through his hair.

"You're not welcome. What the fuck are you doing?" he asked, stretching an arm out across the seat behind her. She kept her eyes trained on the dance floor.

"I just wanted to sit down. I was dancing, I wanted to cool off," she replied, trying to sound casual.

"Tatum. You're a horrible fucking liar."

They were interrupted by a scantily clad waitress. She was carrying a bottle of Louis XIII cognac. A gift for Jameson, compliments of the owner of the club. An apology for any distress caused by the staff or guests. Tate's eyes nearly fell out of her head. At home, a bottle cost anywhere from $2,000 to $3,000. The price in Spain, in Euros, in a nightclub … she was impressed. *Beyond* impressed.

The waitress poured out a shot, to taste. Jameson nodded his approval, so the woman filled up two old fashioned glasses, neat, and then left them alone. For the most part, Tate had avoided alcohol ever since her stint in the hospital, but when someone put a drink in front of her worth $166 a pour, she wasn't *ever* going to say no. Jameson sipped at his drink. She downed hers in one shot.

Before he could interrogate her some more, Tate skittered away and hustled into the bathroom. She had to get herself together enough to ask him about Pet. He must have known she was in Marbella. Maybe he was mad because Pet had almost blown his cover, his secret. Maybe the worst was yet to come. Maybe Jameson's sole purpose in life was to slowly drive Tate mad. He had almost succeeded last time. *Maybe he just wanted to finish the job.*

Five minutes later, she dragged herself back out of the bathroom, not feeling anymore *"together"* than before she had gone inside it. She dragged her feet as she walked down the hallway, dreading going back to Jameson. But just as she was about to exit the hall, she almost rammed into someone.

"I have been waiting to meet you."

For someone so pretty, she sounds like she has a dick in her mouth.

Petrushka was much taller than Tate. Both women were wearing heels, which put Pet at around six-foot-three – easily Jameson's height or taller, and well over Tatum. It made Tate feel even more insignificant. Pet was also even prettier up close than she was in all those pictures on the internet. Tate was getting smaller and smaller by the second.

"I didn't know you were here," Tate blurted out. She knew she had no right to be angry at Pet – Jameson had done everything. Pet had been used just as badly in his little game.

"*I* knew *you* were here. It is why I came here. I had to see you, with my own eyes," Pet replied. Tate swallowed thickly, glancing around.

"I'm sorry, you know. About … how everything happened. I didn't know, just so you know. I didn't know he was bringing you home," Tate stammered.

"It was all in good fun, I think," Pet laughed, as if she knew some sinister joke. Tate was confused.

"Well, I didn't really see it that way."

"That's because you are *garbage*, you couldn't possibly understand the things that people like us do."

Tate was shocked. Here she was, assuming a kind of kinship with this woman. Sure, Jameson had painted a very psychotic picture of the supermodel – but god knew what he said about Tate when she wasn't around; she didn't trust anything that came out of his mouth. Plus, he had used Pet. Didn't that make them, like, sisters-against-the cause? Judging by the pissed-mist rolling off of Pet, the answer was *apparently fucking not.*

"Excuse me?" Tate squeaked, not sure she'd heard right.

"You, you are … are trash. A silly piece of desperate trash. He uses you for his filthy sex, and that is it. He always comes back to me in the end," Pet talked down at her.

Tate narrowed her eyes. This was a woman scared, not gloating. Pet was *threatened by* Tate, that's why she was angry. She wasn't there to brag about what a cruel and sadistic joke it was, Jameson bringing Tate to Spain. Pet was there trying to scare Tate away – *because she hadn't expected to see her.*

"Then why is he here with me?" Tate challenged. Pet flicked her wrist dismissively.

"Because he is perverse. He likes rolling in the mud, he has always been this way," she replied. Tate stepped up close to the other woman, got right up in her space.

"You know what? I couldn't give two fucks what you think. What *either* of you think. He chased *me* here – *not you*, who can't seem to stop chasing after him. So who's really the desperate one? *Now get the fuck out of my way*, before I knock you on your ass," Tate hissed.

Pet seemed shocked. She probably wasn't used to someone swearing at her and threatening her with physical violence. Tate took the opportunity to brush past her. She wasn't about to fight over Jameson. He wasn't worth it, on any level.

Though the idea of bouncing Pet's head off the ground like a tennis ball did hold a certain appeal.

When Tate got back to the VIP area, Jameson was sitting in the same spot, but leaning backwards over the couch a little, talking to the man in the suit. Tate was pretty sure suit-man was the owner of the club, the gifter of the cognac. She sat down beside Jameson, tucking her feet up under herself. She was feeling hot after her run-in with Pet. Flustered. A little giddy. She had just confronted a nightmare, and instead of melting into a self-loathing puddle, she had threatened to beat its ass. She felt amazing.

I can do this. I can win this game. I can knock this game out of the park.

Out of the corner of her eye, she saw movement. Pet was sidling up to the edge of the VIP section. A new security guard was in place, and she was getting the same turn down Tate had received. As Pet argued with the guard, her eyes flicked to Tate, then glared. Tate glared right back. Then Pet reached out, running her fingers down the lapel of the guard's suit. The man laughed, obviously not immune to Petrushka's stunning good looks. It wouldn't be long before she weaseled her way into the sitting area. How awkward would that be? Jameson would probably love it. Just sit back, sip his cognac, and watch the two women wrestle around on the floor. Awesome.

Or he could walk away with her, leaving you a broken mess, floating back in that pool.

No. Tate wouldn't let that happen. Not this time. She was stronger, bolder, *better*; she knew that, now. The only person who would be broken at the end of this would be Jameson fucking Kane. *She would win this game.* Without thinking about what she was doing, Tate reached out and grabbed Jameson's head, roughly pulling him away from his conversation.

"What the fuck do you —," he started to snap, but he was cut off. Mostly by her tongue in his mouth.

She moaned and raised up onto her knees, yanking him even closer. One of his arms wrapped around her, the only thing keeping them balanced, what with Tate suddenly leaning all of her weight against him. His other hand still held onto his drink, keeping it out away from their bodies, obviously trying not to spill anything.

But none of that seemed to catch Jameson off guard or slow him down. He dove in head first, went right along with her and kissed her back, his fingers digging almost painfully into her waist. She broke away to gasp in air, and he pulled her right back in, kissing her like

129

she was priceless cognac, and he wanted every last drop.

Tate squeezed her eyes shut tight and tried not to think. Tried not to notice how all the nerve endings in her lips were coming alive. Tried not to notice how kissing him made every hurt go away, just a little. It wasn't fair, Jameson had caused the hurts. But it was true. She felt like a live wire that needed grounding.

As if he could read her mind – which she was pretty sure he could, he *was* Satan after all – he suddenly gripped her waist even tighter and leaned back into the couch, yanking her around to his front. Tate moved her legs so she was straddling him, and she suddenly, *most definitely,* felt grounded. Right against the massive bulge in his pants. She moaned into his mouth, raking her nails down his chest.

Hope you love a show, Pet. Jameson and I know how to put on a good one.

"A moment, please," Jameson panted, before pulling far enough away to down the rest of his drink. Then he jumped right back into it, trailing his lips along her neck, down to her cleavage. Tate let her head fall back, her arms wrapped around his neck. She slid her eyes back to Pet and smiled before blowing her a kiss.

Petrushka. Went. Ballistic. Started shrieking at the security guard in some language Tate didn't quite recognize, maybe Russian. There was a flurry of activity and several more guards showed up, along with important looking suit-man. All the while, Pet kept shouting, pointing an accusing finger at Tatum. Tate just smiled back, gave a small wave. By then, Jameson had leaned away so he could take in the commotion, though both his arms remained around her waist.

"Your girlfriend is a real catch," Tate commented, watching as the security team began bustling Pet away. Jameson snorted.

"Yeah, and what's even stranger – *I don't have a girlfriend,*" he replied, and then she felt his tongue tracing along the neckline of her shirt. She glanced down at him.

Her heart was skipping beats, she was pretty sure. She had been kissing him for show, to piss off Petrushka. Tate didn't really want to be doing this, not with him. She should let him go, get off of him. Go take twelve cold showers, then fly the fuck back to Boston. She could work out the reappearance of her sex drive with Ang, just like old times.

But she couldn't move.

"*Jameson*," she breathed his name. He lifted his head, but didn't look at her. He kept his eyes on her chest.

"Hmmm?" he replied, lifting a hand and tracing a finger along her breast bone. Down into her cleavage. Pulling slightly at her shirt. She licked her lips.

Do not do this. Do not do this. Do not do this.

"We shouldn't do this," she whispered. He quirked up an eyebrow and finally looked at her, his intense blue eyes boring holes into her head. Into her soul. She had never handled his stare very well. He continued slowly rubbing his finger up and down her skin.

"And why is that?" he asked, his eyes hooded and sexy. Tate cleared her throat, looked away from him.

"Because I don't want to."

"I wasn't the one who just sexually assaulted another person while they were in the middle of a conversation," Jameson pointed out with a laugh.

"Yeah, but I only did that because of *her*," Tate admitted. His finger stilled, then moved, tracing along the edge of her shirt until his whole hand was cupping her breast. She closed her eyes. It felt like it had been so long since anyone had touched her like that. Since *he* had touched her.

"Really. That was a pretty dirty game to play, baby girl," Jameson said in a low voice, his palm gliding back and forth. She took a deep breath and opened her eyes. Stared down at him.

"*I learned from the best,*" she whispered.

He stood up abruptly, but held onto her, so she couldn't fall. Tate's legs went out from under her and she had to stay on her tip toes as Jameson forced her backwards. Out of the VIP. Down the narrow little hallway, past the bathrooms. He stopped by the last door, a large "*SALIDA*" sign casting a read glow over both of them. All the oxygen rushed out of her lungs as she stared up at him.

Satan is most definitely back.

"You didn't learn well enough," Jameson growled at her, his hands on her hips, fingers digging into her flesh.

"How so?" she breathed.

"You're still a horrible fucking liar."

His mouth was on hers, punishing her with his roughness, and she was powerless against him. Like always. Any sort of self preservation flew out the window. *Coherent thought* flew out the fucking window. She wasn't pain, anymore. She wasn't hurt, or memories, or anger. She was just Tatum again. Tatum with Jameson.

Finally.

She moaned and pressed her hips against his, dug her nails into the back of his neck. His hands pressed flat against her waist, then slid up her body until they were covering her breasts, squeezing before they worked their way back down to her butt. She pushed back against him, and he let her move them across the hallway, till it was his back against a wall.

Tate was back on her tip toes, her teeth skimming the corded muscles in his neck. Tongue trailing along his clavicle. Jameson's hand was in her hair, but it was gentle, and he turned them again, so she was once again pinned between him and the wall. She moaned loudly, and his mouth was back on hers like she had called for him. Tate couldn't get enough. She had always been an addict, and he was a drug. She wanted more. More than that, more than he was giving. *All* that he had to give.

She felt his hand on her bare thigh, and then he was roughly grabbing at her, lifting her leg to his hip. Trying to get closer to her, as close as their clothing would allow. She stretched her leg out, pressing her toes against the wall across from them. Jameson sunk his whole body down, kissing his way to her breasts, and then he grabbed her butt, lifting her as he stood up straight. Her legs went around his waist. She felt drunk. She felt *wasted*. She didn't care where she was, or what she was doing. As long as it went on and on and on and on and …,

"You're coming home with me," Jameson breathed against her mouth. Tate nodded, running her hands down his chest, pulling at his shirt, working her way underneath.

"Yes," she whispered, groaning when she felt skin beneath her fingertips. She scratched her nails around to his back.

I know this land.

"No more bullshit," he continued, kissing her throat. He lifted one hand away from her ass, skimmed his fingers along the waist-band of her shorts.

"No," she shook her head, mimicking his movements as she trailed her fingers around his belt.

"I want you. You want me," he stated, moving his fingers to the top of her shirt and yanking it down, exposing all of her cleavage, down to her bra.

"*Yes,*" Tate agreed. Her hands were on auto-pilot, sliding his belt out of its buckle. This was her job, after all. She was so good at it.

"It has been three months, Tate," Jameson groaned, raking his fingers across her breasts.

"*Oh my god.*"

"I'm going to be inside of you tonight. We can't stop this."

"I know. I want …"

She was in a dream. A love-drunk haze, it had always enveloped her when she was in Jameson's presence. Tate had been stupid to think that a simple near-death experience had cured her of it. His lips, his body, his words, none of that could snap her out of it. But his hand. His hand, creeping onto her throat, seemingly of its own volition, *that* stopped her.

He felt it, too. She could see it in his eyes. It was like they were both waking up. Jameson's absolute favorite body part, on *any* woman, was the throat. Tate knew this, because her favorite body part for him to touch was her throat. It was like a calling card, a stamp, *a brand*. At night, she would dream about his fingers around her throat. Pray for them. Sure, before him, she'd had men grab her by the throat. But no one did it *quite* like him. He did it like it was something he *needed* to do, like he had to do it because he *owned* her.

Probably because he does.

Her feet hit the ground with a thud. Tate stared at him, her hands still gripping his belt. One of his hands was still on her ass. The other rested *just* below her throat, pressed across her clavicle, his index finger stretched halfway up her trachea.

Such a sexy word.

"Too much for you, baby girl?" Jameson asked in a soft voice, a smile on his lips as he gently tapped his finger against her throat. She swallowed thickly, tried to collect her thoughts in a flash.

"No. I'm just not going to suck your dick in some Spanish night club," she replied.

Oh, there's some bravado! Almost sounded believable, too! A for effort, you stupid bitch.

"You were about to," Jameson called her out. Tate snorted.

"Then why aren't I?" she asked, letting him go. He finally stepped away, and she hated that she missed his warmth.

"Because. You're scared of me. I'll have to work on that," he told her.

"I'm not scared of you," she argued. He laughed.

"You're terrified. But sometimes, that can make things interesting. Let's go home," he said, and then he just walked away, leaving her standing there alone in a horny, confused, breathless, puddle.

6

SHE CAUGHT UP TO HIM outside of the night club. He was putting on his coat, and taking ground eating strides back towards the marina. She had to jog to keep up with him – no easy feat in the towering heels she was wearing.

"Are we having a race?" Tate huffed out, grabbing onto the bottom edge of his jacket to help keep her balance. Jameson glanced back at her.

"Next time, wear sensible shoes," he replied. She laughed out loud

"Oh, okay. Next time, I'll wear a pair of crocs," she threatened.

"Why do I bother talking to you," he grumbled.

They were back to the boat in no time. He hadn't said anything else, but he did slow his pace. Even so, Tate was still out of breath as they made their way onto his yacht, and she was dying for water when they got onto the deck.

It wasn't too late, not quite ten o'clock, and she looked around for Sanders. There were huge glass doors that separated the galley from the main back deck, and during the day they were usually left open, doubling the living space of the boat. They were still open, and she saw a dark figure in front of the stove. But it wasn't Sanders.

"*Who the fuck is that!?*" Tate hissed, scooting up close behind Jameson and pressing herself against his back. He may have been the devil, but he was also a lot bigger than her, and getting mugged was never a fun experience.

"*Qué estás haciendo?*" Jameson snapped.

A woman came out of the shadows, answering in Spanish. She was young, probably around Tate's age, or just under. Very pretty. A small conversation in Spanish took place, then Jameson walked away while the young woman walked back to the stove area, throwing lingering looks his way. Tate hustled after him.

"Who is that? Where's Sanders?" she demanded in a low voice. Jameson took off his jacket and threw it onto a chair.

"That is a maid. She was supposed to clean while we were gone, but she got here late. She's just finishing up. Sanders is staying at my apartment," he replied.

"Sanders is … I'm sorry. What?" Tate asked, thrown off guard. Jameson sank into a chair at the table, rubbing a hand over his face.

"I have an apartment, in town. While you were on the phone with your *boyfriend*, I told Sanders that he would be staying downtown from now on," he explained. She barked out a laugh.

"Fuck that. If Sanders doesn't stay here, *I* don't stay here," she replied. Jameson grabbed her hand and yanked down, forcing her to stumble. While she was caught off balance, he pulled her into his lap.

"I have never been jealous of another man in my entire life, then you come along, and suddenly every man is a threat. Why is that?" he asked while she straightened herself on top of him.

Her breath caught in her throat. Jameson? Jealous? *Not possible.* He had been angry when she had first slept with Nick, but not because he had been jealous. He had been mad because he had unknowingly shared his favorite toy, that was all. She hadn't asked permission, had only done it to piss him off. And *Sanders!?* Please.

"Don't be stupid," Tate snapped, pulling at his arms as they coiled around her waist.

"*You're* stupid," he countered, and she had a strong sense of déjà vu.

Talk about a role reversal.

"Stop it. Let me up," she complained. She was straining against his hold, and he let go so abruptly that she sprang forward, almost falling to her knees. She managed to right herself, then whirled around on him.

"Your wish is my command," Jameson told her, with a mock bow of his head.

Tate glared and sat down across from him. While she worked at taking her fancy shoes off, the maid wandered back out onto the deck, asking a question in Spanish. Tate didn't need to speak the language to know that every word out of the other woman's mouth was dripping with sexual promise, full of innuendo.

She looked the other girl over, watching as the woman eye-fucked Jameson. She certainly wasn't subtle. It was actually kind of brave, considering the fact that the object of her attention was sitting there with another woman.

"Why isn't Sandy staying here anymore?" Tate asked in a booming voice, cutting right through their conversation as she tossed her shoes over her shoulder. Jameson smiled tightly at the maid before turning back to Tate.

"Because he's in the way," was all he said. The maid stayed on the deck for a little longer, her eyes bouncing back and forth between Jameson and Tate, before she headed back inside the yacht.

"Sandy is never in the way," Tate replied.

"Very rarely," Jameson agreed. "This is a special situation."

"Special how?"

"You get distracted easily. I don't want anyone else here when I decide it's time to fuck you."

Tate was a little shocked. That he would assume he had already won, that he thought she would still be that easy. She wasn't … *was she?* No, she most definitely wasn't. Not for him, at least. She sat up straight in her chair, flicking her ponytail off her shoulder.

"Well, seeing as how that's *not going to happen*, you can just bring him right on back," she replied. Jameson laughed.

"Tate, you can't kiss me like you did in that club and not put out," he informed her. She raised her eyebrows.

"I told you, that was just for show," she bluffed, rubbing at her sore ankles.

"Really. So dry humping me in a hallway, where no one could see us, was just for show," he laid out the facts. She tried very hard not to blush.

"More like a sick curiosity."

"*Tatum.*"

Jameson's voice was full of warning, making her shiver.

"I'm not fucking you. Deal with it."

He rubbed a hand over his face again, but before he could say anything else, the maid called out to him. He grumbled to himself, then answered her in Spanish. A light laugh floated out onto the deck. Tate tried very hard not to glare into the boat.

"It's been a long night, baby girl. You sure I can't tempt you into a blowjob, at the very least?" Jameson asked, a laugh in his voice.

"Hmmm, probably not. But your maid seems more than happy to be of service. *Any kind of service,*" Tate replied, not able to keep the bite out of her voice. He laughed some more.

"Ooohhh, now *that* sounds like jealousy. You don't want me, but no one else can have me? How droll," he taunted her.

"I don't care who has you – most of America, and I'm sure half of Germany, has had you. Go fuck your maid, see if I care," she replied.

"Now, I know you don't meant that," his voice was soft, his eyes wandering over her face. Tate shrugged.

139

"Jameson, why would *anything* you do bother me?" she countered. He leaned over the table.

"I think *everything* I do bothers you."

"Then you're stupid. Go. Maybe she'll do you better than I ever could and you'll finally leave me alone. Make a night of it," Tate suggested.

"Maybe I will," Jameson agreed.

"Maybe you should."

"You never know when enough is enough, Tate. You push me, and then get mad when I push back. It's counter-productive. It doesn't make sense. Why do you do it?" he asked, his head cocked to the side.

Because I like it when you push back.

"Because," she sucked air through her teeth, trying to think of something, anything, to say in response. "I'm not the same person anymore. I don't care what you do, or who you fuck. It doesn't affect my life, not anymore than me fucking someone else affects yours. She wants you. You want to fuck somebody. Who am I to stand in the way? *Go.* I don't care."

Jameson stood up abruptly and walked away from the table. He looked *pissed.* Tate was a little shocked, watching him walk into the galley. Her eye sight had adjusted to the dark some, and she could see what was going on inside a little better.

She watched as Jameson walked up behind the maid, leaned down close to her. He whispered something in her ear, but his eyes were on Tate the whole time. The maid threw her head back and laughed. Jameson smiled as well, then kept talking. Talked until she started moving away, towards the back of the boat. He gave one last look at Tate, then followed, his body crowding close to the smaller woman as they disappeared into the depths of the yacht.

Tate sat at the table, feeling small again. She chewed on her bottom lip, glancing around the deck. She wanted Sanders there, wanted to lean on his strength. She *really* wanted to go inside, press her ear against Jameson's door. Was he really going to have sex with that girl? Right then? While Tate was on the boat? They had done some kinky shit in their previous relationship, but never anything quite like that; Tate was open minded, but she had her boundaries.

What boundaries are there, if you're not together? He can do whatever he wants. Right? **Right?**

Of course, she *had* goaded him. Told him to do it. Tate couldn't be mad about it. She had laid it on thick in the club, then things had gotten pretty intense in that hallway. If Jameson hadn't touched her throat, she had no doubt that sex would have been imminent. She had been ready to take his pants off with her teeth. Probably a bad idea. *Definitely* a bad idea. And she had probably left him more than a little hard-up.

So Jameson having sex with the maid was a good thing. A *great* thing. Saved Tate some hassle, and would probably calm him down for a day or two. Get him to lay off her. Hell, maybe if she was lucky, the maid would be *so good,* he would forget all about Tatum. *Perfect.*

Tate leapt out of her chair like she had been electrocuted and prowled through the boat. She paused at the door to her room, still trying to convince herself that she was just going to bed. But she couldn't do it. She tip toed farther, all the way to Jameson's door. She knew she should let it go, *knew* that him sleeping with someone else was a good thing. Good, good, *great.*

But she was a horrible liar, even when it was to herself.

Tatum fucking *hated* the idea of Jameson sleeping with that girl.

She pressed her whole body to his door, straining to hear what was going on; living in a marina was similar to living in a city. There was always some kind of noise. Boats rocking, buoys squeaking, engines rumbling. Even inside an expensive, hand tailored yacht, noise managed to get in, and she had trouble hearing exactly what was being said.

But Tate could definitely hear voices, muffled as they were. The woman was *definitely* in his room. They were talking. There was giggling. Possibly a groan from him. *Definitely* a moan from her. More giggling. Tate wanted to puke. She pushed away from the door, hurried back to her room. Paced up and down the hallway. Took deep breaths through her nose. Tried to remember a happier time, a time when she would've been excited for him to sleep with someone else.

"... I want to know everything."

"Really? You want to know everything? Like how I tied one girl down ... things like that?"

*"**Exactly** like that."*

She had no control over her body. Tate stormed down the hallway and burst through his door, before she'd even coherently thought about it. His room was large, a huge bed in black sheets taking up most of it. Jameson was standing next to it, and the maid was standing in front of him. Both had turned towards the doorway when Tate made her dramatic entrance. Jameson cocked up an eyebrow.

"Yes?" he asked. Tate clenched her hand around the door knob. Took a deep breath.

"I'm bored," she spit out.

Oh, good one. Very good. Very cool. Breezy, even.

"Hmmm. So hearing about it isn't enough anymore, you want to watch?" Jameson clarified, peeling his shirt off and throwing it to the floor. The maid was asking something in Spanish, but he ignored her, just wrapped an arm around her waist. Tate shrugged.

"There's no TV in my room. You threw my phone overboard. You made Sandy leave. I need something to entertain me," she replied. He chuckled, his voice low and evil sounding, and moved to kneel on the bed, pulling the maid along.

He grabbed the other girl by the back of the head, pulling her close. He said something softly to her, all in Spanish. She laughed, giving Tate a sideways look, before pressing herself against Jameson. Her hands ran up his sides, her lips pressed to his chest. Tate took another deep breath. Willed away the bile in her throat.

He lowered the other lady to the bed, propped himself up over her, but Jameson's eyes stayed locked on Tate's, a curious sort of detachment sitting in his blue depths. A woman was rubbing her body and her tongue against his bare skin, but he didn't seem to really care. He was entirely focused on Tate.

Maid-lady didn't care one bit. She seemed excited just to be there. She moaned, hissed things in Spanish, put her hands all over his body, ignored the fact that anyone else was even in the room. It made Tate angry. That was *her property* the woman was touching. In a previous life, Tate could have happily imagined herself sitting on the sidelines, watching Jameson fuck somebody else. But not right now, not when she hadn't had a chance to reclaim what was rightfully hers.

God, I am so fucked up. Ang is right, I should seek therapy.

Tate slowly walked forward, keeping her eyes on Jameson's. Of course, he knew what she wanted. He *always* knew. He didn't say a word, just crawled over and off of the maid, till he was kneeling at the foot of the bed. When Tatum reached him, he didn't even pause to see what her intentions were, he just wrapped one arm around her waist and yanked her close. His other hand went into her hair, pinning her in place while he kissed her.

Tate raked her fingers through his hair, digging her nails into his scalp, dragging them all the way down to his back. She felt like she was *starving* for that moment. She was well aware of the fact that the maid was now pressed against his back, licking her way across his shoulders. Tate couldn't decide whether it was a turn on, or just a nuisance.

She pulled him forward, pulling him off the bed. He took over, moving her backwards, and they fell across the room, her back landing hard against a wall. She gasped against his mouth, slid her leg up and down his, tickled her fingers down his sides. The maid reappeared then, and stepped up to his side. Tried to become part of the act. Wrapped an arm around his shoulders and kissed at his ear.

But when the maid's free hand slid onto Tate's hip, fun time was over. If she was going to be stupid enough to have sex with Jameson, it was not going to be in a threesome, not after having been denied his body for the last three months. She wanted him to herself. This was not an all-you-can-eat buffet. This was dinner for two. And it was suddenly over-crowded.

I'm so much worse than him. He knows what he's doing – I pretend to be ignorant. Poor girl. Shouldn't have been eye-fucking him in front of me. Tacky.

"She leaves," Tate breathed against his mouth.

She didn't have to say anything else. Jameson pulled away and grabbed the woman by the arm, forcing her away from him. The maid seemed surprised, and she started speaking rapid fire Spanish, her hand sliding up Jameson's chest. He grabbed it, held it away from himself. Tate stepped away from the mix.

"*Vayasé, venga mañana y le pagare el doble de su salario,*" he told her. Tate understood "*salary*" and "*tomorrow*", but that was it.

Maid-lady understood it all, and didn't like it, apparently. She gestured violently at Tate, her voice loud and rough sounding. She stomped back to the bed, grumbling and glaring, grabbing her jacket and slipping on her shoes.

"Hey, don't give me attitude. You saw me get on the boat with him," Tate said, not caring whether or not the woman could understand her.

The maid stepped up close to her, and Tate groaned inwardly. Normally, she never had problems with other women. She got along great with most women. She had never once in her life fought over a man. Now, twice in one night, she was finding herself in heated *"discussions"* over Jameson.

I'm so pathetic.

Tate was fully aware that this little problem was her own doing, but she didn't care – the maid *knew* that Jameson had a female guest staying on the boat. Had seen her sitting on Jameson's lap, but that hadn't stopped the lady from hitting on him. Tate knew the rules, because she *was* the maid; she had been in the same position, had been the slutty-help. If she saw a man with another woman, and that man then hit on Tatum – first woman got first dibs. That's just how the slutty-cookie crumbled. Maid-lady could deal with it.

The Spanish woman got even closer, her eyes narrowed. Jameson was saying something in Spanish, his tone not happy. Maid-lady's voice was getting louder, her arm gestures violent. She was hissing at Tate through clenched teeth, and Tate didn't have to speak Spanish to know that none of it was good. She also knew what the words *"perra"* and *"puta"* meant; not exactly complimentary, and they were being said, *a lot*. Still, Tate wasn't going to do anything.

At least, not until the bitch touched her.

When the woman jabbed her pointed fingers into Tate's shoulder, she lost it a little bit. Her grasp on sanity was tenuous, at best. She pulled away from Jameson, yelling at the woman to fuck off. Maid-lady yelled back in Spanish, pushing again. Tate yelled some more in English, daring the woman to touch her again. Jameson snapped at both of them to shut the fuck up. But when the other woman shoved Tate hard enough to knock her back into Jameson's chest, it was over. Tate was done with being pushed around. By Jameson, by circumstance, by life in general, and by whory-maids in particular.

Tate went to shove the woman back, planting her hands on the maid's shoulders. Maid-lady apparently expected that, and began windmilling her arms. Tate ducked her head. She still wasn't much of a scrapper, hadn't been in many fights. But she could fight like a girl

145

with the best of them, so she swung her arms as well, and it turned into an all-out shrieking, slapping, scratching, hair pulling, cat-fight.

It didn't last very long. One strong pull with one arm, and Jameson had them separated. Tate fell back onto the bed while he picked up the maid, carried her shouting form from the room. The door swung shut behind him, and Tate could only listen as he took the maid out onto the deck.

Tate covered her face with her hands, trying not to think about what she had just done, what she had just taken part in. She felt so stupid. *So stupid*. She wasn't going to do anything sexual with Jameson. She wasn't going to fight over Jameson. She wasn't going to embarrass herself over Jameson. Now, all three had been done in the span of a couple hours.

She heard the door open, but she didn't bother looking. She felt him start to kneel over her. His hands spanned her waist, pushing her. Sliding her back on the bed, over the covers. Then his knees came to rest on either side of her thighs, his hands planted on the mattress next to her head.

"Tate," Jameson's voice was serious.

"*No*," she replied, her voice muffled by her hands.

"Tatum, look at me," he ordered. She shook her head.

"No."

He leaned back and she felt his hands on her own. He peeled them away from her face, then moved them to the bed. Pinned them down. Hovered his mass over her own. She wanted him to let go. To feel his weight on her, pressing her down. She hated him. Hated herself a little.

"Why do you play these little games? You're not very good at them," Jameson told her, his voice soft. She sighed, not meeting his eyes.

"Because I don't want to lose," she replied.

"You *always* lose."

146

"I know. Odds are, I have to come out on top, at least once," she tried to joke.

"I don't want to hurt you."

"You *always* want to hurt me."

"No."

"I'm just a game to you."

"*No.* Tatum, it doesn't have to be a game," Jameson's voice grew quiet, and he lowered his head, his breath hot against her neck. She struggled to remember how to breathe. Tried not to notice how amazing it all was, the things coming out of his mouth.

"I wouldn't be here if it wasn't a game," she replied.

"Yes, you would. Just like you were at my apartment seven years ago. Just like you were in my office four months ago. This isn't going away," he warned her. Tate stared at the ceiling.

"I want it to go away," she whispered. Jameson shook his head, and she felt his lips on her chest.

"*Don't say that.*"

His mouth moved to hers, and there was nothing she could do about it. Sex between them had never been romantic, not even in the end – Tate was pretty sure she'd never had "romantic" sex. But when Jameson kissed her, she could feel it. However the love songs wanted to put it, that's how she felt it. In her heart, in her toes, in her spleen, in her hair follicles, *everywhere*. There was no stopping it. It was going to happen. So why not go with it? Why not just give in?

Just sink down, down, down into that pool. Under, so deep, you won't want to come back.

"*Excuse me, sir.*"

Jameson pulled away, but he kept his eyes locked on hers. Tate stared, wide eyed, right back at him. She had been perilously close to the edge, and he knew it. He had been one step and a few articles of clothing short of winning their little game. He'd almost had her.

It was too close for comfort.

"*Sir.*"

It was Sanders, banging on the bedroom door. Jameson sighed and sat up, resting on his heels. Tate stayed laying down underneath him. Didn't move a muscle. Tried to blend in with the bed spread.

"What are you doing here?" Jameson barked out, running a hand through his hair.

"I assume you are aware that there is a very angry woman on the upper deck, throwing all of your furniture into the ocean," came the reply. Jameson grumbled and slid backwards off the bed.

"It never ends," he growled before prowling to the door.

Tate stayed laying down, long after he left the room. She could hear the shouting now, the lady cursing in Spanish. Then there were soft footsteps, and suddenly Sanders was sitting on the bed next to her. She heard movement, followed by his hand coming to rest on her knee, his touch light.

"Are you alright?" he asked. She shrugged.

"As good as I was the last time you saw me," she replied.

"Pardon me, but that wasn't very good," he pointed out. She finally laughed.

"No, I guess it wasn't, and I'm probably a lot worse now."

"May I ask what happened?"

"Ran into Pet. Almost accidentally had a threesome. Got into a fight. The usual."

Sanders actually laughed at that, and it set Tate off. She snorted and chuckled, and he laid down next to her. While her eyes watered and she shook with laughter, she reached over and grabbed his hand. Squeezed it tightly.

"You do have a knack for getting into trouble," he told her. She nodded.

"That I do. Sandy, tell me what I should do," her voice fell into a breathy whisper.

"You should stop playing games, both of you. Say how you feel, mean what you say," he replied bluntly.

"Anyone else would tell me that I need to figure it out on my own," she told him. Sanders snorted.

"Then it wouldn't happen. The solution seems very simple to me, I don't understand what the problem is," he said. Tate sighed.

"Because it's not simple, Sandy. I don't trust him."

"But you trust me?"

"Yes."

"Then trust me when I say this isn't a game to him."

She wasn't able to pick his brain anymore, though, because Jameson strode back into the room. He was still shirtless, and now had claw marks going down his chest. *Sexy.* Tate started laughing again, the hand pressed to her mouth doing nothing to hide it. Jameson glared at her, then at Sanders.

"*You.* What do you want?" he demanded. Sanders sighed and sat up.

"I was listening to my Bach. Petrushka showed up at the apartment," was all Sanders said. Tate laughed even harder.

"I can't catch a fucking break," Jameson groaned, sitting down on the bed on the other side of her.

"I will retire to my room here, for the night. Tomorrow, you can speak with the management of the building," Sanders informed him before getting up and walking out of the room.

"You can stop now," Jameson said, but Tate still couldn't get herself under control. It wasn't until his palm pressed against her thigh that she came out of it. She scrambled out from under his touch, practically slithering sideways off the bed.

"It's been a long night. Sandy's right, we should go to bed," she said quickly, her nerves evident in her voice. Jameson chuckled.

"Scared, scared, scared. You used to be so tough, baby girl," he told her. She pulled at her clothing, straightening herself out, not wanting him to see how much his words affected her. How badly her hands were shaking.

She *hated* being afraid.

"Yeah, well, a week in a psych ward can cure you of just about anything."

Then she strode out of the room, not even giving him a backwards glance.

7

JAMESON WAS FRUSTRATED.

He was horny, he was angry, and he was upset, but mostly, he was *very frustrated*.

Things were not going well.

He tried being nice. It was almost physically painful for him to do so, but he tried. *For her*. It didn't work. He tried impressing her, showing off for her, even ignoring her. He let her get away with murder, things he never would have tolerated in the old days. And still. *Nothing*. Tate still looked at him like he was the devil.

For the first time ever, Jameson worried that he wouldn't be able to win her over.

Her body, though, was a different story. It still reacted to him the same way it always had. Ready. Willing. He felt if he could just touch her enough, just taste her enough, her defenses would melt away and he could lay siege to her. Win her. Claim her.

He just wanted to be absolved of his sins. He wanted his old life back. He didn't want to be obsessed with her, but he was, plain and simple. She ruled his senses. Tate hadn't learned how to do it yet, but Jameson knew when to call a spade a spade. He wouldn't waste time wallowing in denial, trying to convince himself that he didn't want her. Despite all appearances, he was much more of a go-with-the-flow kind of person.

Now if only she could learn to do that, life would be so much simpler for both of them.

So he was in a particularly dark mood when he made his way up top the next morning. Both Sanders and Tatum were already awake, dining at the table. He wasn't sure who had cooked – usually he had breakfast delivered. Tate had her mirrored sunglasses on, and she had contorted herself to fit her whole body, legs and all, in her tiny chair. She was laughing at something Sanders was saying, smiling broadly. Jameson's hand twitched, and he once again had to remind himself that she wasn't ready for him to touch her. Not in the way he wanted to touch her; not in the way she needed to be touched.

"I was just going to wake you," Sanders said, noticing his approach.

"I'm sure," Jameson grumbled, pouring himself a cup of coffee.

"Someone sounds cheery this morning," Tate teased him. He glared at her.

"Long night."

"Poor baby."

"Shut the fuck up."

"*Ooohhh*," she almost moaned. "You're going to be extra fun today, aren't you?"

"Piss me off more than I already am, Tate, and I'll show you how '*fun*' I can be," he warned her.

She kept her mouth shut, but she smiled to herself as she sipped her coffee.

"If you are ready," Sanders spoke up, "we could head to the apartment."

It was an offer of escape, and Jameson took it gladly. It was hard to be around Tate, sometimes *too hard*. He wanted to slip into old roles, old habits. She wouldn't let him. It was like ice skating up hill.

After they had grabbed jackets and other necessities, he and Sanders headed off the boat. Not a moment too soon – Tate was stripping off her clothing to reveal a bikini, and Jameson knew he was staring at her like a hungry wolf. He was about to follow her up to the top deck, where he would continue her efforts and help her take off the bikini, preferably with his teeth, but Sanders coughed loudly, dragging his attention away.

"May I ask what happened last night?" Sanders asked, his voice casual as they walked to the Rolls-Royce. Well, casual for Sanders.

"No," Jameson replied, sliding into the passenger seat while Sanders got behind the wheel.

"She mentioned a threesome," Sanders continued, pulling the car out of its spot and heading into traffic.

"No threesome, sorry to say."

"You tried?"

"Jesus christ, Sanders, are you a girl now? What's with the gossip? *No,* I did not try to orchestrate a threesome. If I wanted one, I would have one. Tate laid out a dare. I called her bluff. I wouldn't have slept with that woman, and I knew Tate would stop it. *That's it.* No more questions," Jameson explained.

Sanders made a humming noise, but didn't say anything else.

At the apartment building, Jameson had a chat with the manager. *No one* was to be allowed into his apartment, or even onto his *floor.* Only himself, Sanders, and Tatum were the exception. Though with the way things had been going, he wasn't entirely sure he'd ever get a chance to bring her there. The manager apologized profusely for the mistake – they were training an entirely new security team, and Ms. Ivanovic was very convincing. It was generally known that she and Jameson had been involved together. It wouldn't happen again.

Jameson warned him that it had better not.

He wasn't ready to deal with Tate quite yet, so he took Sanders to lunch at an outdoor cafe. It had been a long time since it had been just the two of them. Since well before Tate had entered the picture. It was quiet. Peaceful. Nice. Jameson sighed, feeling a little restored. He sat back in his chair, just people watching, while Sanders finished his salad.

"Sir," Sanders' voice interrupted his thoughts.

"Yes?" Jameson asked, folding his arms.

"Things do not seem to be progressing very well."

"I am well aware of this."

"She still thinks you're the devil. She thinks you did everything on purpose, planned it from the start."

"*I am aware.* I'm working on it."

"Doesn't look like it."

Jameson was a little shocked. Tate was a bad influence on Sanders.

"You don't help, you know. You have become a very effective cock blocker," Jameson snapped. A blush crept up Sanders' neck, but his face remained impassive.

"Winning her heart is one thing. Using her for sex is another. I won't allow it," he replied.

"Your sentimentality makes me sick, and the thing Tate and I do best is use each other for sex. Just let me do things my own way," Jameson instructed. He took out his wallet and threw some money on the table before standing up. Sanders followed suit and they walked away from the cafe.

"Are you sure that's a good idea?" Sanders asked, for the millionth time. Jameson rolled his eyes.

"Am I ever not sure, Sanders? Just stay out of the way, let me reach her, and the rest of this month will be a cake walk," Jameson told him. Sanders made a sound like a snort, only more dignified.

"I think you are forgetting yourself. Forgetting the past," he pointed out.

Ego, down a notch. Sanders: 1

"I have to, Sanders, if I want to function and move forward. I laid out the deal, she took it. It has to be this way," Jameson replied.

"Is this really about a deal? A *game?*" Sanders pressed.

"Of course. It's what it's always about between us. Only bigger. With smarter players," Jameson laughed. He stopped in front of a building, stretched his arms above his head. Yawned.

"I have a question," Sanders stated, standing at his side.

"Yes?"

"When are you going to realize it's not a game?"

Jameson swallowed thickly. He wasn't a stupid man, he knew his ego wasn't entirely bulletproof. He was very good at hiding how he felt – so good, in fact, that even he didn't know what he was feeling half the time. But sometimes, just sometimes, Sanders could create a crack. Rip right through the layers to reveal a piece of Jameson that he hadn't known was there.

"I need *her* to think it's a game, but *I know* it's not a game," Jameson replied in a soft voice, refusing to meet Sanders' eyes.

"*Good.*"

They started walking again and were silent for a while. During that time, Jameson was able to cover himself back up. Don his armor. He needed to focus. He couldn't worry about anything besides what was in front of him: getting her back. Then he would worry about what all his fucking feelings meant.

It was a little hard to have focus, though, when he was sporting a hard-on 90% of the time.

Maybe I should hire a hooker …

Tate woke up with a start. Someone was touching her. She shoved her hat back off her forehead and looked down. Jameson was sitting on the edge of her lounger, running his fingers down her leg. She wondered how long he had been there.

"What are you doing?" she asked through a yawn.

"Touching you."

"Obviously. When did you guys get back?" she asked, her leg starting to twitch.

"About an hour ago."

"An hour!? Why didn't Sanders wake me?" she snapped, sitting upright.

"Because he isn't here. He's in town. It's just me for now," Jameson told her. He still hadn't looked at her. His voice was calm, soft. Almost zen like, even.

She had never been more nervous around him than she was right at that moment.

What the fuck is he planning!?

"Oh. Well. Are we going to go see him?" Tate asked, licking her lips. Jameson didn't answer, and she pulled her legs away from him, moved to sit cross-legged.

"I hadn't planned on it. It's New Year's Eve," he told her. She nodded.

"I know. I was going to ask what the plan was, if there was a plan," she replied.

"There will be fireworks. I thought we could watch them together," he said.

"No swanky party? No dinner?" she laughed.

"Well, the lobster plan didn't work out so well for me. I don't want to waste anymore of my money," Jameson explained. Tate snapped her eyes to his, ready to be angry, but she realized he was teasing.

"I told you it wouldn't happen."

"Yes. But I was very close."

Grrrrr, this man.

"Close doesn't count."

He got up and walked away from her, stood by a railing. They were on the very top deck, the roof of the boat. Standing over the wheel house. She had never been in the room, never seen any crew. She wondered if they would ever take the yacht out, if he would need to hire a crew to do so.

"I thought we'd take the boat out. We can watch the fireworks from the ocean."

That's right, Satan's psychic. You always forget.

"Sounds nice. I think last night was too much party for me," Tate laughed. She had woken up determined to put on a bright smile about the whole incident. Old-Tatum would have laughed about the whole thing, so new-Tatum would, too.

"Really? And I thought it stopped just short of being a real party," Jameson replied, then abruptly walked away, heading down the stairs.

Tate frowned after him. She wasn't sure what kind of game he was playing. He had been moody all morning, and now he was all quiet and introspective seeming; i.e., *not normal*. She didn't like it, not one bit. She could handle scheming Jameson. Conniving, cruel, sadistic, devilish Jameson. All-of-the-above Jameson. But confused Jameson? Troubled Jameson? *Hurt* Jameson?

She didn't know that man at all.

Tate didn't see much of him for the rest of the day. If she hadn't known better, she would've thought he was avoiding her. Pretty ironic, considering she had finally come to terms with being in his presence. The crawl-out-of-her-skin feeling wasn't as bad anymore.

Of course, it helped that while the men were gone, she had found a corner market and bought a pack of cigarettes. She had chain smoked until she thought she was going to pass out. She had even had one cigarette while lounging on the top deck. An act of defiance. Still counted, even if the devil wasn't present.

Sanders came for dinner, but he was also oddly tight lipped. They made idle chit chat, but when Tate mentioned him coming on the boat to watch the fireworks, he shook his head. He really did get sea sick, he confessed. And he didn't care about fireworks or New Year's. It was just another day. He was working on a 3D puzzle at the apartment, and wanted to finish it.

When she realized he wouldn't be there as a buffer, Tate's bravado deserted her. The puzzle started to sound like more fun than a ride on a yacht under fireworks. Tate chewed at her fingernails, desperate for a cigarette. But she knew she couldn't, not while Jameson was prowling around the boat. So she borrowed Sanders' phone and hid up on the top deck.

She tried calling her sister first. They hadn't spoken since before Tate had left for Spain. They weren't exactly best friends yet, but they did check in with one another fairly often. But Ellie didn't answer. Tate tried calling Nick. His calm, happy-go-lucky nature usually settled any nerves she had – but he wasn't answering, either. She started to grind her teeth and dialed one more number.

"Why hasn't she called me!?" Ang's voice barked the moment the line connected. Tate smiled.

"It's me," she laughed. He snorted.

"Oh. Well. Same question," he said.

"There was an … incident. I lost my phone. Happy New Year's," she said quickly.

"Yeah, yeah, same to you. Have you fucked him yet?" he snapped.

"Jesus, Ang."

"What? I have a radar for that kind of shit with you. It's coming,

I can feel it. Don't do it," he warned her.

"I don't exactly plan on it," Tate replied.

"But it's a possibility?" Ang read between her words. She chewed on her bottom lip, trying not to think about the night before. She rubbed her thighs together.

"Not in my mind," she answered evasively.

"Enough of this bullshit. Tell me everything that has been going on, so I can tell you exactly why you're being stupid," he ordered.

"You're awfully bossy now. You used to be fun," she told him.

"Watching your best friend try to kill herself can do that to you. Spill."

Tate suddenly had a very acute sense of how Jameson must have felt, every time she threw that night in his face. Only her guilt was worse. Jameson deserved to be hassled for his part in everything that happened. Ang hadn't asked for anything, she had dragged him into it.

So she told him everything. Told him about the first kiss, about Jameson throwing her purse into the ocean. Told him about the phone call with Nick, though she conveniently left out what a heartless bitch she had been, just said how Jameson had thrown her phone into the ocean, as well.

Told him about her run in with Pet. It was the only part of the conversation Ang stayed entirely quiet for, and at the end, he congratulated Tate on how she had handled it. But then when she talked about making out with Jameson and practically giving him a lap dance on a VIP sofa, Ang's congratulations were gone and he called her a stupid slut.

"If you're desperate for sex, I get that – it's been a while. It's probably grown over down there. But for god's sake, find someone else. Sanders, anyone, hell, *I'll* fly over there," he told her. There was a sound in the background, then Tate could tell the phone was being muffled. Her ears perked up.

"Ang. Is that your girlfriend?" she asked. He grumbled.

"We're not talking about me, we're talking about —," he started.

"No, no, no. Your girlfriend is there! I can hear her! How does she feel, hearing you talk about flying all the way out here to fuck me?" Tate asked.

"She doesn't care."

"I have to meet this woman. Put her on the phone!" Tate laughed.

"No. Listen. This is all history repeating itself, Tate. I'm not trying to be a Debbie Downer, or a bossy boots, or whatever. I just ... I would die if anything happened to you, and I'm not there to save you this time," his voice grew quiet. Her heart cracked a little.

I am such a horrible person, and my punishment is life with Jameson.

"I know," she whispered, then cleared her throat. "But I had no idea what I was dealing with last time. My eyes are wide open now. I know what I'm dealing with, and I have Sanders. I promise, I won't do anything I don't want to do."

"That leaves a pretty wide scope," Ang snorted. She laughed.

"Once upon a time. Honestly, Ang, am I boring now? Jameson kept calling me a Stepford-wife," Tate told him. There was a pause.

"Normally, agreeing with him would make me wanna puke, but he's got a point. You *were* like a Stepford-wife. All that boring clothing your sister bought you, I almost wondered if she was doing it to be mean," he laughed. The girlfriend piped up in the background, but Tate couldn't hear what she was saying.

"God. Well, you will be happy to know I have bought an entirely new wardrobe," she told him, looking down at herself and plucking at the tight tank top she was wearing. "Most of it is see-through, and most of it is ridiculously tight. They probably won't let me through customs."

"Good. I've missed your tits."

She burst out laughing, and a shadow fell over her. Tate looked up and realized Jameson had joined her. He smiled down at her and her laughter died in an instant.

"What's so funny?" he asked.

"It's Ang. Talking about my tits," she replied.

"Don't say '*tits*' to him, it'll probably make him all rape-y!" Ang yelled down the line.

"May I?" Jameson asked, holding his hand out for the phone. Tate's jaw dropped open.

"I don't think Ang wants to speak to you," she said quickly.

"No, *Ang* most certainly doesn't want to fucking speak to him," Ang agreed. Jameson rolled his eyes and plucked the phone out of her hand. She groaned and turned away, leaning against the railing and looking out over the dark horizon.

"*Angier.* How are you?" he asked. He always stretched Ang's name out, like a sneer. Tate couldn't make out the words Ang was saying, but she could tell they weren't nice. "That's lovely language, I'm sure my proctologist would get a kick out of that idea. Anyway, I have a question for you." Jameson paused, and there was more yelling from the phone. Tate chewed on her nail. "If you're finished ... *if you're finished*, I wanted to say – my birthday is in a week. I am taking Tatum and Sanders to Paris. I wondered if you'd want to join us."

Tate spun towards him so quickly, her foot slipped out from underneath her. She started to fall and he grabbed her by the waist, hoisting her up against him. She righted herself, but Jameson didn't let her go, staring down at her as he listened to whatever Ang was saying. She pushed at his chest, but he didn't move.

"What are you doing?" she hissed. She vaguely remembered before they left Boston, Sanders had said something about them taking a weekend in Paris. But that was before his little Jameson-surprise-party. She figured it had been part of the ruse, to get her to leave.

"Of course I'm serious. Very serious. She misses you. Despite what all of you think, I want to make her happy. So, I am offering you an all expenses paid vacation to Paris," Jameson barked into the phone.

He wanted to make her happy? Tate almost snorted. He wouldn't even begin to know how.

He used to be very good at making you happy.

"Give me the phone," Tate demanded, reaching for it. He leaned his head away, but kept a grip on her waist. They stumbled backwards, her pawing at him, him pulling away.

"This is an expiring offer, *Angier*. Take it or leave it. I know she wants to see you. It's up to you," Jameson said. She slithered around him, and he was forced to switch hands, trading off the phone. She almost nabbed it, but then he tightened his grip around her waist and picked her up with one arm, clutching her to his side. "Yes. Yes, you can. Of course. What? Don't fucking insult me, *Angier*. I'm offering you a gift, but I won't fucking ... okay. *Okay*. Thank you." Tate was squirming back and forth, making it hard for him to keep his footing, when he abruptly ended the call. He pressed a button on the phone and dropped it into a chair.

"What the fuck was that all about!? I didn't even get to say goodbye!" she shouted at him.

"I just agreed to pay for *your* best friend, a man you fuck on a regular basis, to come to Paris for *my* birthday. I think a little gratitude is in order," Jameson informed her. She shoved at his chest, trying to pull away.

"Fuck off. I haven't fucked Ang since you asked me not to," she snapped, and they both paused. Tate hadn't meant it like that; she had made it sound like she still wasn't sleeping with Ang because of Jameson. But that wasn't true.

Was it?

"Very considerate, baby girl," Jameson murmured, smoothing her hair away from her face.

"Oh, get over yourself. I haven't slept with *anyone* since that night. The idea of sex kind of makes me want to puke," she told him.

"You didn't seem so adverse to it last night."

He let her go, and she stumbled backwards. She straightened out the bright maxi skirt she was wearing, adjusted her tank top. Glared at him. It wasn't fair. He was the reason she hadn't had sex in so long. He shouldn't get to have first go. Ang was right, she should go find someone else. *Anyone* else.

"Yet it still didn't happen," Tate pointed out. He quirked up an eyebrow.

"You know, I find it hard to believe that you haven't slept with *anyone*. I know your baseball player is somewhat of a saint, but he's still a man. Is it still boring with him? Are you still holding his hand?" Jameson asked, disdain dripping from his words. Tate laughed.

"*Jealous*. And nothing with Nick is *ever* boring," she taunted. It dawned on her that he honestly thought she and Nick had some sort of actual relationship going on; Jameson was *actually jealous*. She wanted to laugh.

Stupid Satan, don't you know you've ruined me for other men?

"Somehow," Jameson whispered, leaning close to her, "I highly doubt that."

And then he left her, making his way downstairs.

Tate grabbed the phone and followed after him. She gave Sanders his cell phone back, then he said goodbye. She hung onto his sleeve, all the way down the plank. Pleaded with him. Begged him to stay. He refused. He was working for the devil, after all. She glared at him as he walked back to the car.

She milled around below deck for a while, tried reading in her bedroom. She felt the boat move, knew when they had left the dock. She wondered if there was a whole crew of people wandering around, or if Jameson could really operate the whole thing on his own.

After about an hour, her curiosity got the better of her. She wandered upstairs. Out the back of the boat, she could see Marbella, getting smaller and smaller. Just twinkling lights on a coast. In the distance, a couple other lights bobbed around. Other boats, barely pin pricks against the dark sky.

She didn't see or hear any other people, so she made her way to the upper deck. It was barren – Jameson hadn't replaced the furniture that the scorned maid had thrown away. Tate thought about continuing on up to the very top deck, but instead she made her way into the wheelhouse. Jameson was leaned back in a large chair, one foot propped on the edge of it, the other leg stretched out so his foot was against the dash. Very relaxed. The lights were off in the room, and he was staring out over the sea.

"What are you doing?" Tate asked, moving to sit in another large chair that was next to him.

"What does it look like I'm doing?" he countered, not looking at her. She smirked at him.

"Is it safe, operating this thing all by yourself?" she asked. He nodded.

"Safe enough. I'm not taking us out very far," he replied. She leaned back.

"Why don't you hire a crew? I was surprised that you didn't have a chef on board, or a full time maid," she told him.

"Same reason I didn't keep them at home."

Jameson didn't like people. Plain and simple. In Weston, he had a cleaning service that came out on the weekdays, every day after he left for work, but that was it. No full time, live-ins, though his house was built for it, had the room. So she wasn't too surprised that he refused to even hire a captain for his boat.

"What time is it?" Tate yawned, leaning her head back. She saw him move, and then his wrist was held out towards her, his fancy watch facing her.

"Just after ten," he answered anyway.

SEPARATION

There was a heavy silence between them. Something had happened that morning, though Tate didn't know what. It was almost as if Jameson had suddenly woken up with a conscience, and it was bothering him. He seemed upset, and she knew she was the reason.

It wasn't fair. She should be upset. She was the one people looked at funny, like she was crazy. She was the one who spent a week in a hospital. She was the one who got ripped in half. Jameson was still in one piece. He wasn't allowed to feel upset. *It wasn't fair.*

So why do I want to make him feel better!?

Those were the thoughts Tate didn't like, the confusing ones. Sure, it was all a game, and she knew she should be rejoicing in the fact that she had gotten to him. If Jameson was actually upset, to the point of showing it, then he cared. That meant when she won his game, he might be ripped in half a little, as well. Finally. Happy days! She hadn't even had to try that hard, and her goal had been achieved.

So how come all of a sudden, none of that seemed so important anymore?

In fact, it all kind of made her feel sick.

"Jameson," Tate sighed, feeling very tired of their game. "Maybe we should just stop —,"

"Do you remember the maid outfit?" he interrupted. She looked over at him.

"Excuse me?"

"That maid outfit you wore. Remember?" he asked.

Oh, their little games. She had bitched about doing her own laundry. Sanders did Jameson's clothing, but refused to touch hers. Bras and panties gave him the vapors. Tate hated to do laundry. Jameson had made a deal with her. If she could go a whole day without touching him, he would hire someone to dry clean all of her clothing, *every* day. If she lost, she had to be his personal maid for a whole day, and clean *whatever* he wanted. Seemed like an easy win.

Wrong. Not only had it been the warmest day in September, the

165

sun blistering hot, but he had just gotten back from a business trip. Tate had wound up watching him sunbathe, *nude*, while he told her all about a particularly steamy encounter he'd had with a waitress in a bathroom at Tavern on the Green. Tate didn't even make it through ten minutes of him talking before she was on top of him. *All over him.*

He came home the next day with a slutty maid costume in tow. She hadn't expected it to last long, but Jameson had stronger will power than she did. Tate wound up cleaning the whole bottom half of the house before he ripped the outfit off of her.

Fun times.

"I had forgotten about that," she laughed softly.

"I could never forget that day."

"Why are you doing this?" Tate asked, glancing at him. Jameson kept staring ahead, but he reached out and pushed some buttons. Pulled some levers. The boat slowed, came to a stop.

"Because I want you to remember."

"Remember what?"

"That things used to be good between us. They used to be fun," he told her. "Remember that sometimes, just maybe sometimes, I wasn't the devil."

She took a deep breath and stared out over the ocean.

"All I remember is a swimming pool," she whispered.

"Excuse me?"

"This isn't going to work, Jameson," she blurted out, suddenly jumping out of her seat. He looked totally caught off guard.

"Huh?"

"*This.* You can't just ... bombard me with old, sexy memories, and ... what? *Ooohhh,* swoon, I fall all over you? It doesn't work like that!" she snapped at him. He stood up as well.

"Then tell me how it does work, Tate. Because obviously noth- ing *I'm* doing is working," he replied, standing close to her.

"But that's just it! There's *nothing* you can do. You ruined it, and now it's over. Do you really want to go another three weeks, just to hear that? It's over, Jameson. *It's over,*" she stressed. He stared down his nose at her.

"See, if I believed you, I would agree. It would be a waste of time. But you're still such a horrible liar, Tate. Things will *never* be over between us," his voice was soft.

She let out a frustrated yell and stomped out of the wheelhouse. Stomped downstairs, all the way back into her bedroom. She didn't want to hear anything else he had to say. Fuck him. *Fuck Jameson Kane.* She hated him.

Hate it when he's right.

Of course, Tate knew that; somewhere, deep in her brain, she had always known that things weren't over between them. Which was why she had been a nervous wreck for the last two months. Her subconscious had known it wasn't over, and had just been waiting for him. Had always known it. Had known it the first time they parted ways. Had known it the second time. When would conscious-Tate clue into the fact?

Pool. You were in a pool. He brought her into your home. Brought her between you. Didn't care. **He does not care.**

She grabbed her purse and steamed back out onto the deck. As she was digging something out, she saw Jameson coming down the stairs, so she scooted away, made her way to the bow of the boat. There was only so far she could go to get away from him – they were in the middle of the ocean, and none of the bedroom doors had locks.

No escape. Well played, Mr. Kane. Well played.

"You better leave me the fuck alone," Tate yelled when she heard him approaching. "I need this right now."

She lit up the cigarette and took a deep, deep drag. Closed her eyes and slowly exhaled. *There.* That burning sensation in her lungs, that's what she wanted. Smoking was still new to Tate. She didn't do it because she craved it, or because she liked it. She did it because it hurt a little, every time she inhaled.

Something is so very wrong with me.

"Tatum. Put out the cigarette and come talk to me," Jameson ordered. She laughed and turned towards him.

"What's the point? You never listen. How about you have a conversation with yourself, then just answer the way you want me to answer, and we'll call it good," she hissed, moving past him.

The deck on the bow of the yacht was large, and came to a sharp point. Shiny silver railings and glass panels surrounded it, except for two breaks, where ladders folded out down either side of the boat. She went to stand back away from the railing, under a slight awning. They glared at each other, her smoke curling up between them.

"I have been *trying* to listen. For the first fucking time ever. But you're not *saying anything*. Now put the goddamn cigarette out," Jameson told her. Even though she was too far away, she blew a stream of smoke at him.

"*No.* And I don't have to *say anything*, I didn't ask to be here. I was brought here, taken here, tricked into coming here. I don't want to talk to you, I don't want to hear anything you have to say. *I don't want to be here,*" Tate replied. He narrowed his eyes.

"We had a deal. You agreed to play. You're not allowed to lie, or fake anything," he reminded her.

"I haven't lied or faked —,"

He slammed his hand down on the railing, hard, making a gong-like sound. He was *angry*. It had been a long time since she had seen him that mad. She felt her insides turn to mush, her brain turn to putty.

"*Don't fucking lie to me.* You wanted me in that club, and you wanted that to happen in my bedroom. I have let you pretend like you didn't. You dared me into taking that maid. That was *all you,* yet I let you blame me. I am tired of taking your shit. My patience is running out," he growled at her. She guffawed.

"You're tired of taking my shit? *My shit!?* Mister, you haven't even begun to eat shit for the things you did to me! And you're calling *me out* on breaking the rules!? *You fucked your psychotic supermodel girlfriend and then brought her into our home!* How's that for a broken fucking rule!?" Tate screamed at him.

Suddenly Jameson was storming towards her, thunder in his eyes. She pressed herself against the glass door behind her, trapped. He stood in front of her, and she swore she could almost see smoke coming out of his ears. He. Was. *Pissed.*

"I *did not* fuck her. I have apologized for bringing her home. Now stop fucking screaming, and put out the goddamn cigarette. *I will not tell you again,*" he hissed at her. She shivered and raised the cigarette to her lips. Took a deep drag.

"*Make me,*" she whispered, and then blew a smoke ring in his face.

Jameson grabbed her around the waist, and Tate shrieked as she was hoisted into the air. Thrown over his shoulder. She yelled at him to put her down, pounded on his back with her free hand. She was tempted to grind the cigarette into his shoulder blade, but she didn't think she was ready for that kind of punishment.

"*Goddamn Tatum.* Always fucking pushing me," he growled.

"*Stupid fucking Jameson,* always where he isn't wanted," she snapped back.

He didn't respond. He reached the edge of the bow, and she thought he was gong to put her down. Or spank her. Or fuck her senseless. Something. What she didn't expect was for him to throw her. Into the air. Over the railing. She screamed and hit the water, ass first.

"When are you going to learn not to push me!?" he called down to her, after she had resurfaced.

Tate hacked and coughed up salt water, bobbing along. It took

Jameson a second to open the little compartment that hid the stairs, so it felt like an eternity before she hauled herself out of the water. She slowly made her way up the side of the boat. Her skirt, with all its excess material, weighed a ton. She flopped onto the deck like a fish, shivering and scrambling across the surface.

"*There is something ... so very wrong ... with you,*" Tate gasped for air, pushing herself onto her knees.

"Considering that there isn't very much *right* about you, either, I'm going to ignore that comment. C'mon, it's freezing, let's get you —," Jameson started, grabbing her by the arm. She shrieked and slapped his hand away, hurrying to her feet. She skipped out of his reach, circled around till she was safely away from the railing, putting him between her and it.

"*Don't fucking touch me!* You don't get to touch me! You don't believe that I haven't slept with Nick? Why would I *ever* believe you didn't fuck her!? That's all you do, fuck people! *Fuck you!*" she yelled at him.

Tate could feel her sanity unraveling. He'd always had that effect on her. It was like they weren't in Spain anymore. They were in his house. It was that night. She wasn't high in the bathroom with Dunn. Jameson wasn't flirting in the kitchen with Pet. They were back in his bedroom. Only this time, he wasn't walking out on her. This time, he was holding his ground. He was talking to her. Fighting for her.

The way it should have been.

She felt ill.

"Baby girl, are you really worried —,"

"*Don't call me that!* You make me sick! *God*, fucking touching her, touching me. I want to be sick," she hissed at him.

"I touched dozens of women while we were together," Jameson reminded her. Tate narrowed her eyes and stepped up close to him, tilting her head up so he could see the anger on her face.

"And I only ever asked you *not to touch one*. Just one. And you

170

couldn't even manage that. *You're* the stupid whore. You loved calling me that. A slut, a whore; but really, you're a bigger whore than I ever was. *Whore,*" she swore at him.

He lifted his hand then. Slowly. Traced a finger down her neck, from under her chin to the hollow of her throat. It was a hint, a shadow, of what he really wanted to do. He was holding himself back. The air was vibrating with the tension between them. She could feel it. Someone was going to get hurt that night. Tate just had to make sure it wasn't her.

"You know, you should *really* watch the way you speak to me," Jameson said softly, his finger taping against her collar bone.

"I'm not scared of you," she whispered. He leaned close to her, pressing his hand flat against her chest.

"*Liar.*"

She shrieked and shoved him. As hard as she possibly fucking could. He lost his footing, stumbled backwards. Right into the gap in the railing Tate had crawled through only a moment ago. *Good.* She shouldn't be the only one to take a dip. She hoped he hit the water flat on his fucking back. Be bruised for a week.

Something wasn't right, though. Her eyes had recognized it instantly, but her brain took a second to catch up. Jameson wasn't a man that could easily be knocked off balance, especially when he had been ready and waiting for her to push him. He had taken a step back, to brace himself, and his foot had landed on a pile of chains. Slipped inside them, got tangled in them. He couldn't get any purchase, so he went over.

Tate suddenly remembered talking to Sanders that morning, him saying that someone would be working on the boat. Something was wrong with one of the anchors. In the wheelhouse, she hadn't seen Jameson release any. She didn't know much about boating, but she knew that most people dropped anchor when they stopped a boat. Jameson hadn't done it because the chain for one of the smaller, front anchors wasn't attached to the yacht. Now that same chain was wrapped securely around his ankle.

Jameson hit the water hard, on his back, just as she'd cursed him. Tate dropped to her knees, but she wasn't quick enough and the anchor was yanked out of its cubbyhole in the side of boat. It flew after him, falling into the water at the exact same spot he had, disappearing in the splashes.

She shrieked, laying flat. God, had it hit him!? It wasn't a big anchor, but it was big enough. And it was a long way down. Oh god, had she just killed Jameson!? Typical. That would be just like him – he finally talks to her, *really* talks to her, and then goes and dies.

Stupid dick.

Tate screamed his name, pounding her hand on the deck. He didn't resurface. She pulled herself to her knees, raked her fingers through her hair. He still didn't come back. She thought she was going to throw up. She had killed him. They were alone on a boat in the Mediterranean. Everyone knew they weren't getting along, that Tate was very angry at him. No one would believe it was an accident. She would go to jail for murder. Sanders would be an orphan.

I'll never see Jameson again.

And that thought, more than anything, absolutely terrified her.

She scrambled over the side of the deck, making it down a couple rungs before she lost her grip and fell into the ocean. She couldn't see shit, but Tate dove under water as far as she could. Resurfaced. Went back. Screamed his name. Over and over, screamed his name. She had never wanted to hear his voice as much as she did in that moment. Wanted to hear him yelling at her to shut the fuck up. Yelling at her to stop fucking screaming.

"Stop fucking screaming."

I've gone crazy. I killed Jameson, and I've gone crazy.

She went still, treading water, looking around her. There was another sound, a cough, and she looked up. Jameson was standing on the deck, staring down at her. She gasped and fell under the surface of the water. Struggled to swim back up. She was having trouble – her heart seemed to have fallen out of its cavity and was now somewhere in her stomach.

She gagged and broke the surface, gasping for air. She couldn't see anything, her hair was covering her face, but something grabbed her arm. Strong fingers wrapped around her forearm, hauled her up against the boat. Pulled her onto the ladder. She found the railings and clung to them, wiping her hair out of her face as best she could with her shoulder.

"Dead … I thought you were dead ..," Tate gasped. Jameson was on the ladder next to her, leaning out over the water.

"If you want to kill me, Tate, you're going to have to try a little harder. C'mon," he urged, curling an arm around her hips and pushing her upwards.

When she got to the top, she stumbled away from the railing, pressing a hand to her heart. She stood with her eyes closed, trying to catch her breath. She had thought he was dead. Gone forever. And that had terrified her. More than jail, more than murder, more than anything. Not seeing him, ever again. Extinguishing him. If Jameson was gone, what would become of her?

Stupid girl. It was never a game.

"I thought you were dead," she breathed, turning around to face him. He was walking towards her, running his hand through his hair, shaking the water out of it.

"Not quite," he laughed.

"But … I saw the anchor, I thought it hit you. You didn't come up," Tate said.

"It didn't hit me, I didn't die. The anchor, unfortunately, *did* die. The chain wasn't attached to the boat. It's somewhere on its way to the bottom now," Jameson sighed, almost sad sounding as he glanced behind him at the water. Tate was a little blown away.

"You're sad about losing an anchor, and you almost *died*. Where the fuck did you go!? I screamed at you for forever!" she demanded.

"It dragged me under the boat – when I came up, I almost smacked into the bottom of the hull. I swam to the back, came up those stairs," he explained. She shoved at his chest, albeit gently this time.

"It didn't occur to you to fucking say something!?" she snapped.

"No. You had just shoved me overboard, *with an anchor chained to my ankle*. I didn't think you really gave a fuck," he replied. Tate shoved him again.

"Of course I give a fuck! I was freaking the fuck out! I thought you were dead! Why didn't you say anything!?" she shouted, slapping her hands against his chest.

"You were screaming enough for the both of us. I'm surprised the *Servicio Maritimo* isn't out here, the way you were carrying on," Jameson told her, grabbing at her wrists. She yanked away.

"Well, I thought you had died, you stupid fuck! Do you have any idea how horrible that feels!?" she shrieked at him. He glared down at her.

"Yes, *you stupid fuck*, I know *exactly* how that feels!" he yelled back.

She gasped, and it was like a dam inside her broke. A wall collapsed. A series of explosions, bringing down all her defenses. What a horrible world it would be, if she couldn't wake up and play with Jameson. Fight with Jameson. *Be* with Jameson.

Tate practically jumped on him, her mouth on his before her feet had even left the ground. He knew it was coming – he *always* knew – and his arms were around her, holding her up. Holding her to him.

Jameson stumbled towards the door, pressed her against the wall while he struggled with the door handle. She kept trying to lift her legs, but her stupid skirt was in the way. When they got inside,

174

she let go of him long enough to shove the soaking wet material off of her body, and then Jameson grabbed her again, his hands on her ass, guiding her legs around his waist.

Tate groaned, letting her head fall back while he kissed her neck. He walked them downstairs, holding onto her the whole way. His shirt had a tear at the back, from his adventure with the anchor, and she pulled at it. Ripped a seam across the top, let her hands dive inside, let her nails score across his skin. He hissed, and his lips were replaced by his teeth. They pushed and pulled at each other, bumped into walls, ricocheted off, stumbling around in their need for each other.

He kicked open his bedroom door, breaking the frame, and Tate was suddenly *very* glad that he had left Sanders on shore. Jameson held onto her hips as he turned around, sitting at the foot of the bed while she pulled her tank top off. His mouth immediately went to her cleavage, while his hands slid up to her shoulder blades.

She pushed him away, forced him back so she could rip his shirt off. It felt like she was in hyper-drive. If she slowed down, not all of her molecules would stop with her, and she would burst into a million pieces. How would Jameson ever find her then?

"This is happening," he breathed, his lips moving across her face as he reached around and undid her bra. "*Please, please, please, please ...*"

*Is Jameson Kane **begging**!?*

"Yes," she breathed back, tossing the bra to the other side of the room. His hands gripped her hips and he rolled them over, moving them up to the center of the bed.

"This was *always* going to happen," he told her, working his way down her body. Tate nodded and stretched out underneath him, gripping at the blankets above her head.

"Yes," she agreed.

She felt his teeth low on her stomach, scraping against her underwear. Then he was biting at the satin, pulling it over her hips. He worked it all the way to her knees before he stood up, yanking them past her feet. He dropped his pants to the floor and then he was covering her again, his hands everywhere.

"I'm sorry I threw you over overboard," he whispered. Tate managed a laugh.

Is Jameson Kane **apologizing**!?

"I'm not sorry I pushed you," she replied. He snorted.

"Yes, you fucking are."

"*Yes.*"

His fingers kneaded into her flesh, almost massaging her. It had been so long since he had touched her like that; she practically leapt at the feel of his hands. He left scorched flesh in his wake, a burning sensation in her soul. When his fingers were swimming in and around her, all over her, reaching deep inside of her, she gasped and cried out. Arched away from the bed as his lips covered her nipple. Then he was moving between her legs.

It flashed across her mind that maybe this wasn't the best idea, jumping into sex with Jameson when only an hour ago she had been ready to tell him she wanted to go home – near death experiences were no excuse, she of all people knew that.

But then he was demanding entrance, and Tate had never been very good at denying him. Probably because she never wanted to. His erection pressed against her, pressed inside of her. She dug her nails into his back, hard, and raked them across his shoulders while she gasped. Jameson groaned loudly, pressing his hips tight to hers.

"Fuck," he whispered, his forehead dropping to her breast bone. She wiggled her hips against him, rotated her pelvis in a circle, and he groaned again.

"Yes," she whispered back. Chanted. "*Yes, yes, yes, yes.*"

He moved out, then pushed back in, and she cried out. Even she was surprised by her response to him. In previous times, Tate had always been up for some good sex. Orgasms typically came easily and readily for her, she was very lucky, she knew. But usually *some* work was required.

Not this time. She felt like she was going to explode, *immediately*. Like a corked bottle, full of fine champagne and effervescence. Her breathing hitched and she knew she was whimpering, whining. Praying.

"Holy shit, Tate," Jameson whispered, one of his hands covering her breast. She moved her hand over his, squeezed.

"Please. Please, god, please," she begged, not even able to move anymore. She felt tiny tremors beginning to run all under her skin.

Suddenly, he was rolling them again. She felt dizzy as she tried to steady herself, her eyes shut tight while she clung to his shoulders. He sat upright with her straddling him, then he put his hands on her knees. He pushed them wider, causing her to slide lower on his shaft. She sank her teeth into her bottom lip and the tremors turned into all over shaking as he slid so deep inside of her, there was no going back.

"It's okay, baby girl," Jameson whispered against her ear as he moved his hands to her hips, urging her to move. Rocking her hips against him. She groaned and let her head fall back, her eyes fluttering closed.

"Jameson, I'm … I'm …" she gasped, running her hands into her hair as they picked up speed. He always filled her up, so much. There wasn't enough space for both of them. Just him. Why didn't she ever remember that? She was going to explode.

"*It's okay,*" he urged, fingers biting into her flesh.

When his teeth clamped down on her nipple, she lost her fucking mind. Actually screamed. One hand went to his head, pulling his hair while at the same time holding him to her. It felt like she came *forever,* shaking and gasping for air on top of him. Her body turned to jell-o, all of her muscles dissolved.

When the biggest part of her orgasm had subsided, Jameson laid down, taking her with him. Tate panted against his chest and his arms came to rest around her waist, his fingers drawing lazy circles in her skin. She shuddered and pressed her face against him, ran her teeth along a muscle.

Something was different. It was *so* different. She couldn't put her finger on it at first. Sex between them was always amazing, so the orgasm didn't shock her. He hadn't come, but that wasn't necessarily a surprise, either – Jameson usually liked to wring a couple orgasms out of her first, before giving her one of his own. It had been a lot quicker than normal, but they had all night, so it wasn't that. Sure, it had been a little quiet, but …

Tate's eyes snapped open and she grew still on top of him. They were *never* quiet during sex. Jameson was the most talkative man in bed she'd ever met – and that was saying something, considering she used to sleep with Ang on the regular, and he *never* shut up.

Jameson used words the way other people used toys; vibrators, whips, ropes. Backed up by his hands, so demanding in their grab and pull. But not this time. Tate felt amazing, like she was glowing. God, he'd been so gentle. What the fuck did that mean!? It certainly wasn't anything like the sex they used to have, back in Boston. She suddenly felt ill. Jesus, they weren't … they didn't … they hadn't just *made love*, had they!?

You're losing again, baby girl.

"Get up," Jameson suddenly urged, slapping her on the ass. She was still reeling from her moment of introspection, and just fell off of him as he started to sit up.

"Huh?" she asked as he got off the bed.

"Get up, let's go," he said, grabbing her arm and yanking her to her feet. She almost didn't make it, and he grabbed her around the waist.

"I'm sorry, wait. What's going on?" Tate asked.

SEPARATION

"You were laying there thinking, never a good thing. Stop it. Follow me," Jameson said, then he was pulling her across the room.

"I was only —," she started to argue.

"Shut up, Tate. Don't ruin this."

He led her across the large room, into his master bath. She had never been in there, and was a little stunned. There was a huge circular jacuzzi tub. Did Jameson take baths? There was also a large, glass enclosed shower stall. He turned both taps on, then pulled her into the shower while the tub filled up.

"What are we doing?" Tate asked, slicking her hair away from her face. He grabbed her hips and pulled her close.

"Getting reacquainted."

"I thought we just did that," she laughed.

"No, we had sex," Jameson replied, pinching her chin between his fingers and forcing her to stare at him. "Now that it's out of the way, maybe you'll hear me."

She swallowed thickly and pulled herself free of him. The sex hadn't been quite as scary as she thought it would be, it hadn't quite broken her. But talking – now that was *really* dangerous. If he started saying things she'd always wanted to hear, she wouldn't be able to handle it. He would really win, once and for all.

It's still a game. Sex doesn't change anything. It has to be a game. You'll never be anything more than that to him, and if you ever forget that, he'll put you back in that pool.

Tate turned around and leaned into him, pressing her back against his chest. Jameson moved and she moved with him, standing under the spray of water. She felt his hands in her hair, working the water over the strands. She sighed, resting her head on his shoulder.

"I've never been on a yacht before," she commented. He chuckled, his hands moving back down to her hips.

"Really? I would've assumed your family had one," he replied. Tate shook her head.

"There's like a family boat, parked in the Hamptons, but I never got to go on it. Yours is nice," she told him.

"My god, she says something nice to me. I didn't think it would ever happen again."

"Don't get used to it."

"Tatum, I want you to know, I always —,"

Stop him. It's too much. You'll overflow. Shut down. Break down. Fall apart.

"Have you owned this boat long?" she interrupted, lifting her head away from him. He sighed.

"Years. I bought it after I left Harrisburg," he answered.

"Did you —,"

"Tate, since when do you give a fuck about boats?" Jameson demanded. She laughed and stepped away from him.

"Since you tricked me into staying on one. Very dirty game, Mr. Kane," she teased him.

"*I'm not playing any game.*"

Tate almost swallowed her tongue. She didn't know what to say to that, so she chose to ignore it.

"Your bath is full," she told him.

"*Our* bath. C'mon."

It was big enough to fit both of them. She asked for bubbles, and he gave her a dirty look, but he did turn on some jets. Tate pressed him against the side of the tub and then settled herself in front of him, between his legs. He wrapped his arms around her waist and she fought down a feeling of panic.

How can someone who bears such a striking resemblance to Satan be so lovable!?

"God, this feels good," she groaned, sinking down so the water was up to her chin. Jameson's hands crept onto her shoulders, began massaging her.

"Good. I thought you'd like it. I had it installed before you got here," he told her. She perked up.

"This tub is new?" she questioned.

"This whole bathroom was completely remodeled," he answered.

"Why?"

"It was too small before, I wanted enough room for both of us to move around."

"You had awfully high hopes."

"Only the highest."

"Seems kinda extravagant," Tate told him.

"You deserve it," Jameson whispered in her ear.

She couldn't handle him talking to her like that, not if she wanted to win this little game. They'd had sex, and they would most definitely be having sex again – like in the next five minutes – but that didn't mean she had lost. That didn't mean she couldn't still walk away unscathed. It was *just sex*.

Right. Sure it is.

Tate pulled away from him, turned around and laid against him. Jameson kept trying to talk – it was obvious he wanted to tell her things. Things she wanted to hear. Things she probably *needed* to hear. But she wasn't falling for that trick again. She ran her tongue along his skin, her hands along his body. The devil was surprisingly easy to distract and soon enough, neither of them were thinking about talking.

See? That wasn't so hard. Now, just don't think about tomorrow …

8

TATE SNORTED AND ROLLED ONTO her stomach. Stretched her arms out. When she didn't encounter another body, she opened her eyes. She was alone in the bed. She propped herself up, looked around. She was in a sea of black sheets and pillows, and completely alone. The drapes were drawn over all the windows, but one was letting a slice of bright sunshine into the room. She rolled over onto her back.

After their bath together, Jameson had wrapped her in a blanket and moved them upstairs. They watched fireworks from the bow. Had sex on the top deck. By the time they headed back downstairs, Tate was emotionally and physically *drained*. Jameson led her to his room and she collapsed on his bed. But right as she was dozing off, she felt his fingers walking down her spine. Lightly scratching back up. Scratching was good, so she had woken up. Played with him a little longer.

You're going to lose.

Tate shook her head and slid to the edge of the bed, throwing the sheets aside. She had work to do. She had to harden her heart. Prepare herself. There was still three weeks left in Jameson's little game. Sex was going to make it a lot harder for her to resist him, and now, thanks to a stupid anchor with a loose chain, *not* having sex was out of the question. They'd had sex all night, and she was already wondering where he was so they could start again. Not good. She *could not* lose.

She heard voices outside, and she was caught off guard. They were in the middle of nowhere, how were there people on the boat!? Tate tip toed to the window and peeked out. She was looking at his speed boat. Beyond it, another boat. They were back in the marina. She glanced around, looking for a clock. It was almost noon! Jameson had driven the boat back into town while she was sleeping.

She found his robe and put it on before wandering upstairs. But Jameson wasn't there. He wasn't anywhere on the deck, or up in the wheelhouse. But while she was up there looking, Tate saw where he was; he was on the other side of the speed boat, sitting in a tiny row boat, messing with its engine.

She wandered back into his room, smelling at the edge of the robe. It smelled like him, of course. She had always liked his smell. Expensive cologne and aftershave. Rich. Male. Heady. It gave her an idea.

She padded over to some built in wardrobes and yanked open the doors. One was full of normal clothing – jeans, t-shirts, polo shirts, shorts. The other held his suits. That was the Jameson she knew, the one she recognized, the one she could handle. Tate pulled out a shirt, ran her fingers down the sleeve. *Balenciaga.* She shivered and let his robe fall to the floor before pulling the shirt on, reveling in the feel of a $400 garment resting against her skin. She looked for a tie next. The first one she grabbed was a Barney's, but she figured her shirt deserved something even more high class, so she pulled out one by Ann Demeulemeester. *Ooohhh,* $250. Jameson might shit a brick.

She pulled her hair up into a knot on top of her head, then wiggled into a pair of bikini bottoms. Done. Tate skipped upstairs, then tip toed down the gangplank, hoping Jameson wouldn't see her. He didn't, and she made her way over to where he was working. His back was towards her, and he was completely absorbed in what he was doing. The top of the engine casing was off, and he was practically elbow deep inside of it. She shivered and sat down on the edge of the cement, dangling her legs over the side. She cleared her throat.

"I wondered when you'd make an appearance," he said, not turning around.

"You should've woken me up," Tate replied.

"I know how you are, you were probably freaking out when you woke up. Frankly, I'm amazed you're not halfway to the airport right now, running back to Boston. *Fuck,*" Jameson hissed, yanking his hand out of the mess as if he had touched something sharp.

"What are you doing?" she asked with a laugh. The row boat was old, wooden, with peeling paint. A piece of shit. It had two bench seats stretching across the middle, and a pair of ancient oars rested in the bottom of it.

"I bought this off a guy this morning. I figured you and Sanders could use it to tool around in, if you wanted. *If* I can get this motor working," Jameson explained. She laughed again.

"Oh, I'm sure Sandy will love this plan. Permission to come aboard?" she asked.

"By all means."

He didn't offer to help. *Shocker.* Tate slid off the cement, trying to balance on her toes. When she felt secure, she let go and stepped into the boat. It rocked under her, but didn't throw her, so she sat down on the open bench. Straightened out her tie. Rolled up her sleeves.

"Why don't you just by a new engine?" she asked. He snorted.

"Because this one might still work. I know you think I'm some rich asshole, Tate, but if something can be fixed, I don't just go out and buy a new one anyway," he snapped. She raised her eyebrows.

"Nice tone. Sounds like someone else woke up freaking out this morning," she called him out. Jameson finally laughed.

"This motor is a bitch. I finally get you to be compliant, and then something else gives me shit. Story of my life," he joked, finally turning around.

Tate wasn't sure who looked more shocked, him or her. Jameson's eyes were wide as he took in her outfit, but her jaw dropped as she took in what he was wearing. Glasses. Jameson. *In glasses.* They were narrow black frames, and the glare from the sun hid his blue eyes.

"You wear glasses!?" she exclaimed.

"Contacts. The question is, what the fuck are *you* wearing?" he asked.

"I never knew you wore contacts, and I never saw a pair of glasses in your house," she argued.

"They were in there, I assure you. Why are you wearing my clothing?" Jameson asked again.

"I'm sorry, I can't. *Glasses,*" Tate mumbled.

It changed his face so much. He looked so serious. Scholarly. Like a sexy professor. A whole new encyclopedia of fantasies and fetishes poured through her head. Did she pack a pleated skirt? How quickly could she get one? Would Jameson be into role playing? He would be, once he saw her dressed up as a naughty school girl ...

"Tate," he snapped his fingers in front of her face. She reached out and slid the frames off of his face. Inspected them.

"Why are you wearing them now?" she asked, turning them over in her hands.

"*Someone* shoved me into salt water, then I slept in my contacts. My eyeballs feel like they've been stepped on," he replied, glaring at her. Tate glanced at him.

"Do you need them to see?" she asked. Jameson shook his head.

"I'm not blind, I can see. They just help," he replied, his eyes wandering down her body. She licked her lips and glanced at the oars.

"Let's take this baby for a spin," she suddenly suggested. He laughed.

"I suppose you didn't notice, but all this shit around my feet? That's the engine. This baby isn't going anywhere," he assured her. Tate rolled her eyes.

"And what are these?" she pointed out, tapping a pointed foot against an oar. He raised his eyebrows.

"You want me to row your ass around this marina?" he clarified.

When Tate tried to put the oars in the water herself, Jameson's manly pride kicked in and he took over. She was sitting with her back to the bow, so she leaned back, resting her elbows on the sides of the boat while she put her feet in his lap. She put his glasses on and closed her eyes, soaking in the sun.

"See? This is nice," she told him, sighing. He grunted.

"Easy for you to say. I'm doing all the fucking work," he pointed out. She laughed.

"What are all those muscles for, just show? *Row faster,*" she said saucily.

"*Watch it.*"

He kept it up for quite a while, she was impressed. But after they were well away from the harbor, Jameson had to stop. He had sliced his finger open on the engine earlier, and a small stream of blood was running down his forearm, mixing with the engine grease that was coating him from finger tip to elbow. He let the waves carry them farther out to sea while he inspected the wound.

"We should've brought an anchor," Tate commented. Jameson flicked his eyes to her.

"So you could finish the job?" he asked. She laughed.

"Big bad Jameson, so scared of me," she teased.

"I'm always scared of you. What's with the outfit?" he asked. She slid her hand down the tie, waving the end of it at him.

"You don't like?"

"I like it very much – hence why I bought it. Looks good on you."

"Thank you."

"Tate. I'm letting you wear clothing that probably costs more than your entire wardrobe. I rowed you out to the middle of no-where. What's your game?" he asked. She sat upright, made a pro-duction of straightening the tie.

"As Freud would say," she started, putting on a heavy Austrian accent, "*tell me about your mother.*"

"Excuse me?" Jameson asked, sitting upright. Tate adjusted his glasses on her nose, looking over the top of them to see him.

"Tell me about your relationship with your mother," she asked, again in an accent.

"Why the fuck do you want to know about my mother?" he de-manded. Tate sighed.

"Jameson, you wanted to prove to me that you're not the devil, right? Had some big grandiose plan to convince me that being with you would be better than anything that could possibly be waiting for me at home. We stay on your boat, we hardly ever go anywhere, unless I bitch. We fight. We have sex. So far, I can't see how anything is different from before," she pointed out.

"You never used to have a problem with the way we were at home," he countered. She glared.

"It became a big fucking problem right around the time you brought your *girlfriend* home."

"Which I have been trying to tell you, I nev—,"

"I don't care. I'm bored, this is all *boring*. More of the same. You don't wanna answer my question? Fine. Let's go back so we can sit around and do *nothing*," Tate challenged him.

"Boring, huh? When has your baseball player ever shown you

this good of a time? Does he talk about *his* mother?" Jameson asked, his tone snide. She cocked up an eyebrow.

"I've already *met* his mother."

It wasn't a lie, Nick's mom had come to Boston one time. Tate had bumped into her in the hallway.

Her ploy worked. Jameson stared at her for a second, his lips set in a hard line. She expected him to argue. To tell her to go fuck herself. She didn't necessarily expect him to give right in, she had planned on having to needle him. But then he moved, kicking pieces of machinery out of the way and sitting on the floor of the boat.

"Come here," he said, reaching a hand out for her. She took it.

He helped her to sit between his knees, then arranged her legs so her feet were on either side of his hips, her knees bent. He rested his hands on her legs, feathering his fingers along the insides of her thighs. Tate wasn't sure what was going on, but she was beginning to feel short of breath. To go from not touching him for so many months, to him touching her whenever he felt like it, took some adjusting. She tried not to drool.

"Your mother," Tate reminded him.

"Why do you want to know about my mother?" Jameson asked.

"I don't know anything about you. Why not start there," she answered. He nodded, looking out over the water.

"My father had some passport trouble, while he was traveling. She worked at the embassy in Argentina. That's how they met," he started.

"Your parents met in Argentina? That's neat," she said. He glanced at her.

"Yeah, '*neat*'. He stayed long enough to get her pregnant. When she realized she was having a child, her family kicked her out," he explained.

"Your mother was actually from Argentina?" Tate was a little surprised. Jameson smiled at her.

"*Soy Argentino, señorita,*" he replied. He was part Argentinian. Well. Who knew?

"I had no idea."

"I look like her."

"She must have been pretty," Tate replied, and he laughed at that one.

"She was *very* pretty. She got ahold of my father, he brought her back to America. They got married. Six months later, I came along. Nine years later, she died from lung cancer," Jameson encapsulated everything. Tate rolled her eyes.

"Did you not get along with her?" she asked. He looked surprised.

"We got along great. Why would you ask that?" he questioned. She shrugged, leaning against the bench behind her.

"I don't know. Trying to figure out why you like to treat women the way you do," she responded. Jameson laughed.

"You think I like to treat women like shit because I hated my mother?" he clarified. She shrugged again.

"Maybe."

"You hate your mother – is that why you *want* to be treated like shit?" he pointed out. She blinked in surprise.

"I … no. I don't know," Tate hadn't really thought about it.

"What's your favorite color?" Jameson suddenly asked. She was caught off guard again.

"Huh?"

"Your favorite color. What is it?"

"I don't know. Black? Gold?" she prattled off. He nodded.

"Why do you like gold?" he pressed.

"Are you okay?"

"Shut up and answer the question. Why do you like the color gold? Specifically. Think about it. *Why,*" he stressed. She looked at him like he was crazy, but she thought about it.

"Because … I like it. When I look at it, it pleases me, aesthetically. I don't know why, but it just does," Tate explained as best she could. Jameson nodded, digging his fingers into her thighs and dragging his nails up towards her knees.

"When I call you a '*stupid cunt*', it pleases me, physically. I don't know why, but it *just does,*" he copied her answer to make his point. "Why do people always need a reason? I hate my mother, so I treat women like shit? You hate your dad, so you find guys to treat you like shit? *No,* Tate, I didn't hate my mother. I got along great with her. Loved her very much.

"I'm not acting out my psychological problems in bed. It is possible to like kinky shit just because you like it. If it seems like I treat women like shit, it's because I treat *everyone* like shit; women, men, orangutans, *everyone*. I'm not some damaged person, I'm just *spoiled*. I'm used to getting my own way, and when I don't, I tend to throw a temper tantrum. I have no problem admitting this – I have been getting my way long enough to expect it to just happen, and I have enough money to normally ensure that it *does* happen. It's as simple as that. So, sorry to disappoint you, I'm just plain old fashioned kinky. I like weird sex, simply because I like how it makes me feel."

Temper tantrum. I thought bringing Pet home was some well thought out, elaborate plan to hurt me because he's a sadistic bastard. But he's really just a spoiled brat. A goddamn temper tantrum …

"You should really work on that whole spoiled thing. Your temper tantrum nearly drove me insane," Tate managed a laugh, though she felt very much like crying. Jameson nodded.

"I know. I think about that everyday. You have very effectively taught me that it is one thing to want things my way," he started in a soft voice, staring her very directly in the eyes. "But quite another to ignore the ways of everyone else. I hurt you, and I'm still finding it difficult to forgive myself. If you had died, Tate …, there are no words. I would have been very sad. And not just because I had done something bad, I want you to know. I would have been sad because my world is a very lonely place without you."

So many unshed tears. Tate was glad she was wearing his glasses, she felt like they were hiding her emotions a little bit. She took deep breaths through her nose, tried to stay calm. They were very sweet words. Words that soothed the gaping hurt in her soul. But the devil is very good when it comes to dealing with damaged souls.

I wanted to learn about him so I could hate him more. I didn't expect his answer to make me want to forgive him. Cheating bastard.

"We were talking about your mother," Tate drew the conversation away from the heavy stuff. Jameson sighed and looked back over the water, wearing a look on his face that she couldn't quite decipher. Annoyance? Hurt?

Those two shouldn't look similar ..., only on you, Satan.

"My mother and I got along great, she was an amazing person. My father wasn't exactly big on being involved in family issues. He wasn't even there when I was born. My mother is the one who named me," he told her.

"Oh yeah, you said your middle name was her last name," Tate remembered the first time they had run into each other in Boston, at his firm's opening party.

"Technically, *Kraven* is part of my last name. I have several middle names."

"You have more than one middle name?"

"Yes. I'm a thoroughbred," he joked.

"What's your full name?" she asked. He sighed and dragged a finger back down her thigh, following its path with his gaze.

"*Mi nombre es Jameson ... Santiago ... Agustin ... Kraven Kane,*" he said it slowly, tracing the first initial of each name on her skin.

He's branding me.

"You have five names," she commented softly. He nodded and glanced at her.

"I know. It took a long time to memorize, when I was little," he chuckled. She couldn't imagine him ever being little.

"*Santiago*. I like it. Can I call you Santi?" she teased.

"Only if you want to get slapped."

"Ooohhh, tempting."

"Is this really okay, Tate?" Jameson asked, going back to scratching his nails up and down her legs.

"What do you mean?"

"*This*. Day before yesterday, you were over me. Last night, you were ready to say you wanted to go home. Today, you're sitting here, flirting with me, half naked in my clothing. I am a little suspicious," he warned her.

"Sometimes, I just need a good fucking to put me in my place," she laughed.

"*Tatum.*"

"I don't know," she was finally serious. "I'm just tired, Jameson. I'm tired of fighting, and I'm tired of arguing, and ... and I missed you. I hate to admit it, but I did."

She watched him carefully while she talked, tried to judge whether or not he believed her. His eyes were narrowed, wandering over her face. She swallowed thickly and stared right back. Prayed for him to believe her.

He should – you're technically telling the truth. Weak bitch.

"So. That's what you wanted to talk about? My sexual proclivities?" he asked, his fingers starting to massage her. Tate shrugged.

"Yeah, amongst other things."

"I never knew they bothered you."

"Obviously, they don't – I love them. I was just curious, if there was something else there," she replied.

"And that's why you wanted to ask about my mother?" he asked. She nodded.

"Yeah. I don't know, I used to wonder if you hated women. I

SEPARATION

thought maybe there was a reason," she told him. Jameson laughed
and grabbed her ankle, lifted her leg up so he could nibble at her calf.

"I don't hate women, Tate. I *love* women," he said, kissing his
way to her ankle. "I love the way they feel, their skin, their smell. The
way they *taste*, the *sounds* they make."

"Clearly. I just wanted to get to know you better," she continued.
He sat her leg down and grabbed her by the hips, scooting her even
closer to him.

"So what else do you want to know, baby girl?" he asked, his eyes
hooded as he looked down at her. Tate licked her lips and ran a finger
along the collar of his shirt.

"Mmmm, how many women have you fucked since me," she
breathed. Jameson laughed and moved his hands to her neck, slowly
undoing his tie.

"Hmmm, how many, how many," he wondered out loud, pulling
the tie over her head and tossing it behind her.

"Less than ten?" she asked. He looked upwards, like he was
thinking hard, and took the glasses off of her.

"I lose track of these kinds of things, so easily," he mumbled. He
sat his glasses down beside the engine parts and then went to work
on the buttons of her shirt.

"Less than twenty?" Tate pressed. It had started out as a tease,
but now she wanted to know. *Needed* to know. Jameson finished
unbuttoning and spread the shirt open, running his hands over her
breasts.

"Tatum," he whispered, leaning her backwards till she was laying in the bottom of the boat.

"Hmmm," she purred, lifting her hips as he slowly pulled her
bikini bottoms away.

"I haven't slept with *one single other woman* since you."

With words like that, she would give him anything. They could
play all the games they wanted, and he would always win. It was his

193

board game, his dice, his cards. She never stood a chance against him.

Tate had slept with a lot of guys in a lot of interesting locations, but she could safely say that in the middle of the day, on a tiny row boat, in the middle of the Mediterranean, was a first.

"Your color has improved," Sanders commented, when he came to see them later in the day.

"You think? I've been soaking up as much sun as possible," Tate replied, holding out her arms to examine her skin.

"I wasn't talking about your tan," he told her. She laughed.

Jameson had set a table up on the top deck. Very intimate. However, he obviously hadn't counted on Sanders crashing the party. He had glared at him the whole time while they all ate. It made Tate laugh. Jameson had finally stomped away, in search of something stronger than champagne and water.

"It was a good New Year's party," she replied. Sanders quirked up an eyebrow.

"Really? I was under the impression that it was just the two of you," he said. She smiled at him and waggled her eyebrows.

"It was."

"Good. *That* took long enough," Sanders said, looking out over the ocean.

"Sandy," she started, glancing at the stairs, listening for Jameson. "Why do you think Jameson and I are so good together?"

"Because you are," he replied simply. She rolled her eyes.

"Seriously. Us being together is obviously a big deal to you. But, he doesn't want a girlfriend. I told you, he's never gonna really care about me. We're not gonna, like, *be* your parents, Sandy. He's going to leave me at some point," Tate warned him. Sure, she planned on leaving Jameson before that ever happened, but she didn't think that needed to be said out loud. Sanders cleared his throat.

"I don't think of you as my parents. I have parents. Jameson is my guardian. You are my best friend," he corrected her. She smiled brightly, pleasantly shocked.

"Really? *Me?* God, I love you, Sanders," she gushed. He still wouldn't look at her.

"I want you two to be together because you make Jameson happy. He makes you happy. If you would both stop trying to *assume* what each other are doing and thinking, and just *ask* each other once in a while, things would be much better between you," he informed her.

"You should be a marriage counselor," she pointed out.

"Oh god."

"I just don't think it's that easy, though. He's playing a game. At the end of this month, what, we're going to ride off into the sunset together? I don't think so. I'm not holding my breath for him to change," Tate said. Sanders shrugged.

"That shouldn't be a problem, because he already has."

Before she could question him further, though, Jameson came back up the stairs. Her eyes got wide as she saw the bottle he was carrying. He stared back at her while he took his seat, putting the bottle in the middle of the table.

"Scared?" he asked, giving her a wolf grin. She snorted.

"Terrified," Tate answered honestly, her eyes traveling over the black and white label.

"I would just like to say, I think this is a bad idea," Sanders piped up. Jameson glanced at him.

"No one asked you. Besides, this is for me," he replied. Sanders cleared his throat and stood up.

"I think I should leave. I have everything arranged for Paris, sir.

We leave in seven days?" Sanders clarified. Jameson nodded, leaning back in his chair.

"Yes. Did you book the hotel room for *Angier*?" he asked. Sanders nodded.

"I did, and one for myself. Are you sure you don't want us all in one suite?" he double checked.

"Positive. I never need to share a dwelling with *Angier*. My generosity has its limitations."

"It seems to me that it would be more cost effective if —," Sanders started, but Jameson held up a hand.

"We'll talk about it tomorrow. Go home," he snapped. Tate wondered what the big deal was with not wanting to share a suite. It was already surprising enough that he didn't keep Sanders on the boat. Why the need for so much privacy?

I knew it. He's gonna sell me into sex slavery.

"Very well. Good night. Good night, Tatum," Sanders said, then hurried down the stairs.

"That guy," Jameson grumbled.

"Is a very, very good guy," Tate finished for him. He snorted.

"He's something, that's for sure. So, I figured, since we're conquering your fears," Jameson started, and he reached out and grabbed the bottle of Jack Daniel's. Unscrewed the cap. Tate licked her lips.

"I haven't had any serious kind of alcohol since that night," she warned him. He nodded.

"I know. Sanders kept me well informed. You don't have to drink tonight, but I wanted you to have the option. I just want you to … feel safe. Around me," he told her, not looking at her as he poured a shot.

"Oh my god, Jameson," she laughed. He glanced at her.

"What?"

"That was really sweet."

"Fuck off."

"And I have never felt safe around you, so you can stop trying," she teased him.

"You once told me that I didn't scare you," he reminded her, sipping at the whiskey.

"That was a long time ago. A Danish beauty and a temper tantrum have taught me otherwise," Tate replied. Jameson sighed.

"Never gonna stop, are you."

"Probably not."

He took the shot in one go, and then poured another. She raised her eyebrows, and it occurred to her that she had never seen Jameson drunk. Not once. He liked to drink, and drank often, but never to excess. She was suddenly very curious.

"How about," Tate started, sliding the bottle towards herself. "For every shot I take, you take two." Jameson narrowed his eyes.

"Sounds dangerous."

"*Chicken.*"

He took his second shot, staring at her the whole time.

"Alright. Let's do this."

She poured herself a shot, tried not to smell it. She knew if she smelled it, it would be that night all over again. She shuddered and tried not to think about it. Tate looked at him, concentrated on Jameson's eyes. He'd had new contacts delivered to the boat and his glasses were hidden away again. She could see his baby-blues without any hindrance. She stared at him while she took the shot.

"One down. You owe me two," she informed him.

He snorted and took them back to back.

I'm so fucked.

Her tolerance was much lower than it used to be, Tate knew, but she had also eaten a large dinner. She took another shot a couple minutes later, then one more more about ten minutes after that; she figured she wouldn't need to do anymore. She'd had three shots – Jameson, eight. After his last one, she could definitely see a difference in him. She tried to focus, keep her head clear. She was a little drunk, but only just a little.

"Feel it yet, baby girl?" Jameson asked, sitting his shot glass upside down.

"Yes. Had enough?" she asked back, nodding at his glass. He shrugged.

"I think *you've* had enough," he replied. He hadn't taken his eyes off of her for about ten minutes. They were glued to her face. He wasn't slurring, but his eyes were hooded, his posture relaxed. He kept his arms folded across his chest.

"I think so, too," she agreed, laughing lightly. He ran his tongue across his bottom lip, slowly, and she swallowed a groan.

"Are you drunk enough to let me be bad to you?" he asked.

"You're *always* bad to me."

"Baby girl, you haven't seen bad in a really long time."

You ain't just whistlin' dixie ...

"Jameson," she breathed. He raised an eyebrow, his eyes on her lips.

"Hmmm?"

"Do you think I'm pretty?" Tate asked, then hiccuped. He burst out laughing.

"Are you serious right now?" he asked in return. She nodded, hiccuped again. Maybe she was more than "*just a little*" drunk ...

"Yes."

"What a stupid fucking question. Of *course* I think you're pretty. You're goddamned stunning, Tate. I think you're one of the sexiest fucking women I've ever met," Jameson replied bluntly. She beamed at him.

"Thank you. What's your favorite part of me?" she asked, leaning on the table.

"God, you're one of *those* kind of drunk girls," he groaned. She shrugged.

"Unfortunately. My ass?" she guessed.

"*Your pussy.*"

"Something visible, please."

He thought for a while.

"I love your lips, how they look, what you can do with them. Your eyes, when you put all that shit on," Jameson began to stand, leaning over the table. "But your body ... *mmm*, Tate, *your body.* Everything from your neck to your knees, I want to *completely devour.*" He swept his arm across the table, sending all the glasses and plates and silverware crashing to the ground.

"Good answer," Tate whispered. He grabbed her by the back of the neck and pulled her forward, forcing her onto the table top. She knelt in front of him.

"What did you think, the first time you saw me?" she asked as his hands raked through her hair.

"Which time?"

"At your office building, at that party."

"I thought, '*I want to fuck that caterer.*'" She laughed at him. "Then when I realized it was you, I thought '*I want to fuck Tatum O'Shea.*'"

"What did you —,"

"*Stop talking about stupid shit.*"

He kissed her. Sloppily, which was a new experience, coming from Jameson. His lips covered her own, almost entirely, and she could taste the whiskey on him as his tongue filled her mouth. He pulled her roughly against him as his fingers dug into her scalp. Pulled at her hair. Made their way to the back of her neck, where he gripped hard enough for her to the feel the burn of friction. She leaned against him, and the table lurched forward, causing him to stumble to the side. Tate flattened herself as much as she could, not relishing a fall into the ocean from that height.

"We shouldn't do this," she panted. Jameson nodded, stepping back up to the table and grabbing her arm.

"I know, com'ere, I'll throw the table overboard," he suggested, trying to pull her down. She laughed.

"No, that's not what I meant. We shouldn't do *this*, not while we're drunk," she explained. Now he laughed.

"Fuck that. You don't get to sit there and just talk about shit like that. I'm going to fuck you tonight," Jameson told her plainly.

"Um, I think I have a say in it, and I say, *no thank you*," Tate replied with a snicker. He pulled her close and swayed towards her.

"You really think you have a say in it?" he breathed in her ear.

"I *know* I do," she said back. He shook his head and clucked his tongue, stepping away from her.

"Stupid, stupid girl. Always making me prove you wrong," he sighed, heading towards the stairs. She gaped as he disappeared down them, leaving her sitting on the table top.

"Excuse me!?" she asked out loud, looking after him.

Was that it? He was just giving up? It was sexy banter. Tate was fully prepared to fuck his brains out. He just had to work for it a little. Had things really changed that much between them? She slid off the table and followed him.

She made it to the stairs in time to see Jameson reach the upper deck. He was lifting his arms over his head, peeling his shirt off. He dropped it to the ground and kept moving. She hurried down the stairs, grabbing his shirt as she swept across the deck.

He took off one shoe at the bottom of the next set of stairs, and another shoe as he went below deck. Tate kept following, wondering how far this show was going to go, picking up the trail of items he was leaving. He pulled his wallet out of his pocket, tossed it over his shoulder. Then his phone hit the floor, right outside his bedroom door, which still didn't shut because of the broken frame. He undid his pants and managed to step out of them before he got to his bed, where he promptly moved to kneel on the mattress. Jameson slowly turned to face her, but he wasn't looking at her, busy concentrating on removing his watch.

"Tatum," he said, his voice syrupy thick. Like a lion purring. She dropped his clothing to the floor.

"What?" she asked, leaning against his door frame.

"Is it my turn to ask questions?"

"Depends on the questions," she replied. He finally loosened his watch and dropped it off the side of the bed.

"How many men have you fucked since me?" he asked. He yawned and linked his fingers together, stretching his arms above his head. Every muscle he had flexed and strained with the act. Tate's mouth went dry in an instant.

"I'm, uh …"

"Staring. You're staring," Jameson told her, stretching his arm across his chest, gripping it by the elbow. Different muscles stretched and moved.

"Yes, I think I am."

"Answer the question, please."

"How many times have you fucked Pet, since me?" she countered. She couldn't stand the thought, couldn't bear the idea. In her tipsy state of mind, things were even blurrier than normal. She didn't want to hear that he had touched the other woman. Or *any* other woman. Tate wanted to be the one. His only one.

Scary thought, baby girl. Still sure it's a game?

"How many times have you fucked Nick, since me?" he responded.

Even in her drunken state, Tate knew better than to answer that question. She had told Jameson that she hadn't slept with anybody, but he still assumed that she and Nick had a relationship. It kept him on his toes; jealous, distracted. *Nervous.* She needed that kind of energy, if she wanted to win.

"I don't know why you're so insecure, Jameson. It's always a '*who's got a bigger dick?*' contest with you," she evaded answering.

"I know it's not a contest – if it was, I've already won, so I'm not worried. I'm not insecure, just curious. I haven't touched Petrushka, *inappropriately*, since last June. *Before* you and I even ran into each other, I'd like to point out. Now answer my question," he demanded. She snorted.

"You spend a month with her in Berlin, pretending to be her boyfriend, and you didn't hit that, not even once?" Tate challenged him, the liquor making her bold.

"Not even once. And I wasn't pretending to be anything. I wouldn't need to pretend to be her boyfriend to get her to fuck me," he corrected Tate. She rolled her eyes.

"Yes, I'm clearly well aware of how good you are at *not* being a boyfriend and fucking people," she snapped.

"You never said it bothered you. In fact, you said it was fine. If something changed, and it wasn't fine, you should've said something," Jameson told her in a soft voice. He then slowly leaned forward onto his hands, basically doing a push up.

"I *did* say something. You just never said anything back," she reminded him. He rolled and stretched out onto his back.

"You want to be my girlfriend, Tatum?" he asked, his voice light.

"No."

"Sure sounds like it."

"I don't think I have what it takes to be Jameson Kane's '*girlfriend*.'"

"Hmmm, I think you were built for it."

As he laid there on the bed, wearing only Etiquette Clothier boxers, looking like something out of a sexy men's magazine, Tate had a realization. Jameson Kane was trying to seduce her. He had never really done that before, not back in Boston. Back then, she had always been easy pickings. She had never even pretended to not want him, so it had never been an issue. Now here he was, half naked, spread out like a buffet, and saying things she had always wanted to hear.

Resisting Jameson had been impossible when she had been trying to convince herself that she hated him. As she made her way across the room and crawled onto the bed with him, she wondered if she would ever truly be free of him.

Or if she even wanted to be free.

9

ATE MADE HER WAY UP top when Jameson disappeared into an office that she hadn't known existed. He did actually have to work, he informed her, especially the way she was racking up the bills. Turned out when he had thrown her purse overboard, he had very thoughtfully removed his credit card first. She then used it to go on another shopping spree. Thirteen handbags later, he held her down and forcibly took the card from her hand.

It was almost a week later, and things were not going well. Or *too* well. Tate couldn't tell anymore. The lines between game and not-a-game were blurred beyond recognition. They played, they flirted, they had sex. Jameson took her out, he showed her off, he didn't look at any other women. In Boston, he had always been gallivanting off under the pretext of work, but really just on missions to find some ass. She kept expecting it to happen in Spain. Nope. He only seemed to have eyes for her. He was almost sweet. Almost un-Satan like, even.

God help me.

They were going to Paris in two days, and Tate felt like she was unraveling. She had never been very good at sorting out her emotions where Jameson was concerned, and things hadn't gotten any easier. He caught her crying in the shower the day before; luckily, he was self-centered enough to think it was because she was upset with him, and he kissed the tears away. Touched the hurt away. He had no idea that she was crying because she was upset with *herself*.

*Stupid bitch. Weak bitch. **Easy** bitch.*

Every morning, Tate told herself that it was still a game, that she was still in charge, that she could still leave. And every day, Jameson made her forget everything. By the time she fell asleep at night, she was almost happy. Almost glad to be there. Glad to be with *him* again. Couldn't really imagine going back to her old life. Life without *him*.

You're losing, you're losing, you're losing.

Of course, she would see Ang in Paris – he was arriving a day or two after them. Tate was counting on him to be like a booster shot to her psyche. Help her get her head back in the game. Ang loved her. Ang hated Jameson. It would be perfect. She needed him to remember all the bad stuff for her, and remind her, because she wasn't too good at remembering anymore.

The bad stuff was fading away. That pool in her memories was draining. New memories came to mind when she was around Jameson. Memories of him holding her in the bathtub, telling her she was worth it. Him sharing with her while they were on the rowboat, explaining that he was a spoiled brat who had behaved poorly. Him touching her while they slept together, whispering to her how glad he was that she was there.

Too much. This man is so much more than me.

When Tate got outside, she moved to the very back of the boat. Jameson was locked away below deck, but she wanted privacy. There were sets of stairs on either side of the back deck, leading down to a platform that rested right above the water. Tate moved to that and sat down, dangling her legs in the water. Jameson had bought her a new phone, but had apparently thought it was funny to leave all the settings in Spanish. She was determined to figure it out, without his help, but it was proving harder than it looked. She wished she could phone Sanders for help, but she couldn't figure out how to call *anyone*.

"*Fucker*," she cursed, shaking the phone, tempted to have it join her old phone.

"Trouble?"

Tate looked up, and it was the guy from the boat down the way. The one she had met her first night there, who had invited her onboard to his party. She had been in Spain for two weeks, but she hadn't seen him again. She smiled, shielding her eyes with her hand.

"Phones, I hate them. How are you? I never saw you again, and I wanted to say thank you, for letting me on your boat," she said. He squatted down across from her and shrugged.

"Oh, no big deal, you don't have to thank me. We flew home for a couple weeks, now we're back here for a while. How is Mr. Kane?" the guy – she struggled to remember his name – asked.

"Mr. Kane is fine," Tate laughed. "*Jameson*. He's somewhere inside."

"I was worried about you that night. He seemed a little … shall we say, testy," *Bill*, that's his name, Bill said. She laughed again.

"His bark is worse than his bite, don't worry about it," she assured him, though she wasn't sure about that statement at all.

"Oh, good. I always wanted to introduce myself, but he seems a little … standoff-ish. A lot of us around here, we like to throw block parties. Sometimes we go out and tie the boats together, make a day of it. Never thought he'd be interested," Bill said.

An idea flashed across Tate's mind, and her breathing quickened. She stood up. It was a bad idea. A bad, bad, *bad* idea. Jameson would be *so* mad. But maybe that's what she needed. A good slap in the face reminder of what a tyrant he was, of how "*testy*" he could be, when things didn't go his way.

"Oh, I think he'd be very interested. What are you doing right now?"

Jameson looked at his ceiling, wondering what the fuck was going on upstairs. The noise had been escalating for a while, but he hadn't thought much about it. Tate was always getting into something. At home in Weston, it hadn't been unusual to hear a bang, crash, smash, clank, followed by *"I'm okay!"*, several times a day. He had learned to ignore it. But this was a bit much. It sounded like she was walking clydesdales around the deck.

When he made his way upstairs, he was in for a shock. People. His boat was full of people. People he didn't fucking know. People he didn't *want* to fucking know. Sitting on his furniture. Drinking his alcohol. Someone had dumped a bunch of pool toys on one of his couches, and was that a *Budweiser cooler* parked at the edge of his deck!?

Jameson began pushing his way through people. He found Tate towards the bow of the ship, and stalked up behind her. She was talking to someone vaguely familiar. The man from the boat party that first night. Jameson ignored him and grabbed her by the arm, spun her around.

"What the fuck do you think you're doing!?" he demanded. She smiled up at him.

"Throwing a party!" she laughed.

I've gotten too soft. Let her get away with almost killing you, and look what happens. She thinks she fucking owns you.

"I'm sorry, mate," the guy interrupted, stepping forward. "This is partly my fault. We got to chatting, I told her about some parties we've thrown over the years. She said they sounded like fun. One thing led to another."

Jameson stared down at the man. Who was this insignificant person, and why was he talking to him? He turned back to Tate, who had lost her smile. She was still staring at him, though, with a very different look in her eye. He ignored it.

"Tell everyone to get the fuck out, *now*," he growled. She snorted, but before she could answer, her new best friend interjected again.

"Of course, I'm so sorry. I should've talked to you, I'll —," he started, when Tate held up her hand.

"No, everyone stays. If you're gonna kidnap me and make me stay in Spain, then you can at least let me make friends," she snapped. Jameson cocked up an eyebrow. New boat buddy lifted both of his in shock.

This is a new attitude …

"I haven't kidnapped you, nor have I kept you here. You are free to leave whenever you want. Now. Get these fucking people —," Jameson tried to demand again. Tate laughed.

"Are you scared of a little party, Jameson? I remember you used to *love* parties. Remember the last party you threw? Was pretty amazing. I can't remember ever having been to a *'party'* quite like that one before," her voice lowered into a hiss.

He wanted to slap the smile off of her face. Jameson felt his usual desires begin to run rampant just under his skin. He had kept them on a tight leash, for her. She was stretching that leash to its limit. He dug his fingers into her arm, and was rewarded with a slight wince.

Good.

"You want a party? *Fine.* Everyone can stay," he said. Tate seemed surprised.

"Really? You're not gonna pitch a bitch-fit?" she asked.

Strike two. At some point, I've got to start making her pay.

"Not at this moment. Bill," he remembered the other man's

name, "care to join me upstairs? I've got a fine cognac not fit for most of these plebeians."

Bill practically fell over himself, climbing up the stairs behind Jameson.

Jameson didn't much care for socializing. He had been born into a wealthy family, so from before he could even remember, people had been using him for that wealth. Money stayed – people came and went. Which sounded more appealing? Of course, there were always exceptions to the rule, like Tatum and Sanders. But for the most part, he just preferred his own company. So listening to Bill prattle on and on about how he'd read every article ever written about Jameson, or Kraven Brokerage, or Kane Holdings, or Kane, Inc., or all of the above, made Jameson want to shoot himself a little bit.

He had to keep reminding himself that it was all for her. He was doing it for Tate. She was so close to giving in, he could feel it. Sure, it was obvious she was trying to hold herself back, but he'd put a couple of cracks in her armor. In the bathroom, in the rowboat. One more good crack, and she would go to pieces, fall back into his hands.

Jameson finally managed to escape Bill, his new one-man fan club, and went back downstairs. There were a lot of attractive women mingling about, and Jameson wondered how Tate would feel then, if he took another woman downstairs. It would serve her right. Teach her a lesson.

He found her on the back deck, near a makeshift bar someone had set up. She wasn't drinking, but she did look like she was having a great time, and he was surprised to feel some of his annoyance wash away. It was happening more and more. Things that normally upset him, got under his skin, weren't so bad anymore. Tate's presence calmed him. Made things better. Making her happy, made him feel better.

It made him more than a little nervous. He had wanted to get Tatum back in his life so he could ease his conscience, appease his guilt. Jameson wasn't stupid, he knew that when he did something wrong, he should admit fault and apologize. He just rarely ever happened to be wrong.

He had also wanted her back so he could play with her some more. They had been good friends, had great times together; some of the best he'd ever had in his life. Why throw that away? It wasn't every day he found a woman who would tolerate his prickly real life personality *and* his heavy-handed attitude in bed. Tate not only tolerated those things, she *adored* them. Yin and yang. Puzzles pieces. All that shit. They just fit.

Jameson hadn't, however, counted on wanting her so bad that no one else even existed outside of her. He found himself thinking that he couldn't care less if he never fucked another woman again, as long as he could just be close to Tate. Just touch her whenever he wanted. If she said that, said she wanted monogamy between them, he thought he might actually say okay. For the first time ever in his life, he could almost picture it.

Stupid sentimentality. Stupid heart. It made him sick. *Monogamy!?* And while he was drunk, hadn't he admitted to her being the perfect girlfriend for him? What the shit was that!? Instead of infecting her with his dark needs and wants, she had cured him and turned him into a kitten at her feet, into a love drunk fool. *Love sick* fool.

Fuck me.

"*Tatum*," Jameson barked out, sidling up next to her. She glanced up at him.

"You've been gone a while. This is Tracy. Tracy, this is Jameson Kane, he owns the boat," Tate introduced him to the woman she had been talking to. He nodded, and the busty blonde smiled enthusiastically.

"Oh, I know who you are, I just can't believe I'm here. Fabulous boat, Mr. Kane, I've admired it for quite a while," Tracy bubbled, stepping right up to him, completely cutting Tatum out of the conversation. Tate started to laugh.

"Fantastic. Tate, a word," he growled, then he dragged her inside.

"I wondered how long you were going to last," she snickered while he shoved her into the galley.

"Is this some sort of fucking game?" Jameson demanded.

"Ooohhh, we haven't really played a game, a *real* game, in a long time. Sounds fun," she laughed. He narrowed his eyes. Something was off. She had been weird ever since the day before, when he had found her crying. She was talking like her old self more than ever before, but almost in an odd, rehearsed way. Like she was forcing it.

"I don't want to play games with you," he said.

"All you know how to do is play games," Tate countered. He folded his arms across his chest.

"What the fuck is your problem? Is there something you're not telling me?" he asked. Her eyes slid away, glancing out at the party.

"No," she said softly.

"*Liar.* Something is going on in that brain of yours. That usually doesn't bode well for me. If you're pissed off at me, tell me, so I can apologize for whatever stupid shit you're upset about now," he snapped. Her eyes locked back onto his.

Looks like she's not the only one slipping into old habits.

"That wasn't very polite," she said in a cool voice.

"I'm not a very polite man. Look, Tatum, whatever weird shit you have going on in your head, just let it out. This party, the shower the other day – *something* is going on with you. I can't apologize, and I can't make it right, if you don't tell me," Jameson stressed. She laughed.

"*You?* Apologize?" she cackled. He stepped up close to her, forcing her back against the cupboards.

"I have apologized to you every fucking day. Me *bringing you here* is an apology. I don't know how else to say it, to show it. What the fuck do you want? A goddamn sky-writer? I'll hire one. Whatever it takes, just *tell me*. I'm sorry, Tate. *For everything*. More than words can express. Now either accept it, or get the fuck over it," he demanded.

He *was* sorry. That night had been a very enlightening experience. Jameson wanted to hold Tate down and slap her around and call her mean names, but he *never* wanted to hurt her, ever again. Seeing Tatum in that hospital bed, seeing how close he had come to losing her …, well, they were clichés because they were the truth – he hadn't known what he'd had, till it was gone. He couldn't bear the thought of her being gone for good. She had to understand that, somehow.

She has to understand that.

Tate was silent for a long time, her eyes wide as she stared up at him. For a moment Jameson thought he had won. Thought maybe, just maybe, brutal honesty had done what flirting and sex and games hadn't been able to do. But then something different welled up in her eyes. Not emotion, not resistance, something …, different. She stood on her tip toes, leaned even closer to him.

"There's a tone of voice I haven't heard in a while," she purred. He cocked up an eyebrow.

Ah, distracting me. Haven't quite won her over yet, I guess.

"If you want me to get nasty with you, Tate, then it can be arranged," he told her. She laughed.

"You've had a week to be nasty to me. Haven't seen it happen yet."

"Because I've been trying to be *nice*," Jameson reminded her. She snorted.

"Really? Seems like your version of 'nice' is most peoples 'dickead', mixed with a little boring," she taunted him.

"It's as nice as you're ever gonna get from me," he warned her. She rolled her eyes.

"I don't want *nice*. I want *you*," she stated.

212

He wasn't sure who was more shocked by her words, Tate, or himself. She obviously hadn't planned on blurting that out. It was the first *real* kind of statement she had made regarding any sort of way she felt about him. It wasn't much, but it was something.

It was like her words set fire to his blood, and Jameson didn't even think, just grabbed her by the arm and propelled her down the hall. He shoved her through the first door they came across, a sliding door that hid a water closet – just a toilet and a small counter with a mirror. A *tiny* counter top. There was barely enough room, but he pushed Tate in ahead of him and then slid the door shut behind them.

"What's your fucking problem today?" he growled, grabbing her hips and shoving her up onto the counter.

"*You,*" she snapped back, pulling at his shirt. He yanked it over his head.

"If you wanted me to fuck you, you could've just asked. You didn't need to throw a goddamn party," he told her, pushing her short skirt up and out of the way before pulling her underwear down her legs.

"*Jesus,* you're so boring now," Tate's voice was snide while she wrestled to pull her own shirt off.

"*Shut your fucking mouth.*"

God, he wanted to tear a piece out of her. Jameson loved it, loved *this* – he felt like he was suddenly possessed. He couldn't get his pants down fast enough, couldn't get inside her fast enough. He didn't hesitate, just slammed into her as hard as he could. Tate shrieked, covered her mouth with her hand, then moaned loudly.

"Yes, god, *this,*" she groaned, letting her head fall against the mirror.

"Fuck, Tate. Maybe a little louder, I'm not sure everyone can hear you," he hissed, digging his fingers into her hips. She chuckled.

"Shy, Jameson? *Embarrassed?*" she taunted.

"No. By the time I'm done with you, the people at the other end of this goddamn harbor are going to know you just got fucked," he warned her.

"Doubtful."

"*Bitch.*"

He hadn't really done it since they'd started sleeping together again. Not that he hadn't thought about it, but he was very aware of how skittish she was now, so he tried to keep his touch light. But fuck that, not today. Jameson was done being nice. Mr. Nice Guy was boring. The word had barely left Tate's mouth and his hand was in her hair, yanking her forward. Pulling at her roots. She shrieked again, and there was no doubt that anyone inside the boat would know exactly what was happening in that bathroom.

"Care to say that again?" Jameson asked, pumping into her hard and fast, not caring if one, or both, of them got hurt. She moaned.

"God, I missed this," she breathed, her nails digging into his skin. She was going to come soon, he could feel it. She was so much easier now. Getting her to the edge took so little, it was amazing. Like watching fireworks, every time.

"Stupid *slut*, I think this was your goal the whole time," he whispered. At the word "*slut*", he felt every muscle she had clamp down on his dick, and he couldn't help the groan that escaped his lips.

"No, no it wasn't," she moaned, her hands moving to her breasts, squeezing.

"I think you like this, Tatum. I think you like everyone hearing what a *slut* you are for me. If I had known that, I would've thrown a party a long time ago, you goddamn *whore*," Jameson swore. She rubbed her lips together and finally looked at him, her gaze heavy.

"I do, I love it," she panted before leaning forward to kiss him. He pulled harder on her hair, breaking the kiss.

"Of course you fucking do. You love *everything* I do to you," he informed her, and she nodded, making a high pitched whining sound.

So close.

"I do. I really do. God, so much," she groaned loudly, beating her hand against the wall. It felt like the whole room was shaking, falling apart at the seams.

Kind of like me.

"Such a lucky *cunt*, I treat you so fucking good. So fucking lucky. *Fuck*," he started to growl.

"*So good.* Jameson … Jameson, *please*," she whispered, and he didn't have to ask her what, because he already knew what she needed. He *always* knew. He let go of her hair and grabbed her by the throat. Shoved her back against the wall and squeezed. She shrieked and raked her nails down his arm.

"*So fucking lucky,*" he breathed.

He didn't really care that they were in a tiny bathroom and she had to practically turn herself into a contortionist to get his dick inside of her. He didn't care that there were dozens of strangers probably listening to them have sex. Jameson's entire universe, at that moment, was her. Feeling every inch of her. Wanting to make her come hard enough that she would never want to run away, ever again.

"*You're* the lucky one," Tate managed to taunt as her whole body started to shiver. He squeezed tighter on her neck, pulled her forward. Pressed his forehead to hers while his free hand gripped her thigh so hard, he felt like he was going to go right through her.

"And what makes you think that?" he growled.

"You're lucky I even let you inside of me, because of the two of us, you're the real *whore*," she told him with an evil chuckle. Jameson closed his eyes, dug his nails into her skin.

"Goddamn, Tate, your fucking mouth. *Fuck.* I wish there weren't people here," he groaned, pumping harder. *Harder.* As hard as he possibly could.

"Why?" she breathed.

"Because I *really* want to come on your face."

Apparently just the idea was hot enough for her, and she screamed again, bursting apart. Just exploded around him. He'd had sex with a lot of women in his life, and Jameson considered himself very good at it. Not bragging, just fact – he could pull an orgasm from most women the way a person wrung water from a sponge. Easy. But it was always a different experience with Tatum, the way she shook and moaned and carried on; she always made him feel like he had accomplished something. Climbed a mountain, solved a mystery, *became a man*.

As he came right behind her, dragging his nails down her throat, it was like clarity bloomed behind his eyelids.

This is most definitely not a game anymore. This woman … she owns me.

10

THE NEXT DAY, THEY MOVED into the apartment with Sanders. Jameson was going to have the interior of the yacht redecorated. Tate had made a comment that all of the black was depressing. So he was having it all changed. For her.

Scary.

She tried to ignore it. Tried to ignore the shift in her universe. When he curled around her at night, slept with her tucked against his chest, she tried to ignore how happy she was inside, just to be near him. When he bent her over the console next to the steering wheel and showed her who the captain was, she tried to ignore how happy she was that things were back to normal.

*This is **not** normal. YOU'RE LOSING.*

"Whatever you're thinking, don't," Sanders' voice cut through her thoughts. Tate glanced up at him. The bedrooms on the backside of Jameson's apartment all had small, private, wrought iron balconies. She had wrestled a chair onto the one off of Sanders' room.

"What?" she asked, feigning innocence. He stared at her.

"You're happy. Don't ruin it."

Tate glared.

"*He* ruins things. Why can't I?" she asked.

"He made them better, didn't he?"

"That doesn't just erase what he did."

"No, but you have to move forward at some point. You have to trust him at some point."

That was the problem – Tate didn't think she could. Sure, it was easy to forget that small fact when they were rolling around in his big bed; fucking in a bathroom at a club; going down on him under a table in a restaurant. But whenever he left to take a phone call; gave Sanders a private look; went somewhere without her, she almost had a panic attack. Was Jameson planning something? Was he calling *her*? Meeting up with *her*? Tate couldn't stand it. She was going crazy.

"I don't know, Sandy. I just don't know," she mumbled, pulling her feet up and resting her chin on her knees. He squatted down next to her.

"Is there something you're not telling me?" he asked in a soft voice. She sighed.

"No, not really. I just … I don't know if I'll ever be ready for a man like him," she laughed a little. Sanders nodded.

"Understandable. But if that is how you honestly feel, then you need to tell him. You two, you only communicate through sex. Maybe you should try using words. They work very well for the rest of us," Sanders suggested. Tate laughed for real.

"You're amazing, Sandy. I fear the day some woman steals you from me," she laughed, wrapping an arm around his shoulders. He cleared his throat.

"I don't see that on the horizon any time soon. And just so you know, the entire time we have been here, he has not been in contact with Petrushka. I can show you phone records," he told her. She sat back, surprised.

"Seriously?"

"Of course. I have been taking care of all his bills, and that includes his cell phone bill. I also have regular access to his phone. *He has not called her.* If you won't believe him, and you don't believe me, then I can show you proof," Sanders offered her. Tate groaned and put her face in her hands.

"Between the two of you, it's amazing I even made it out alive the first time," she grumbled.

"That is not funny," he snapped. She sighed.

"No. Sorry."

"What are we talking about?" Jameson asked, walking through the doorway.

"Phones," Sanders replied truthfully. Tatum laughed.

"Phones?" Jameson double checked.

"Yes. I spoke with Mr. Hollingsworth today," Sanders cleverly changed the subject, and she lifted her head at the mention of Ang. "He requested a bigger hotel room. He said it was part of his, and I quote, *'list of demands.'*"

"Christ, that man. You are not allowed to fuck him while he's here," Jameson informed Tate, pointing a finger sternly in her face. She laughed again.

"You ruin all my fun."

"Fine. Change the reservation, put him on the same floor as us," Jameson said, and Sanders nodded before striding from the room.

"You sure it's safe to let me be that close to him?" Tate teased. Jameson rolled his eyes and pulled her out of her chair.

"Actually, I wanted to talk to you about that," he said, leading her out of Sanders' room.

"You wanted to talk about fucking Ang?" she asked with a laugh. They headed into the master bedroom. On the boat, Tate had still maintained a separate room, though she had spent most nights in Jameson's room. Not in the apartment. He simply had Sanders load all her luggage straight into his bedroom.

"No. If there is one thing in life I will never want to talk about, it's *Angier's* sexual prowess," he replied, glaring at her as he took his wallet out of his back pocket before sitting down on his bed.

"You're really missing out," she said, sighing melodramatically as she crawled onto the bed to sit behind him. He removed his watch, tossed it onto the night stand. She knew his routine. She couldn't help herself, she had always been a loyal subject for Satan. She coiled her arms around his shoulders.

"Tate," Jameson said, as she feathered kisses along the back of his neck. He leaned into her, his fingers creeping around her wrists.

"Yes?"

"Where would you like to go after this?" he asked, pulling her hands away from his body.

"What, like for dinner?" she asked, scooting closer so she could wrap her legs around his waist from behind.

"No. Like Italy, or Austria," Jameson replied, linking his fingers through hers.

Tate stopped breathing. He meant after. Like *after*, after. He was already planning on where the next stop was, the next vacation. In Jameson's mind, he must have already won. No questions asked. It was just obvious, apparently, that she would be going wherever he went.

It made her feel a little lightheaded. She licked her lips and pressed her cheek against his back. Listened to his heart beat. Italy. Austria. Would he take her to his home in Denmark? Or how about Turkey? Hell, why not go big – India.

I don't care, as long as I'm with him ...

"Jameson," she breathed, and she felt his muscles twitch. "Let's get through this trip, before we plan another one."

It was evasive, but it was the best answer Tate could give him. Give her heart. She didn't know what she wanted anymore. Things were too blurry. Jameson said he wasn't playing games – maybe he was telling the truth. Maybe it was time for her to start believing him.

He started to lean backwards, forcing her onto her back as he twisted around to face her. He laid on top of her, his head on her breasts while her legs were still wrapped around him. She combed her fingers through his hair while she tried very hard not to cry.

Would it be so bad to just give in? Satan can be a very giving lord and master ...

"Whatever you want, Tatum. I'll do whatever you want."

One tear escaped. Nice was always so much worse than mean.

Tate woke up some time in the middle of the night. There was shouting. The sound of something breaking. She propped herself up on her elbows, trying to wake all the way up. A light flicked on, and she saw Jameson, leaning up on one arm, his hand against a lamp. He was glaring at his bedroom door.

"What the fuck is that?" he grumbled.

"I don't know," Tate replied.

There was a loud crash, followed by a shriek, and Jameson was out of the bed in a flash. He yanked on some underwear and a t-shirt before storming out of the room. With the door open, she could hear better, and could tell that one of the voices was Sanders. Was someone attacking Sanders!? Tate leapt out of the bed as well, ready to commit murder.

But she was still struggling to yank on one of Jameson's t-shirts – if she was going to kick ass, she wasn't going to do it naked – when she figured out who the other voice belonged to; realized the language they were speaking wasn't English. Wasn't Spanish. *Russian.* Jameson's voice came in above the fray, and from then on it was all German.

Tate sat down heavily on the bed, clasping her hands together.

Her whole body was shaking with the effort of trying not to blow up. She glanced at the door, then stared at the wall. There was more shrieking. More German. Then finally, English.

"Oh, is it because *she* is here!?" Petrushka's voice yelled. Sanders answered in Russian. Jameson snapped in German. "No! This was *my* place, before it was ever hers! You are letting trash into my home, Kane. *Garbage.* I won't allow it!"

I hear you, bitch, loud and clear.

Tate found herself in the hallway before she even realized she was moving. Broken glass coated the living room floor. Sanders stood with his back to the hall. He was wearing a pajama set, and his normally perfectly styled hair was standing on end. Jameson was attempting to manhandle a very angry, wiry supermodel out the open front door. There was more cursing in German.

"I hear you," Tate blurted out. Sanders whirled around, but no one else seemed to have heard her.

"Please, go back to bed, we have it under —," he immediately started. She held up a hand.

"*I can hear you,*" she repeated herself, louder. Pet stopped thrashing around in Jameson's arms, long enough to find Tate and glare at her.

"Good. I want you to hear. I want this whole building to hear! There is garbage in this apartment! An American whore! An American whore, and a Russian peasant!" Pet was shouting, struggling against Jameson, swinging her arms at Tate like she thought she could hit her from that distance. Tate stepped in front of Sanders as if he had been shot at, wrapped her arm around him from behind her back.

"Talk to him like that again and I will *end* your career," Tate threatened. As always, she was fair game. Jameson was fair. Sanders was on a different plane from mere mortals, and if that bitch-snake so much as looked at him again, Tate would rearrange her features.

222

"*Everyone* stop talking! Sanders! Call the goddamn front desk!" Jameson roared, and then he practically threw Pet into the hallway. She lurched forward, screaming in German, but he slammed the door in her face. Slid the bolt lock into place. Sanders scurried off to find a phone.

"What. *THE FUCK*. Was that?" Tate asked. Pet continued to beat on the door, screaming things in different languages. Jameson had his hands in his hair.

"*That* was fucking crazy. She *does not* like you," Jameson replied.

"Whose fault is that? She doesn't even know me," Tate snapped. He stared at her like *she* was crazy.

"You're mad at *me?*" he asked. She folded her arms.

"How did she know we were here, Jameson?" she asked back. He actually laughed.

"You're shitting me."

"We've been at the boat, this whole time. She would've known that, after you weren't here last time. Why wouldn't she go to the boat? How the fuck did she know we were here?" Tate demanded.

"Oh, clever, clever girl, Tatum. You've figured out my master plan. I called Pet, asked her to break into my home, attack Sanders, and destroy half my shit, all just to piss you off," he replied, his voice soft. Easy. *Scary.*

"You *are* Satan," she reminded him.

"Watch it, Tatum. I am not in the fucking mood," Jameson warned her. The banging hadn't stopped and Tate groaned.

"Can you please shut your girlfriend up?" she snapped.

"I don't *have* a girlfriend."

"I called security," Sanders said, breathing hard as he hurried into the living room. Tate turned towards him, then gasped.

"Did she hit you!?" she demanded, grabbing Sanders by the collar. His face was red on one side, and his hair didn't look like bedhead, it looked like it had been pulled. He pressed his hand to his cheek.

"She … she forced her way inside," Sanders replied. Tate turned around and strode towards the door. Jameson moved to stand in front of it.

"Stop it. *I* will deal with this," he told her.

"She hit him! I'm gonna tear her fucking face off!" Tate snapped. Jameson put a hand on her chest, keeping her away from the door.

"*You* hit him once, and I didn't hit you back," he pointed out. "Let me handle this."

"By all means," Tate sighed, her voice sounding dejected as she took a step back and gestured for him to open the door.

She stood politely aside, casting a sad glance back at Sanders. Jameson watched her for a second, then pulled the bolt back. Turned the knob. Started yelling at Pet to shut the fuck up as he swung the door open.

Tate sprang forward and went through the door like a runner after a starter shot. She barreled into Pet and they both hit the wall. Tate wasn't a fighter, didn't count that time with Jameson's maid as a real fight, but suddenly she felt like Muhammed fuckin' Ali. She was gonna crush this bitch.

They bounced off the wall and Pet grabbed a handful of Tate's hair, yanked her away. They careened in a circle, and Tate got her arms around Pet's waist. Using her legs, she propelled them back into the wall. Pet slammed into it, shrieked, and lost her grip on Tate's hair. They both fell to the ground and rolled around. Pet was taller, but Tate was heavier – she wound up on top. She straddled the other girl's waist and grabbed her by the hair.

"If you ever touch him again, I will kill you!" Tate screamed, slamming Pet into the ground. The supermodel swung her arms, slapping Tate in the face.

"*Sie sind Müll!*" Pet yelled. Tate slapped her back, then struggled to hold onto her wrists.

SEPARATION

"I DON'T SPEAK GERMAN, YOU DUMB CUNT!"

Before she could land another blow, arms were around Tate's waist, plucking her into the air. With the weight off of her legs, Pet immediately started kicking, so Tate kicked right back, landing a solid blow to the other woman's thigh. She was rewarded with a shriek of pain.

"Stop it," Jameson's voice was low in her ear. She ignored him.

"Don't you ever fucking come back here!" Tate screamed while Jameson hauled her backwards. "Don't you ever fucking talk to him again! Don't talk to him, don't touch him, *don't come near him!* Do you understand me!? He didn't come here for you! *He came here for me!*"

At some point, the fight had stopped being about Sanders, and had become about Jameson.

So when, exactly, did you lose to him? Stupid, stupid, girl.

Luckily, Jameson had the penthouse apartment, so there was no one else to witness Pet's psychotic break. Or Tate's. As security spilled out of an elevator, Jameson pulled her back through the apartment's doorway, all while she and Pet were still screaming at each other. Sanders slipped out into the hallway, explaining the situation to the guards.

"Calm the fuck down, Tatum," Jameson urged. She yanked at the arms he had around her, tried to get a grip on the floor with her toes. There was so much adrenaline pumping through her body, she felt like she was going to have a heart attack.

"No, no, I'm not done! Let me go! That bitch almost killed me once, I owe her!" Tate shouted, kicking her legs wildly. His arms only got tighter around her, twisting and pulling her t-shirt up so it bunched up beneath her breasts.

"She didn't do that, *I* did that. Blame *me*," he instructed her. Tate swung her whole body from side to side.

"I already do! But you won't let me hit you!" she yelled.

He barked out a laugh, which set her off, and suddenly she was caught in a bout of hysterics. There was a cough from the door, and Jameson turned them towards it. Tate figured she was quite a sight, only in a pair of tiny underpants and her shirt little more than a tube top, Jameson holding onto her like she was possessed by the devil.

That happened a long time ago, baby girl.

Sobering thought.

"Mr. Kane, we're very sorry. The man downstairs, he got confused. She said she was your fiancée, said she lost her key. He gave her one. The owner of the building and the manager have been called, they are headed down here. I'm sure you'll want to speak to them," a security guard said from the doorway.

"My man out there, Sanders, can deal with it. His name is on the lease," Jameson explained. Tate squirmed in his arms, but he still held onto her.

"Very good. We are taking her away now. If you need anything, have any questions, don't hesitate to call my office, anytime," the guard urged.

"Give the number to Sanders," was all Jameson said, turning away. The guard said goodbye and made his way back into the hall.

"Let me down," Tate breathed, digging her nails into his wrist.

"No."

"Put me down," she hissed again. He walked all the way down the hallway with her, carrying her back into his bedroom.

"*No.* You need to calm down," he told her.

"Well, that's not gonna fuckin' happen, so you should just put me down," she snapped. He let go of her abruptly and she teetered forward, a little shocked.

"Quite a little show you put on, Tate. I particularly liked when you were on top of her, your ass in the air," Jameson told her, his tone even and calm. She stopped breathing for a second, then shook it off. She grabbed a hair tie from off the nightstand, roughly yanking her hair up into a ball on top of her head.

"I'm sure you did like it. I should've charged," she growled at him before stomping over to her luggage. There was clothing strewn around, and Tate began picking stuff up, throwing it all into the suitcase.

"Didn't know you were still into that. What are you doing?" he asked, moving to stand behind her.

"Packing, what the fuck does it look like I'm doing?" she snapped.

"And where, may I ask, are you packing to go?" Jameson continued.

"Anywhere. Anywhere that's not here, anywhere that's not around *you*," Tate replied.

"And why are you running away?"

"Because! I don't want to be here when the next surprise visit pops up!" she yelled at him.

"I did not plan this. You heard that guard, she lied to get in here. I can promise you, it will *not* happen again," Jameson assured her.

"I couldn't give two shits if it did. I'm gonna take Sanders and we are getting the fuck out of here, and you and Ms. Denmark can have your sick, weird, love-hate relationship on your own fucking time," Tate swore, bending at the waist and shoving the last bit of clothing into her bag, trying to force the suitcase shut.

"Awfully mean talk for someone who was just fighting over me," he pointed out, and she felt his hand run over the edge of her hip. She wiggled away from him.

"I wasn't fighting over you!" she yelled, straightening out her t-shirt, trying to regain some dignity.

"Sure looked like it," he called her out. She felt a blush creep into her cheeks.

"Well, you weren't doing anything about her! One of us had to be a man," Tate sneered at him. Jameson laughed and stepped up close to her.

"Maybe I should take lessons," he replied. She nodded.

"Maybe you should."

"Tatum?"

"*What!?*"

He pulled her close, and she jumped on him. They fell to the ground, pushing and pulling at each others' clothing. He ripped her shirt, but she figured it didn't really matter, because it was actually his shirt. The panties, though, were slightly disappointing. She had spent a lot of his money on them.

"I thought you were running away," Jameson taunted while she yanked his boxers down his legs.

"Shut the fuck up," she snapped, dragging her teeth along his thigh as she crawled back up his body.

"I think that's my line."

"You know, I can think of better uses for your mouth than being clever."

"My, my," Jameson chuckled, laying flat on the floor and putting his hands behind his head. "Someone wants to wear my shoes, apparently. Go ahead, Tate. Be the heavy. Let's see how good you are at it."

Tate was angry, and she wanted to take it out on somebody. She was angry at Pet, and she was angry at Jameson, but most of all, she was angry at herself. She was still hyped up. It was like Petrushka was there in the room, and Tate suddenly had something to prove. She wasn't in the mood for his attitude or his smart-ass comments.

"Please. You have it so easy," she sneered at him, hooking her nails into his chest and then slowly dragging them down. He hissed.

"You think so?" he whispered, his eyes falling shut. She scratched her hands back up to his shoulders and repeated the process.

"All you do is say a couple dirty words, get grabby with your hands. Big fucking deal," she pointed out. He managed a laugh.

"According to your pussy, it's a *very big* fucking deal," he teased.

"You think that's so special? I can do what you do."

"Doubtful."

Tate glared at him and then paused for a second. Of course she was lying through her teeth. It was getting to a point where all Jameson had to do was breathe in her direction, and she had to change her panties. But he didn't really need to know that, she figured. She wanted to make him sweat. Make him nervous. Make him *angry*.

"*Fuck you,*" she breathed. His eyes opened to look at her, and she smiled down at him. "That wasn't so hard. I can see why you like it. *Fuck you*, Kane."

"Watch your mouth," he warned her. She laughed and slowly dragged one of her hands up her body.

"*You* watch your fucking mouth," she threw it back at him. She scratched her way up past her breasts, across her clavicle, and then slowly wrapped her fingers around her neck. Of course it didn't feel the same – Jameson owned that part of her body, her hand was just visiting. But still.

"What's your game, baby girl?" he said softly.

"Mmmm, no game," Tate whispered back, letting her eyes flutter closed while her free hand found its way between her legs.

"Whatever this is, it isn't very fun for me," he pointed out, moving his hands to her thighs. She snorted. It may not have been "*fun*" for him, but he was obviously enjoying it – she was straddling his hips and could feel his hard on pressing against her ass.

"Stop talking, *whore,*" she cursed at him, and then gasped, moving her fingers between herself and his stomach. Sliding between her wetness and the sweat on his skin.

"What the fuck did you just say to me?" he demanded.

"*Whore*. As in, *shut your fucking mouth, whore,*" she mimicked him, and then gasped again, raising up higher on her knees. She dug her fingernails into her throat, and while it still wasn't as good as Jameson, she could see the appeal of being him. She had wanted to play with him, make him as angry as she had been, but she wasn't angry anymore; she was too close to coming to really feel any sort of way.

"Alright. Play time's over. Stop it, now," he insisted. She groaned and let her head drop back, her fingers pushing harder against herself, inside of herself. It all felt so different. Angry, not angry. Her in charge, but not really in charge. With him, but not really with him. She just wanted to stop thinking for a second. Stop feeling. Just be numb.

"I think you're forgetting who's in charge right now," Tate panted, wiggling her hips against him. His hands moved to her waist and held her in place.

"Stop. I'm not doing this just cause you're pissed off at her. *You won*. She doesn't matter, she's out there. I'm in here. *With you*."

Too nice. Nice words are always the worst.

"*Liar*," she moaned.

"That's it. I'm not fucking around, Tate. Get the fuck off me, or —," he started to threaten.

"*Stop fucking talking*."

She may have taken the imitation too far, though, when she slapped him across the face, shocking herself a little.

Hmmm, might have pushed it with that one.

His reaction was instantaneous. Jameson's hand was in her hair, pulling so hard she was forced to look straight up and arch away from him. He sat up abruptly, and in a somewhat fluid motion managed to stand up, letting her slide to the floor. But he didn't let her stay there long; with his grip in her hair, he yanked her to her feet.

"Just because you're angry doesn't mean I have to be; why the fuck do you always want to piss me off?" he hissed, pressing his face against hers.

"Because then I know I'm dealing with the real you," she gasped.

"Shut the fuck up, Tate."

230

He bent her in half, slammed her down against the mattress. She was still trying to push the blankets out of her face when he slammed into her. She shrieked, dragging her claws down the covers. She felt one of his hands in the middle of her back, pressing her down. Holding her in place. His other hand gripped onto her hip, pushing and pulling her against his thrusts.

Like my body even needs to be told what to do when it comes to him.

"See? Better, so much better," Tate groaned, closing her eyes and focusing all of her energy on feeling him.

"*Everything* I give you is better. Is the *best*. When are you going to get that through your fucking head?" Jameson snapped.

"Never," she breathed.

She wanted to taunt him, to tease him. Wanted to make him mad enough to step outside himself, mad enough to *really* treat her bad. But she couldn't get a word out. He was pounding so hard, she couldn't catch her breath. She wasn't sure what was going to happen first – orgasm, or fainting.

If you're really lucky, both. Because if you needed any further proof that you're never getting away from him, you have it now – slamming into you, over and over again.

Tate screamed when she came, beating her hand on the mattress, begging him to stop. Begging him for more. She was vaguely aware of voices outside the bedroom door, remembered that security was still wandering around the apartment, and she started coming harder. Gasping for air. Sobbing for it.

"Who's the *slut* now?" Jameson growled, pressing flat against her back as his hips picked up speed. She managed a laugh. Choked on a sob.

History just keeps repeating itself, on and on and on and on and on ...

"For you, Jameson. Just for you," she whispered, stepping back in time, to seven years ago. A lifetime ago. Not long enough ago.

"Only for me," he whispered back, and then he was coming, too.

Houston, we're so far beyond having a problem that we're just completely fucked.

11

TATUM HAD BEEN TO PARIS before, when she was fifteen, on a school trip. Standard, touristy stuff. She liked the city, thought it was very beautiful. It was hard, though. The most romantic city on earth, and she was there with Jameson. Hmmm.

The morning after her stint as an MMA fighter, she had woken up to him sitting at the foot of the bed, talking softly on his phone. His voice *did not* sound happy.

*"If you ever come to my home again, I will get a restraining order. If you ever touch Sanders again, I will have you arrested. And if you **ever** hit her again, **I** will be the one who hits back. She is here to stay, she is part of my life. You are not. **Get used to it**."*

Tate was touched, but at the same time, she also felt kind of bad. Jameson had dragged Pet back into the mix. What had he said the other day? He hadn't slept with Pet since last June. Then he had wined and dined her in Germany during his little sabbatical. The woman was a raving lunatic, a complete psychotic bitch, no argument there, but Jameson was the one who had invited her back into his life.

They didn't speak much about the whole situation the next day. The living room was magically clean, though Sanders looked suspiciously tired. He slept on the plane ride to Paris, and Tate leaned against him, hugging his arm to her chest. He also didn't say much of anything about the incident. There was so much silence going on, she felt like it was deafening.

Their hotel room was amazing. Views of the Eiffel Tower, balconies, a sitting room. He hadn't gotten a penthouse suite, at Tate's request. She thought it was just too much, considering that whenever they were together anywhere, they spent most of their time in a bedroom. Plus, that way, Ang's room and Sanders' room could be on either side. Tate had a shoulder to cry on either way she turned, and she had a distinct feeling that a huge crying fit was imminent.

She had spoken to Ang a couple times since New Year's, but only briefly. Short enough conversations that she was able to get away without confessing her sin to him, which she was grateful for. She spoke to her sister a couple times, as well. Her baby was due in a little over two months. It was going to be a boy. Tate wanted to ask her all about it, but her sister was surprisingly short on the phone, as well. They were still working on the whole let's-be-friends-because-we're-sisters thing, but it was obvious that it wasn't working out too well.

Tate had only called Nick twice. In a lot of ways, he was the worst, because he would be the most understanding. They had never dated, but she still kinda felt like she had cheated on him. Why couldn't she have just liked him? Life would be so must easier, if she would just be a nice, normal girl.

"Hi," Tate said softly into the phone when he answered.

"God, it's good to hear your voice. I feel like I haven't talked to you in forever!" Nick laughed. She smiled, stretched her legs out. She was sitting in the hallway outside of the hotel room.

"I know, I know. It's been … crazy. There was a whole super-model-smack-down episode, it got weird," she said.

"Oh god. What have you gotten yourself into now?"

She gave him an abridged version of the fight. Nick laughed as

Tate got heated up all over again, describing how she had tried to tackle Pet. He agreed that it sounded like the other girl had deserved to get her ass beat, but he didn't condone violence; though he did wish he had been able to see it.

"It was most definitely a show," Tate laughed.

"Everything you do is a show," he chuckled.

"Hey!"

"When are you coming home? I miss you," he said plainly. She chewed on her thumbnail, glancing down the hallway.

Italy, Austria, hell – pick a vacation, any vacation.

"I'm not sure, but you'll be the first to know," she assured him.

"I hope so. Tate, I've been thinking. A lot," Nick started. Warning bells went off in her head.

"That's never a good thing," she joked, trying to lighten the mood. He didn't laugh.

"I know that you and Jameson have a history that goes way back. I know you and I haven't really known each other that long," he began. She swallowed thickly.

"Nick, don't —,"

"*But,* I really think we'd be good together, and I like you, *a lot.* Enough to wait," he said.

This all sounded horribly familiar, only in this picture, Tatum was Satan, and Nick was the poor fool in love. All they needed was a dark library and a roaring fireplace.

I am going to one of the darkest recesses of hell. Good thing I've already been there once.

"Nick, you don't know what you're saying. I'm not a good person. Just … just wait till I come home, and then we'll talk," she urged in a quiet voice.

"*Get him out of your system,*" Nick continued. "Whatever you need. And I will be here. I understand."

Tate felt like she was going to be sick, and as if that wasn't bad

235

enough, the elevator doors at the end of the hall opened. A man in a dark suit stepped off. Strode towards her, his steps sure. Confident. She licked her lips, staring up at him.

"I know. I just don't want to hurt you," she said, watching as Jameson came to a stop next to her.

"You won't. I know what I'm getting into – do you?" Nick countered. Jameson squatted down next to her, adjusting his cuff links as he did so. A suit. He was back in a suit.

Ah, there's my Satan.

"I haven't the faintest clue," Tate whispered.

"Time to go, baby girl," Jameson said softly, holding his hand out.

"Be smart, Tatum," Nick warned on the other end of the phone.

"*Never am,*" she replied, then hung up the phone. She put her hand into Jameson's, allowed him to pull her to her feet.

"Important phone call?" he asked. She shrugged, dusting her hands off on her pants.

"Nick. Checking up on me," was all she said. Jameson snorted and took off back down the hall.

"How is your boyfriend doing?" he asked as she trailed behind him.

"Jealous?" she taunted, wrapping a scarf around her neck. Paris was a lot colder than Marbella. After they had settled in at the hotel, she wound up having to buy even more clothing to match the change in weather. She wasn't sure how she was going to get all her new stuff home.

"Always jealous," Jameson replied, pushing the down button for the elevator.

"At least my boyfriend never broke into your apartment and attacked Sanders," Tate countered. He laughed.

"I would like to see him try. Could he even find Spain on a map?" he asked as they stepped onto the elevator.

"You don't even know him, have never met him, and you're insulting his intelligence? My god, Jameson, you *are* jealous," Tate gasped. He cleared his throat, his eyes trained on the doors.

"I don't like it when other people touch my things," he explained in a low voice. She laughed.

"That was almost sweet."

"Almost, huh. Close one."

They went to dinner. Once again, Tate felt a little dressed down. Jameson was wearing a suit that probably cost more than her first car. She was wearing low-rise skinny jeans and a racer-back tank top, paired with a slim leather jacket and scarf. They never quite matched, but Jameson never seemed to care, so she decided she wouldn't care, either. After seeing the name on the reservation, the maître d' didn't even look twice at her, anyway.

Sanders was already at the restaurant, and they all ate together. There was actually a lot of laughter. Jameson had a very dry sense of humor, and half the time she couldn't tell whether Sanders was being deadpan or serious, but she cracked up anyway. They talked, they shared food. It was fun.

After they were done, they headed back towards their hotel, but a different hotel was having some sort of event. Loud music was pouring into the street. Tate grabbed Sanders' arm and dragged him inside. Jameson eventually followed. She was pretty sure they were crashing a wedding reception, but she didn't care. She was two steps away from selling her soul to Satan, what could it hurt to crash someone's party?

Sanders wouldn't hardly move, so Tate was forced to dance by herself for most of the time. She made friends with a bridesmaid, danced around with her for a little while. Jameson finally danced with her, after a slow song came on; she got shivers as he slid her hand into his, wrapped an arm around her waist. She hadn't danced like that since a cousin's wedding, when she was a lot younger. It was almost more intimate than dancing the way she was used to, arms wrapped around her partner's neck. Jameson stared down at the her the whole time, moving her around the floor. She found it hard to breathe.

When they got back to the table they had commandeered, it was to find that Sanders had also made a friend. Unwillingly. He was standing next to the table, very tight lipped, as a very drunk woman leaned near him, murmuring in French. Tate laughed and walked up next to him.

"What is she saying?" she asked. Sanders kept his eyes pointed straight ahead.

"She likes my suit," he replied through clenched teeth. Tate snickered and ran her finger under his lapel.

"You like? *Très bon, oui?*" she asked the woman.

"*Oui, is est très, très beau – il ne danse pas?*" she replied. Tate didn't speak a word of French, but she was pretty she understood "*dance*".

"Only with me," Tate laughed, pulling on his arm.

"No, I don't want to dance, Tatum. I don't …" Sanders tried to resist, but she'd already pulled him into the thick of the dance floor.

"It's okay, Sandy. Just act like no one's watching. No one cares if you can't dance," she assured him, holding his hands as she bopped from foot to foot.

"I know how to dance," he told her. She stopped moving.

"Really?"

"Just not like that," he said, glancing around at the younger couples on the floor, who were all bumping and grinding.

"Then like how?" she asked.

Sanders sighed and pulled her close. She found herself in the same position she had been in with Jameson moments before, Sanders' arm around her torso, his hand pressed against the skin on her back, just under her bra. He took a deep breath and glanced around.

"Just do as I do. Follow my movements, my body," he instructed. She smiled.

"Kinky."

He snorted, then he was pushing her backwards. If Tate had ever thought about it, ballroom dancing was right up Sanders' alley. Strict rules, stiff frames, precise movements – that pretty much described him. He all but carried her across the dance floor. She was surprised at how strong he was; in his suits, he looked so slender and trim. The arm around her, though, was like steel.

She felt like a little kid. She was completely delighted. After she stepped on his toes a couple times he started counting. Very softly, almost under his breath. It took Tate a second to realize that he was counting the steps for her. After that, it got a little easier. He spun her around, and when the song came to an end, he even took her into a small dip.

"I hope that was enough for you," Sanders said as they broke apart. Tate clapped her hands together.

"Are you kidding!? I wanna go again! Sandy, I think I just fell in love with you a little!" she laughed.

"That would make things very awkward," Jameson's voice came from behind her. She turned around and smiled up at him, but he was staring at Sanders.

"It's a lie, anyway. I fell in love with Sanders the first time I ever saw him, when he was looking at me like I was a two-dollar-hooker," she joked. Sanders nervously adjusted his tie.

"I thought you were worth at least ten dollars," he replied.

Even Jameson laughed at that one.

Back at the hotel, after Tatum had fallen asleep, Jameson climbed out of bed. Put on some clothes. Made his way next door, to Sanders' room. The younger man was awake, sitting on a couch, a laptop open on the coffee table. He glanced up.

"Good evening," he said simply. Jameson nodded, heading over to some windows.

"What time does Angier get here tomorrow?" he asked. Sanders glanced at a paper that sat next to him.

"Noon. I have arranged for a car to pick him up and bring him back here. I assumed he would want to rest after his plane ride, so I booked a late lunch for you and Tatum, then have arranged dinner, downstairs, for all of us," he ran through the itinerary.

"Sounds good."

"I must say," Sanders started, "it was a very nice gesture, inviting Mr. Hollingsworth. I was very impressed."

"Were you?" Jameson asked, glancing down at him.

"Yes. You did something nice, just for her. You normally don't do things like that; it is a happy improvement," Sanders explained.

"You like to see her happy, don't you?" Jameson questioned.

"Of course I do. Why I wouldn't I?" Sanders asked, going back to his computer.

"Sanders. Are you in love with Tatum?" Jameson asked bluntly.

He wasn't sure which was more shocking, the fact that Sanders didn't laugh away the question, or that the fair skinned man suddenly turned bright red. Jameson couldn't remember ever seeing Sanders fully blush before; couldn't remember him ever really looking embarrassed. Uncomfortable, yes. Embarrassed, *no*. This was not good. If Sanders was in love with Tate, it would be a *big* problem.

"*No*, I am not in love with her," Sanders answered before getting up off the couch and hurrying away.

Oh wow, this is interesting.

Jameson had known Sanders since he was thirteen, and in all that time, he had never seen the young man show any interest in women. He had wondered if Sanders was gay for a while, but then it just seemed more like he was asexual. He didn't really show a sexual interest in *anything*. So the fact that Sanders was getting all red and fidgety over Tate … it was *interesting*. Jameson followed him.

"Are you sure about that? Are we going to have to duel at dawn? Or maybe just ask her to choose between us," he teased. Sanders turned around.

"This is ridiculous. I am not in love with her, but even if I was, we wouldn't duel because you would never fight over her. And I wouldn't ask her to choose between us, because I know who she would pick. And it *would not* be you," Sanders snapped. Jameson's eyebrows shot up.

"Awfully sure of yourself there," he said in a soft voice. Sanders let out a sigh.

"It is easy to be sure of myself when I know I'm right. It's not modesty, or bragging, if it's the truth. I am not in love with her. I care about her, a lot. She talks to me, because I'm me. Not because of you. Most people ignore me when you're not around. I *appreciate* her. That is it, though," Sanders explained.

"Alright. It's a problem I never foresaw as happening, but I would hate for a woman to ever come between us," Jameson said, and Sanders nodded.

"Me, too. Luckily, I tend to find your taste in women appalling," he added, and Jameson burst out laughing.

"Really? I thought I had pretty good taste – Pet is a model, and Tate's a knockout," he laughed as he headed towards the door.

"They have all been very beautiful, but Petrushka is psychotic, and the first time Tatum came over, I thought she was a prostitute. She's lucky she is so nice and funny, it is her saving grace," Sanders explained, and Jameson started laughing even harder.

"Have you mentioned any of that to your *bestie?*" he cackled.

"No. Unlike *some people*, I know what tact is and how to employ it."

Jameson laughed for a while at that one, even after he'd left Sanders' room. He had tact, he just chose *not* to employ it most of the time. Sanders was wrong on another note, too. Jameson *would* fight over her.

It was a scary realization, but his instant, gut reaction to thinking that Sanders was in love with Tate, was to end his relationship with Sanders. That said something, right there. When Dunn had made a move on her, then later had sex with her, Jameson had wanted to kill him. *Still* wanted to kill him. *That* said something. Bringing her to Spain, *said something.*

He would most definitely fight over her.

Jameson crept back into the bedroom, careful not to disturb her. She was laying on her stomach, her arms stretched out to either side. As he crawled into the bed, she grumbled in her sleep and scooted closer to him. He laid on his side, his eyes wandering over her back. There was a bruise near her shoulder. They had gotten adventurous in the shower, wound up falling to the floor. She had gotten mouthy, and he knew there was now a bite mark on her breast. Fun times.

What have you done to me?

He pressed his palm flat against her back, feeling her warmth. She nuzzled even closer, pressing her face into his chest. She had evaded his questions about what they would do next, where they would go. He couldn't figure out why. She had to know it wasn't a game anymore.

It occurred to Jameson that maybe, just maybe, he was done playing games.

Tate was very excited to see Ang. She wanted to go to the airport, but

Jameson wouldn't let her. He'd already had some sort of breakfast or brunch-y thing planned. Ang was going to get to the hotel and be allowed to relax, did she understand? Jameson apparently didn't want to deal with a cranky Ang. Tate could understand. Happy, pleasant Ang was openly hostile towards Jameson. She didn't want to imagine cranky Ang.

"Feels like it's been a while since it was just the two of us," Jameson commented as they rode around in a hired car, after breakfast. She glanced at him.

"We spent a whole week on your boat in virtual solitude," she reminded him.

"I know. I got used to it. Having Sanders meddling gets tiring," he said.

"Is that a joke?"

"I know he chirps in your ear. He tells me everything, I hope you realize," Jameson warned her. Tate held her breath a little.

"He tells you what we talk about?" she asked, trying to sound nonchalant. Probably failing miserably.

"He tells me what he says. He is surprisingly tight lipped about what *you* say," Jameson replied. She let out a sigh.

"Good."

"Saying things I wouldn't want to hear?" he asked, glancing down at her. She shrugged.

"Sometimes."

They got out at the Eiffel Tower. There were a million people around, and she almost thought Jameson would get back in the car, but he didn't. They surged through the crowd, Jameson leading the way.

"Have you been here before?" Tate asked, standing next to him when he stopped to look up.

"No, not really. I've only seen it from a distance. I'm usually working when I'm here," he replied. She laughed.

"I came here with a French class, we went all the way to the top," she told him.

"You took French, but you don't speak French?" he asked.

"I only took it for the trip."

They didn't go inside, just walked around. Tate took a lot of pictures. Usually, she avoided taking pictures of Jameson. If things went to shit, which they always did, she didn't want memories captured to come back and haunt her. But she couldn't resist. He was wearing a heavy overcoat with a thick scarf tucked inside it. He hadn't gotten a haircut yet, and the wind was ruffling his thick hair. He looked very serious, and intimidating, and more than a little scary.

He is so fucking gorgeous.

"Stop taking pictures of me. Let's get out of here," he finally snapped. She skipped after him.

They walked around for a while, just taking in the sights. Went down to Napoleon's tomb, and Tate took some more pictures. She could tell he didn't really give a shit about anything they were looking at and was just indulging her. It almost would have been sweet, if he hadn't glared the whole time.

They were heading down the street, ready to call the car to take them back to the hotel, when Jameson stopped. Tate made it almost a block before realizing he wasn't next to her, and she looked back to see what was he was doing. He was standing in front of a window, looking inside it. Then he moved and went into the building.

Huh?

Tate went back and followed him inside. It was a jewelry store. She swallowed thickly, glancing around. A man behind a counter said something to her in French, looking her up and down. He didn't smile. She rolled her eyes at him and continued forward. Jameson was nowhere to be seen, which was odd, because it wasn't a very big store. The man continued to chatter at her in French, then a door in the back of the store opened.

"Mademoiselle! S'il vous plaît," a woman came out, gesturing towards the door. Tate glanced around.

"Me?" she asked, pointing at herself.

"Get in here," Jameson's voice carried out onto the floor.

Tate got in there.

He was standing in front of a large wooden desk, looking down at something. The woman came in, as well, and walked to the far side of the desk. Tate stayed near the door, wondering what was going on – was she really being sold into sex slavery? Jameson spoke in a halting sort of French, pausing to search for the right words. The woman nodded, then adjusted something on the desk.

"This one," Jameson said, pointing down. Then he looked over his shoulder at Tate. "Come over here."

She went and stood right next to him, taking in the sight before her. Several pearl necklaces were carefully laid out on the glossy, wooden desk top. Her breath caught in her throat. The woman was picking one up, and almost started to come around the desk, but Jameson held out his hand. Said something in French. The woman handed the necklace over to him.

"What is going on?" Tate demanded.

"I told you that you needed real pearls," he said, turning her away from him and clasping the strand of pearls around her neck.

"Yeah, and I also remember you telling me they cost like $50,000," she reminded him.

"I said *some* cost that much," he corrected her, turning her back to face him so he could look at her. He shook his head and reached around her neck, took the necklace off. The woman held up another strand for him.

"So these ones don't cost $50,000," Tate clarified. Jameson nodded, holding the other strand up against her collar bone.

"No. These ones are around €50,000," he told her. She choked a little.

"Euros!? That's like $70,000!"

"Give or take," he said, then nodded at the woman while laying the pearls on the desk.

"What are you doing?" Tate asked, watching as the woman took out a box and a bag.

"Having them wrapped up," Jameson replied.

"Why?"

"Because I just bought them," he answered as he pulled his wallet out of his pocket. She slapped it out of his hand, shocking him. He stared at her like he really wanted to slap her back.

"You can't do that!" Tate snapped.

"And why not?" Jameson asked.

"Because! Why would you do that? Spend that much money on me!? On pearls!?" Tate demanded.

"I told you, you need real ones," he repeated himself.

"I don't 'need' real pearls, Jameson."

"No. But you deserve them."

I could never handle this man. Not in a million lifetimes.

She ran away. It was what she did best, after all. Tate burst out of the store, and kept on running. She felt like her heart was going to explode. She made it a couple blocks before Jameson caught up to her. If she hadn't been so upset, she would've been amazed that he had bothered to run after her. Ran, *period.* She would've paid to have seen it.

"*Stop,*" Jameson said, grabbing her from behind and pulling her to a stop.

"No! *You stop!* You can't buy me!" Tate shrieked at him. People streamed around them, staring. Jameson dragged her into an alley.

"I wasn't trying to buy you, Tatum. I was buying you a *present,*" he growled in her ear, letting her go. She spun around to face him.

"So buy me a fucking card! I am *not* your whore!" she shouted.

"I never said you were. I have *never* treated you like one, not

246

since Boston," he pointed out, staring down at her, his eyes alive with anger. She didn't care. Time was up. She was finally, completely, unraveled.

"You *do* treat me like one! Like some stupid whore you can just yank around whenever you want! Push and pull, beck and call! Why would you buy me a present like that!? You don't care! *You don't care!*" Tate yelled at him. Jameson stood close to her, bringing his face down near to hers.

"I wanted to buy it to show you I remembered. To show you I *do* care," he hissed.

Liar.

She shrieked and smacked him across the face. Jameson let her hit him in the chest a couple more times, but when she slapped him again, he grabbed her by the wrists. Twisted her around and pulled her back into his chest. She struggled against his hold, so he pinned her wrists to her chest. Leaned forward, causing her to bend in half.

Tate kept trying to yell at him, but she was choking on sobs. Jameson's arms around her grew softer. Not restricting. *Holding.* She was aware that he was swaying lightly. Rocking her. She turned her head to the side, away from him, and just cried. For her lost heart. For her broken soul. For her weak spirit.

"Why!? Why did you bring her home? Why did you do that? How could you be with her? After everything. *You promised.* Why did you do that to me!? How could you be with her!? *How could you do that to me!?*" she sobbed, over and over again. His lips pressed to her ear, and it was a while before she could tell what he was saying.

"I'm sorry, Tatum. I'm really, truly sorry."

"You're not. You're not sorry. You treated me like *nothing.* I'm nothing to you," she cried.

"It was only *ever* you," Jameson whispered. "Two weeks ago, four months ago, seven years ago. *This whole time.* Always you."

She cried harder.

12

"I'M MAD AT YOU."

"I know."

"I don't know if I'll ever stop being mad."

"I know."

"Why do you want to deal with that?"

He pulled her out of the car.

"Because I want to."

"That's not an answer."

"It's the only one you're getting."

"That's not fair."

"Life isn't fair, baby girl."

He pulled her out of the elevator.

"You owe me."

"Tatum, I don't think I'll ever stop owing you."

"But you never pay up."

"I don't think I'll ever stop paying."

He pulled her down the hall.

"Why did you do it?"

"I was angry. Mad. Hurt."

"Why didn't you just talk to me?"

"Because I thought you hurt me on purpose. I wanted to hurt you back."

"I didn't even know I could hurt you."

"You're actually very good at it."

He pulled her into the hotel room.

"You scare me."

"I am aware of this. You're still crying."

"You love tears."

"They're not as fun as they used to be."

He pulled her into the bedroom.

"I don't want this. I don't want to be … part of this."

"I don't think you have a choice."

"I know."

"So why fight it?"

"Because … I don't want to end up in that pool again."

"I won't let you."

He pulled her jacket off.

"I don't trust you."

"We'll work on that."

"Sometimes, I think I hate you."

"Sometimes, hmmm. And other times?"

"Other times, I … I think I …"

He pulled his jacket off.

"See, it's those other times. I only pay attention to those times."

"Works out awfully well for you."

"Only sometimes."

"Jameson. This isn't a game. This is my life. I don't want you playing with it."

"Baby girl, sometimes I wonder if it was ever a game."

Oh, Satan. You get me every time.

13

TATUM SNUCK DOWNSTAIRS. IT WAS about three in the afternoon. She wanted to collapse. She wanted to fall into a coma for a hundred years. She wanted everything to be still, and quiet. Last time she'd had thoughts like that, things hadn't ended so well for her.

After her mental breakdown in the alley, Jameson had the car pulled around. Carried her to it. Took her back to the hotel. Treated her nice. Told her things he had been wanting to say. Things he had apparently been *needing* to say.

It hurt her soul.

While Jameson took a shower, she had tried to sneak into Sanders' room, but he wasn't there. Tate knew Ang was at the hotel. His flight had gotten in at noon, plus there was a *"Do Not Disturb"* sign hanging on his door. He was probably sleeping. She wanted to curl up with him. Cuddle. Cry. Figure out what the fuck was wrong with her. See if he would still love her, even after she had sold her heart and soul to the devil.

Getting a key card was easy. Jameson had rented all the rooms, and Tate was listed as a guest under the room numbers. She simply told them that she had forgotten her key. She got a couple of sideways looks, probably because of the short-shorts she had slipped on and the fact that she was barefoot, so she told them she was Jameson's wife. Scary thought. They backed right down and Mrs. Kane was given a key to all three rooms. *Success.*

Tate peeked her head through Ang's door, glancing around. She was surprised at what she saw, and walked all the way into the suite, leaving the door open behind her. The room was a mess. His luggage looked like it had been thrown into the room. There was a small seating area with couches, and all the cushions were askew, one even on the floor. A tall floor lamp was knocked to the ground and broken. Ang's jacket was on the floor, one of the sleeves ripped a little. Tate started breathing fast through her nose. They were in a very nice hotel, in a very nice part of the city, but still. It was a *big* city. Muggings happened, robberies happened.

There was a thump to her left and Tate whirled around. She crept forward a couple steps and she heard it again. *Thump, thump.* Someone was in the bedroom. Tate pressed her hand over her mouth. Someone was robbing the hotel room, right at that moment. They were in Ang's room. *With Ang.*

Fuck that. She rushed back towards the front door. The hotel provided bins full of complimentary umbrellas – Paris had wet winters. Tate pulled out a long one and charged back towards the bedroom. She kicked open the door and let out a growl, holding the umbrella like a bat.

"The cops are coming, mother fucker! You have —," she started to shout, but was cut off by yelling and screaming. She blinked a couple times, trying to adjust her eyes to the sight in front of her.

Oh. My. God.

"What the fuck, Tate!?" Ang was shouting as he struggled to get out of the bed.

He was completely nude, but that wasn't what shocked her –

she had seen Ang naked more times than she could count. No, what shocked Tate was the other person in the room. A woman sat on the edge of the bed, pulling on a shirt in a nervous, frantic manner. Tate stared in wide eyed shock.

"I … you … I …" she breathed, feeling a little like she was going to faint. Ang groaned and started to walk towards her.

"I didn't want you to find out this way, I wanted -,"

Tate lost it. Her mind wasn't exactly the strongest thing on the best of days, and it certainly wasn't one of those days. She let out a shriek and banged the umbrella against the bedroom door. The sound was loud, and caused Ang to jump. Tate let out another frustrated yell as she turned and hurried back into the seating area. There was some muffled movement in the room behind her, then she heard footsteps racing after her.

"Don't talk to me. I don't want to talk about it," she said, her voice fast and shaky. Ang appeared in front of her, now wearing a pair of boxer briefs. He stood in front of the open door, blocking her exit.

"Stop. We have to talk about this, you look like you're going to pass out," he told her. She stared at him for a second and then whirled away, pacing across the living room.

Don't crack. **Do. Not. Crack.** *One breakdown per day, that's all you get.*

"I'm fine. I just have to get out of here," Tate said, raking a hand through her hair.

"Just let me —," Ang started again, walking up next to her. He reached for her arm, but she swung the umbrella up, pointing it at his chest.

"*Don't touch me!*" she hissed at him. "How could you do this? How could you not tell me!?"

"You've been gone! You've been with *him!* How was I supposed to tell you!?" Ang yelled back, holding his hands up like her umbrella was locked and loaded.

"Stop using him as an excuse for everything! This is why, isn't it!? Why you've been weird for so long, why you never wanted to see me!" Tate yelled. He looked at her like she was stark raving mad.

Jameson never looks at me like that. Sanders never looks at me like that.

"I wasn't being weird, Tate, I was just waiting for the right time," Ang said. From behind him, Tate could hear soft footsteps coming down the hallway. She narrowed her eyes and stepped to the side so she could point her umbrella at his guest.

"Well, you sure knew how to pick the right fucking time. *Was this your idea?*"

She was very pregnant, but her sister still looked beautiful. Ellie's honey blonde hair was a disheveled mess around her head, and her shirt had been buttoned wrong, leaving one side hanging lower than the other. She was chewing on her bottom lip.

"Tatum, it's really … not what you think," Ellie insisted. Tate let out a laugh, but it sounded more like a dying cat.

"Not what I think? *Not what I think!?* Then things sure have changed a lot during my little vacation, cause it looked an awful lot like the two of you were *fucking!*" she screamed at them, waving the umbrella around as she spoke.

Ang closed his eyes, sucking air through his teeth. Ellie turned bright red. Tate glared at both of them, gulping in deep breaths of air, the umbrella still held out in front of her like a weapon. She glanced around them. The living room made sense, now. Ang and Ellie must have stumbled in, gotten busy on the couch. Knocked over the lamp. Ripped each others clothes off, and then crashed into the bedroom.

Thank god I didn't come in any earlier.

"Tate. Please. It just sort of … happened. We spent a lot of time together while you were in the hospital. We both missed you," Ang explained, holding his hands out defensively. She gasped.

"This has been going on for over *two months!?*" Tate demanded. He winced.

"It just happened one night," he told her.

"It just *happened* one night!? You both *missed me!?* So, what, you thought sleeping with each other would be like being with me!? That is so fucking weird, and some kind of incestuous, I'm sure," Tate pointed out, pressing a hand to her forehead.

"It's not all always about *you,* Tate," Ang snapped. "We missed you, so that brought us closer together. I get her, and she likes me, I don't know."

"But jesus, in *TWO STATES*, my sister and I have managed to sleep with each others ... *whatevers.* Somethings. *God! She* sleeps with Jameson, *I* sleep with Jameson. *I* sleep with you, *she* sleeps with you. *Fuck,*" Tate swore. Ang went to step forward and she swung the umbrella wide. "*Don't fucking come near me.* You kept this from me, and it's *huge.* I may have gone crazy, and I may have sold my soul, but I would *never* have kept something like this from you."

"You're not my mother, or my girlfriend, Tate. I can sleep with whoever I want to," Ang pointed out.

All of a sudden, and very unexpectedly, her eyes filled with tears. She didn't know who was more horrified, her or Ang.

"You know how I feel about her, what she did to me. You're my best friend. Why did it have to be *her?*" Tate sniffled in a small voice. Ang's face went from angry to heart broken in an instant, but it was Ellie who stepped forward.

"Tatum, he didn't do it on purpose – *we* didn't. Really. And we kept trying to stop, but ... we just couldn't," she tried to explain. Tate glared at her.

"Oh, that makes me feel *so much* better," she hissed.

"Tate, just chill out and let's —,"

Knock knock knock.

Jameson stood in the open doorway. Perfect. Tate cut her eyes to him for a moment, and then looked back at Ang. He looked equal parts guilty and angry. To be called out by Tate was one thing, but to be called out in front of the devil was quite another.

"You should really keep your door shut," Jameson's cool voice rang through the room.

"I don't want him here, not now," Ang's voice was cold and ominous as he stared hard at her. Tate gripped the umbrella between two hands and licked her lips.

"Give us a minute," she said as Jameson made his way into the suite, shutting the door behind him.

"This looks far too exciting to walk away from. What's going on in here?" Jameson asked, his eyes looking over the messed up furniture, the umbrella in Tate's hand, Ang's state of undress. He stopped when he got to Ellie's disheveled form, and he narrowed his eyes, smiling.

"*Get the fuck out of my room!*" Ang roared. Jameson raised one eyebrow, but appeared otherwise unruffled by the outburst.

"*Your* room? I believe *my* name is on the bill," Jameson pointed out. Ang's whole body turned red.

"I don't have to take your shit, *Satan*," he snapped. Jameson laughed; a dark, evil sound.

"You'll take anything I decide to serve you, *Angier*," he growled back.

"That's it, I'm gonna —," Ang started to swear and stalk across the floor. Tate shrieked and waved the umbrella up and down in between them.

"*Stop it!* Everyone just shut the fuck up! You and I used to have sex *all the time*, you're my *best friend*, and you fucked my sister, the person who tried to ruin my life!" she screamed at Ang. Everyone went completely still. Except for Jameson. He kept smiling. She swung the umbrella around and pointed it at him. "And *you!* You're the one who planned all of this! You get some sick, weird, pleasure out of fucking with my head! So *fuck off!*" At last, she swung the umbrella to her sister. "And you! Maybe think of someone else, instead of yourself, for *one goddamn fucking second!*"

Tate was shaking by the end of her tantrum. She was positive her face was beet red, and had no doubt that she looked full-on crazy. Both Jameson and Ang stepped forward, reaching out for her. She shrieked and swung the umbrella wide, causing them to jump back. She took the opportunity to scurry out of the room, down the hall, and into her own suite. She marched right into the bathroom and slammed the door behind her, as hard as she could.

God, I'm like an eight year old. So pathetic.

She slid to the floor, squeezing herself in between the toilet and the bath tub. The umbrella clattered to the floor. She felt crazy. *Ang and Ellie.* Sure, her feud with her sister was over and they had made sort-of-peace – but it didn't change the fact that for a large chunk of her life, Ellie had been a raging bitch. She had made Tate's life a living hell while growing up, and then just one night. One horrible, young, thoughtless mistake, and Ellie ran Tate out of her home. Away from her family. Sure, Tate liked the way her life had turned out, but it still hurt. It never *stopped* hurting. Her father still wouldn't talk to her. And Ang knew all of this, *knew* what Tate had been through because of her sister, *knew* how much it still upset her – and he'd *still* had sex with Ellie. Then *lied about it*, for *two months.*

Not. Okay. It was like a best girl friend sleeping with an evil ex. Horrible.

And Jameson. *Jameson.* He had to have known Ang was bringing Ellie. He *had to* – he had chartered the private plane. He had done this on purpose. To make Tate crazy. To drive a wedge between her and Ang. To rip her apart a little. He would do anything, to be in charge. All his sweet words. *Lies.* He had brought them there, he had to have known. Well, not him entirely. Sanders had made all the reservations. God, did Sanders know!? Tate started crying harder.

She felt betrayed, by *everyone*. How could Ang go two and a half months, and not say anything!? All those phones calls, all those times he had bailed on her; he had been sneaking off to see Ellie – *ditching Tate for Ellie*. So many opportunities to say something.

That's what hurt the most. More than him picking Ellie of all people to date, was him keeping it a secret for *so long*. Despite everything that had happened, Tate had thought they were closer than that; she still told him everything about Satan. She thought he would have returned the favor. Apparently, she had thought *wrong*.

Just like always, stupid girl.

"Tatum, open the door," Jameson's voice was loud. She shook her head.

"Just go away," she sighed, pressing her face into her knees. He banged against the door.

"*Open the door*," he demanded.

"I want to go home," she whispered, wrapping her arms around her legs.

"I am going to count to three, and then I am coming in there, whether you like it or not," he warned her.

"*Please. Just let me go*," she was barely breathing, her lips hardly moving.

There was silence for a second, then a loud crack. The door flung wide open, bounced off the wall. Tate could hear him striding into the room, but she didn't look up. He grabbed her wrists, pulled her up so she was standing. She was waiting for him to tell her to shut up, to calm the fuck down. But he didn't. He pulled her into him, wrapped his arms around her.

"Baby girl, the things you get yourself into," he sighed.

"Why did he have to sleep with *her*?" Tate whispered, sliding her arms around his waist, curling her fists tightly into his t-shirt.

"Life takes some interesting turns – especially when it comes to the people we wind up sleeping with," Jameson pointed out.

"You're not allowed to make me feel better. You're an asshole."

"True. But I'm an asshole who used to be very good at making you feel better," he reminded her. She sighed, pressing her face into his chest.

"And making me feel like shit."

"You like that almost as much."

Not when it's for real.

"Why didn't you tell me?" Tate whispered.

"Because I didn't know."

"Liar."

"He asked if he could bring his girlfriend. I said I didn't care. I didn't ask who the girlfriend was, why would I ever care who *Angier* is fucking?" Jameson asked her.

Liar.

"Sanders knew," Tate breathed. She felt his fingers dig into her hips.

"He didn't. Stop trying to find someone to blame. Shit happens. *Get over it,*" he instructed her.

Shit doesn't happen. Jameson fucking Kane happens.

"Why did you do this? To rip me and Ang apart? To make me hate him, so I would like you more? Or to teach me a lesson? That I shouldn't forget my past? Shouldn't forget what a horrible person I am? Trust me, I'll never forget that. You made sure of that last time," she told him, visions of water dancing through her head. So much water. So cold. All around her. Only this time, there was no Ang to save her.

"You're not a horrible person, baby girl," Jameson whispered. "I'm not playing with you. No more games."

Liar.

It was always games between her and Jameson. She had lost sight of that for a little while. It was easy to do, when a person was surrounded by sweet words and sweeter lies. She felt like being with

Jameson was like living from one panic attack to the next. She didn't know how much more her psyche could take, if she let it go on. It wasn't fair. His ego wasn't even bruised. Wasn't even scratched. Wasn't even *touched*.

Of course it isn't. He's Jameson Kane, the goddamn devil. What did you expect?

14

TATE SAT AT A BAR just off the lobby of the hotel. It was a little after midnight. Sneaking out of the room had been difficult – Jameson was suspicious by nature, and had watched her carefully after her little break down in the bathroom. But after she had calmed down, she had found a way to distract him.

Sex always was my favorite weapon. Time to wield it with a vengeance.

She sipped at her drink, then went back to the what she had been doing – she had a cocktail napkin in front of her, and she was writing tiny notes on it. She chewed on the end of her pen, trying to figure out what else she wanted to add, when someone next to her cleared their throat.

"Excuse me," a voice with a heavy French accent asked, and Tate turned on her stool to see a handsome, older gentleman standing beside her. "Is this seat taken?"

"No, go ahead," she offered, gesturing to the empty seat next to her. The man smiled and sat down.

"It is very late to be having a drink. Are you here alone?" he asked, and she laughed. An evil sound. Almost as evil sounding as

Jameson's.

"Alone enough," she replied, letting her eyes slowly trail over his body. She hadn't exercised her slutty-flirting muscles in a while, but they seemed to be working just fine – the man sat up straighter, adjusted the tie he was wearing.

"Interesting answer. May I ask what you are working on?" he questioned, leaning towards her napkin. Tate laughed again.

"I am working on a revenge plan," she answered coyly. He raised his eyebrows.

"Revenge?"

"Yes."

"And why are you seeking revenge?" he asked. She sighed.

"Because, people I trusted did something bad to me. Continually. I think it's time for payback," she replied. It was almost surreal, the conversation she was having. Of course, her *life* was surreal. Tate was pretty sure her brain had gone on vacation, possibly permanently.

"Ah, *oui*, of course," the man chuckled, and it was clear he thought she was joking. "So what is your plan, *ma chère*?"

"Well, to give them a taste of their own medicine, of course! I'm going to do to them what they did to me," she told him, laughing again.

"And what, exactly, did these people do?" he asked for clarification.

"One of them lied to me, a lot. Then slept with my sister, a lot. This person has already slept with me," she explained, picking up her drink, playing with the straw with her tongue. His eyes followed the movement.

Still got it.

"Oh, that's horrible, *ma chère*. And the other people?" he asked. Tate cleared her throat.

"Obviously, my sister needs to pay."

"Of course."

"And then there's Satan," she added.

"I'm sorry. Did you say '*Satan*'?" he repeated her. She laughed.

"Oh yes. I'm involved in a very interesting relationship with the devil. You see, he won't leave me alone. He likes to play these games, where he tells me one thing, gets me to believe he's a good person, then he pulls the rug out from underneath me. He's the worst," she finished.

The man stared at her, a small smile playing on his lips. He thought she was playing a silly game. He didn't realize he was dealing with a woman who had lost one too many games already. She wasn't about to lose to anyone else. Not him, not Ang, and most-fuck-ing-certainly not Jameson.

Play time is over.

"So what are you going to do, in order to exact your revenge?" the man asked, his voice low and sexy. Tate slid off her bar stool, slowly, and stood so she was brushing against his knees. She leaned close to him, pressing her lips against his ear.

"Anything I want," she whispered.

And then she walked away, leaving him staring after her.

Abso-fucking-lutely anything.

TO BE CONTINUED …

Acknowledgements

So many people to thank. Separation was written in April/May of 2014, and mainly consisted of me hunched over my laptop, yelling at it in frustration. This story did not come easy. How do you make the devil likable!? I didn't want a trilogy, but there were so many things that I felt needed to be said. Sanders had a story that demanded to come out, and Jameson needed some understanding. So thank you to everyone who read it early on, and encouraged me to keep at it.

As I said in the dedication, big thanks need to go to my "street team" – you help me, promote me, answer questions for me, critique things for me, help me figure things out, make me laugh, anything, everything. There are no words. I am very blessed to have met all of you.

To the author friends I've made a long the way. The list isn't very long, but your help and friendship is invaluable.

To EVERY blog that has read and reviewed for me. To ANY blog that has posted something on my behalf and supported me. Without all of you helping Degradation to get where it's at now, *this* book might not ever have been published.

To Becs at Sinfully Sexy Book Reviews – thank you for taking a chance on a book that caught your eye, and on an author that didn't really exist. Seeing Degradation chosen as one of your top reads of the summer, and it came out at the tail end of July, shuffled in amongst other more famous books, more famous authors …, I don't think I'll ever get over it. So thank you for that, and for your continued support.

Once again, to Najla Qamber at http://www.najlaqamberdesigns.com, the amazing woman who designs my covers. You are able to take my millions of e-mails and random pictures, and then turn them into gold. Your designs are better than anything I could ever picture. I'm so glad you were recommended to me, because I think you are truly one of the best cover designers out there.

Of course thanks go to my husband. Shoved to a back burner at times, forced to listen to gossip about the indie world, rants about formatting troubles, jokes about street team antics. There are few people more understanding than my husband. You are an amazing person. Thank you for always listening to me, always supporting me, always encouraging me. Some day, I will buy us that mansion (read: shack on the beach) in Lagos, and it'll all be worth it.

And of course, thank you to everyone who read Degradation and liked it enough to read this book. Bigger thanks if you liked this book enough to continue on to Reparation. And HUGE thanks if you took the time to rate and review this book, or any book I've written. Without reviews, books don't sell. If books don't sell, then we can't write. It's that simple. You keep us in business.

So thank you.

About the Author

Crazy woman living in an undisclosed location in Alaska (where the need for a creative mind is a necessity!), I have been writing since …, forever? Yeah, that sounds about right. I have been told that I remind people of Lucille Ball — I also see shades of Jennifer Saunders, and Denis Leary. So basically, I laugh a lot, I'm clumsy a lot, and I say the F-word A LOT.

I like dogs more than I like most people, and I don't trust anyone who doesn't drink. No, I do not live in an igloo, and no, the sun does not set for six months out of the year, there's your Alaska lesson for the day. I have mermaid hair — both a curse and a blessing — and most of the time I talk so fast, even I can't understand me.

Yeah, I think that about sums me up.

79055992R00162

Made in the USA
Columbia, SC
25 October 2017